Red is for
Remembrance

About the Author

Laurie Faria Stolarz was raised in Salem, Massachusetts, and educated at Merrimack College in North Andover. She has an MFA in creative writing and a graduate certificate in screenwriting, both from Emerson College in Boston. She currently teaches writing and French. Visit her website at teen.llewellyn.com.

To Write to the Author

If you wish to contact the author or would like more information about this book, please write to the author in care of Llewellyn Worldwide and we will forward your request. Both the author and publisher appreciate hearing from you and learning of your enjoyment of this book and how it has helped you. Llewellyn Worldwide cannot guarantee that every letter written to the author can be answered, but all will be forwarded. Please write to:

Laurie Faria Stolarz
℅ Llewellyn Worldwide
2143 Wooddale Drive, Dept. 0-7387-0760-0
Woodbury, MN 55125-2989, U.S.A.

Please enclose a self-addressed stamped envelope for reply, or $1.00 to cover costs. If outside U.S.A., enclose international postal reply coupon.

Many of Llewellyn's authors have websites with additional information and resources. For more information, please visit our website at:

http://teen.llewellyn.com

Red is for Remembrance

Laurie Faria Stolarz

Llewellyn Publications
Woodbury, Minnesota

Red Is for Remembrance © 2005 by Laurie Faria Stolarz. All rights reserved. No part of this book may be used or reproduced in any manner whatsoever, including Internet usage, without written permission from Llewellyn Publications except in the case of brief quotations embodied in critical articles and reviews.

FIRST EDITION
Second Printing, 2005

Book design by Rebecca Zins
Cover design by Gavin Dayton Duffy
Cover image (candle) © Stockbyte
Editing by Megan C. Atwood, Rhiannon Ross, and Rebecca Zins

Llewellyn is a registered trademark of Llewellyn Worldwide, Ltd.

Library of Congress Cataloging-in-Publication Data [pending]
Stolarz, Laurie Faria, 1972–
    Red is for remembrance / Laurie Faria Stolarz.—1st ed.
        p. cm.
    Summary: To come.

    ISBN 0-7387-0760-0
    [1. Witchcraft—Fiction. 2. Magic—Fiction. 3. Dreams—Fiction.
    4. Extrasensory perception—Fiction. 5. Revenge—Fiction.] I. Title.

PZ7.S0000Si 2005
[Fic]—dc22

0000000000
ISBN-13: 978-0-7387-0760-0

Llewellyn Worldwide does not participate in, endorse, or have any authority or responsibility concerning private business transactions between our authors and the public.

All mail addressed to the author is forwarded but the publisher cannot, unless specifically instructed by the author, give out an address or phone number. Please refer to the publisher's web site for links to authors' web sites and other sources.

Any Internet references contained in this work are current at publication time, but the publisher cannot guarantee that a specific location will continue to be maintained. Please refer to the publisher's website for links to authors' websites and other sources.

Llewellyn Publications
A Division of Llewellyn Worldwide, Ltd.
2143 Wooddale Drive, Dept. 0-7387-0760-0
Woodbury, MN 55125-2989, U.S.A.
www.llewellyn.com

Printed in the United States of America

Other Books By Laurie Faria Stolarz

Blue Is for Nightmares

White Is for Magic

Silver Is for Secrets

In loving memory of my grandmother
Anne M. Anderson
1911–1981

Acknowledgments

A great big thank-you to Lara Zeises, my friend and critique partner, who's been a constant source of encouragement. These books would not be nearly as rewarding to write—or read—if it were not for her cheering me on, chapter by chapter.

A special thank-you goes to my husband Ed, who's read every word of all my books, who's always there to offer encouragement, support, and a sense of humor whenever I need it.

A huge thank-you goes to Megan Atwood who, four books later, is more than a fabulous editor to me—she's more like a fabulous friend.

Thanks to my brother Mark for checking bookstores for copies of my books and for leaving reader copies in the lunchroom where he works.

Thanks to fabulous Llewellyn editors Rebecca Zins and Rhiannon Ross for their patience, critical suggestions, and careful attention to detail—this book would not have been the same without every bit of it.

Thanks to all the friends and family members who continue to cheer me on—you know who you are.

Huge, huge thanks to all the fans who continue to support me by buying and recommending my books, by e-mailing me, sending me letters of support and gratitude, and coming to my events. It means more than you know.

Lastly, a great big thank-you goes to my biggest fan, my mother, who, as we grow older and get better, has become even more of an invaluable friend and source of support.

Jacob may have drowned that night,
but I'm the dead man floating.

—SB
(from a transcript with her therapist)

Stacey

I want to go home.

While Amber and I unpack our stuff, Janie, our new room-mate, prattles on about how *her* pinks will clash with *my* reds, and how Amber's rainbow of colors really belong in a room all their own.

What am I doing here?

"Do you love it?" Janie asks me. She's talking about her bedspread. It's cotton-candy pink with swirls of white going through it. She's got the matching bed linens, too, as well as a cloud-covered poster of a bubbly pink heart with big butterfly wings.

"Love it," I say flatly, turning away.

"Don't mind Stacey," Amber tells our cheery friend. "She's had a rough couple of months."

"You too?" Janie asks, clutching her pink teddy bear. "Well, if it was anything like *my* last semester, then *you* deserve a sticker." She pulls a sheet of smiling fruit stickers from her backpack and smacks a happy watermelon on my hand. She does the same to her own hand, only she chooses a laughing kiwi for herself.

"Um, are you okay?" Amber asks her.

"Somebody's jealous," Janie sings. "O-kay, you can have one too." She goes to stick a cheery bunch of grapes to Amber's cheek, but Amber intercepts.

"Unless it's laced with whatever *you're* obviously taking, I'm all set," Amber says.

Janie's freckly face bunches up. She goes to tuck her nut-brown curls behind her ears, out of nervousness maybe, but the length of her hair is way too short. Instead, she readjusts the skinny peach-colored headband that peeks out across her crown.

"She's kidding," I say to Janie, in an effort to play nice.

"Not really," Amber mumbles.

Amber's one to talk. She's a freshman in college, but she still carries around a Hello Kitty lunchbox for a purse, she still wears her hair in a bunch of mini-pigtails, and she still sports Wonder Woman garb on occasion.

At the moment, she's tucking her life-size Spider-Man blow-up doll into bed. She kisses his cheek and then nestles in beside him.

"What's that all about?" Janie asks.

"Getting in a little cuddle time before dinner," Amber explains. "Nothing like a little PDA before PB & J."

"Excuse me?"

"I used to sleep with Superman," Amber continues, "but I ended up being too much woman for him. He exploded last summer. Don't you hate it when that happens?"

Janie's face drops and Amber feeds into her appall, whispering in Spider-Man's ear and licking down the length of his cheek. "Who's jealous now?" Amber growls.

It *almost* makes me laugh. Amber's been trying to get me to laugh for the past four-and-a-half months, but I'm not even sure I remember how. Sometimes I stretch my mouth open to try, but I only want to scream—to wail at the top of my lungs. Nothing seems funny anymore. Nothing even seems remotely interesting. So why did I even come here? How can I even think about studying topics like philosophy and humanity when those things don't even seem real anymore?

"Do you guys have *real* boyfriends?" Janie asks.

"Just Spidey here," Amber says. "My last serious non-inflatable relationship was with this guy named PJ, and it was beyond fizzle city—no challenge, you know. The guy would call me all the time, write me cute little love poems, want to be with me constantly, want to walk me to class . . ."

"Sounds pretty nice."

"It was hell," Amber clarifies. "I mean, at least blow me off a couple times."

"How about you?" Janie asks, turning toward me.

I shrug.

"Ix-nay on the oyfriend-bay questions," Amber whispers to her. "Sort of a sore spot."

"Oh, sorry," Janie says.

I shrug again and unzip the side compartment of my suitcase. I look down at the bottle of pills I've been prescribed, the ones my doctor said would "help take the edge off."

"Are you okay?" Amber asks me. "Do you want to go down to the cafeteria and get some overcooked pasta? Maybe some lamp-heated mac and cheese?"

I shake my head and palm the bottle of pills. "You guys go. I'm just gonna stay here and lie down. I'm not really that hungry."

"You sure?" Amber narrows her eyes on me.

"Come on, Stacey," Janie pipes up. "It wouldn't be the same if you didn't eat with us our first night as roommates. It's like some unwritten freshman rule or something—roommates eat together the first night."

"She does have a point," Amber says.

"Plus," Janie continues, "I can tell you all about my first semester and how they made me room with this psycho Goth chick."

"*You* rooming with a Goth chick." Amber says. "Now *this* I have to hear."

I wipe the moisture from my eyes and do my best to look interested, hoping Janie's cheerfulness will be enough to take Amber's attention off me.

"Be-ware," Janie says. "Her name is Sage and she still lives on this floor. She's basically this psycho Goth girl who does all kinds of witch stuff. Like, last semester, just after midterms, she got arrested for breaking into a cemetery at night and trying to rob one of the graves."

"Rob it of what?" Amber asks.

Janie shrugs and makes a grimace. "Death stuff . . . you know."

"That obviously isn't true," I say, pausing a moment from my bottle of pills.

"Is so. Rumor has it she was trying to collect some decayed fragments for one of her spells. She also stole the plot flowers."

I roll my eyes at how ridiculous the story sounds, at how I feel like I'm in high school all over again.

"A couple weeks after that happened," Janie continues, "some freshman was making fun of her by wearing a string of garlic around his neck to ward her off. Word is she put a hex on him that messed up his brain. He ended up getting all spacey and flunking out because of it."

"Maybe his brain was messed up on something stronger than garlic," Amber suggests.

"I doubt it. He was a really nice kid."

"Sounds like it," I say, somewhat under my breath.

"What's that supposed to mean?"

"It means that none of what you're saying has anything to do with *real* Wicca—more like the hocus-pocus stuff they save for storybooks and cheesy movies. And stupid rumors like this."

"What do *you* know about it? You weren't even here."

"I obviously know a lot more than you about Wicca."

"*Whatever*," Janie says, rolling her eyes. "I don't *want* to know about it. That's why I asked the R.A. for a new roommate, like, the *first* day of classes. Unfortunately, they made me wait it out all semester. I'm hoping this semester goes a whole lot better."

"Boy, are you in for a treat," Amber says, rubbing her palms together.

"What do you mean?" Janie follows Amber's glance and looks toward my night table—toward the crystal cluster rock sitting atop it, as well as the white candle stump and my bowlful of lavender pellets.

"Do you want to break it to her, or should I?" Amber arches her eyebrows up and down.

"What?" Janie asks. "Do you guys know Sage?"

"I'm going to lie down for a while," I tell them again, ignoring the conversation.

Amber mumbles something back to me, but I'm really not listening. "You guys go," I say.

"Don't make me go alone." Amber evil-eyes me, gesturing to our cheerleader of a roommate.

"You won't be alone, silly!" Janie says, eternally perky. "I'll be there."

"Exactly," Amber says. She looks at me. "Please? You really shouldn't be alone."

"I'm fine—really."

Or at least, I will be.

"We'll bring you back something yummy," Janie tells me.

"We're going to the *cafeteria*," Amber squawks, "where the word *yummy* doesn't apply."

More smiling. More nodding. Until they finally leave.

I sift a couple of the green and black capsules onto my palm—Librium, according to the label on the bottle. I swallow them down, despite a dry mouth, and lay back on my bed, hoping the effects don't take too long.

Shell

Shell shines his flashlight over the back porch and makes his way up the creaking wooden stairs. It's freezing out here. A dog howls somewhere off in the distance, but the sound is too far away for him to fear that he's the cause. He lifts an edge of the welcome mat and finds the key—just where Clay told him it would be.

Shell takes it and presses it into his glove, wondering what Lily would say if he didn't go through with it or if

Clay would think him a failure. He swallows hard, his breath smoking out his mouth in a long, visible puff. His fingers shake as he pushes the key toward the lock. Maybe he should have taken the knife that Clay offered him. "It's only for protection," Clay had assured him. "You won't even need it." But he could barely even hold it in his hand, let alone carry it in his pocket.

The lock clicks and he turns the knob, the warmth of the house smothering his chill. He takes a deep breath and moves farther into the room, running his flashlight beam over a stove, a refrigerator with fruit magnets, and a toaster oven. He remembers how Clay told him to look in the dining room for sterling silver dinnerware, in the family room for DVD players or VCRs, and in the medicine cabinet for any prescription medicine that might be worth double on the street.

He heads for what he thinks might be the dining room and shines his light over a photo on the wall. It's a picture of an old couple. They're facing one another, gazing into each other's eyes like getting ripped off is the last thing on their minds.

He shifts his focus toward the mahogany box sitting atop the dining room hutch, wondering if that's where they keep the silver. He takes steps toward it, the wooden floor making a cracking sound beneath his feet. He stops, his heart pumping hard. The clock on the mantel sounds, startling him even further. He presses his eyes closed, counting off the twelve bell-bongs that indicate the hour, reminding himself that he has to hurry up—Clay and Lily must be wondering what's keeping him.

Shell works his gloved fingers at the latch on the box, finally managing to open it. Lying to the side of what must be at least ten place settings' worth of silver is a pocket watch. He picks it up, noticing the ample weight, wondering why it's here—why it isn't inside a safe or jewelry box instead.

It's circular in shape and fits inside his glove. He opens it. The face of the clock has yellowed a bit. On the opposite side, there's an engraving: *To Candace, forever, with love.*

His jaw trembles at the sight of it. He clenches the watch in his palm, noticing that his heart is pounding even harder than before, that he's going to be sick.

He throws the watch back inside the box, shuts everything up, and retreats toward the door he entered. The floorboards creak under his weight. The noise startles him. He stumbles and bumps into a chair; the legs make a scraping sound on the floor.

There's a stir in the other room. He knows they must have heard him. This is a Cape-style house; their bedroom is only a few yards away. He aims his flashlight at the exit door. At the same moment, someone's footsteps begin down the hallway toward him. He ducks under the kitchen table, hoping the floor-length tablecloth will cover him. He knows his choice of hiding spots is ridiculous, but he doesn't have time to think of another viable option.

The footsteps stop just a couple feet away. He wonders if he closed the door, if he locked it back up to avoid suspicion. He's almost sure he didn't. The lamp clicks on in the room. He can see the man's feet as he walks out in front of the table; he can see the baseball bat, resting by the man's ankle.

"Who's there?" the man calls out, a voice peppered by age and interrupted sleep.

Shell doesn't answer. He bites the inside of his cheek to keep from gasping out loud.

"I know you're here." The man moves toward the door, checking the lock, probably noticing that it's open.

Shell wonders if he returned the key to its spot under the mat. Or did he leave it on the table?

"Come out now," the old man says, his voice turning away, toward the dining room. He obviously doesn't know where Shell is hiding.

A woman's voice calls from the hallway. "John?"

Shell thinks it must be Candace.

"Stay in the bedroom," the old man tells her. He moves into the dining room, turning a corner, noticing perhaps that the silverware box has been tampered with. Shell hears the baseball bat clunk to the floor, followed by a gasp. "Candace, call 9-1-1!"

Shell scrambles out from under the table, diving for the door. He goes to turn the knob, but it's locked. The old man must've done it. He hears footsteps running toward him, but Shell doesn't look back.

"Stop!" the man shouts.

Shell turns the lock, yanks the door open, and runs as fast as he can down the porch steps, slipping on a patch of ice and landing smack against his back.

The old man charges toward him. Out of the corner of his eye, Shell sees the baseball bat.

"John!" Candace shouts from the door.

Shell struggles to his feet, remembering what Clay said about keeping his head down so that no one would see his face. He heads toward the woods, hearing the old man slip on the steps as well; his body makes a loud thud against the wood. Shell stops. His first instinct is to help the man, to check that he's okay. He hears the man cry out in pain.

Shell tries to block out the cries, shaking his head, knowing in his heart how wrong this is, how wrong it feels. He moves toward the woods, knowing that the darkness of the forest will hide him, but also knowing that he's going to have a hard time finding his way back to the car.

Police sirens begin in the distance. He'll have hell to pay if he doesn't hurry up. But, then again, he'll have hell to pay anyway—once Clay finds him empty-handed.

Stacey

I roll over in bed and peek at the clock. It's a little after 11. At first I think it's eleven at night, like I completely slept through most of the evening, but then I notice the sun. It paints a thick bright stripe across the scuffed wooden floor of our dorm room. So where did the night go? Did I really sleep that long and soundly? Did I dream anything? I close my eyes a few seconds to try and remember, but it's just black and fuzzy inside my head.

There's a sandwich wrapped up in wax paper and a bag of ripple chips by my bed. Amber must have left them for me. Last I remember, she and Janie were heading off to dinner. I'm assuming they must have gone off to class now. I should probably go, too.

Except I'm still so tired. I reach over and grab my backpack from the side of my bed. I unzip the main compartment, where I've tucked my schedule, and look down at the array of classes—places I'm supposed to be, subjects I'm supposed to learn, people I'm supposed to meet. It all seems so overwhelming.

Maybe I should just go back to bed, especially since it seems as though I've already missed two classes—Life Science and English. I'm almost surprised Amber didn't try to wake me up for them. The girl has been such a mother to me these past four months. What other friend would postpone college a semester so she could look after me? While Chad, Drea, and PJ went off to school, Amber elected to stay with me at the cottage—in the same unit we'd all chipped in and rented last summer.

I just couldn't leave the place. Even now, all I really want to do is turn back. I just want to go back there and sit on the sand. I want to look out at the ocean and wait for Jacob to walk up the beach—to come and greet me with a kiss.

But instead I'm here. I'm here because I made a promise to my mother that I would only take one semester off. I'm here because my therapist told me that if I ever wanted to get over Jacob's death, I'd have to start living again. I'm here because the school offered me a full scholarship after I turned down their admission this past September. Because Amber was enrolled here as well and we could be roommates—at least then one thing in my life could remain constant.

But what does all of that mean when there's a giant part of me that can't accept the fact that Jacob's gone? The part that won't ever be able to say goodbye—that still sleeps with my night-light on, hoping that someway it'll guide him to me?

I glance over at the shell-shaped night-light, still mystified over why Beacon—my *reach* school—even accepted me, let alone why they gave me a full ride. I mean, with all the stuff I was dealing with in high school, it's not like my grades were much better than passable. From what I've heard, the kids here were in the top tenth of their high school classes.

I reach into the side pocket of my backpack and pull out my bottle of tranquilizers. If I just take a couple, I might be able to fall back asleep; I could start fresh and new tomorrow morning. I go to pop the top, but the phone rings.

"Hello?" I say, snagging the phone from Janie's stuffed monkey. She's got Curious George's cousin sitting on the receiver, as though waiting for a call.

"Good morning," some woman says. "I'm looking for Stacey Brown."

"Who's calling?" I ask, noting that I don't recognize the voice.

"This is Alice McNeal from the President's Office."

"Who?"

"Alice McNeal. I'm Dr. Wallace's administrative assistant."

"Dr. Wallace?"

"The president of Beacon University," she clarifies. "Is this Stacey Brown?"

"I overslept," I say.

"Excuse me?"

"It won't happen again."

There's a pause on the other end. "I'm calling," she says, finally, "because Dr. Wallace would like to meet with you."

"What for?"

"Do you have some time today?" she asks, ignoring my question.

I grab my schedule, noticing that I have my Holistic Health class from 2 to 2:50. "How about 3:30?" I ask.

"That should be fine," she says. "His office is in Ketcher Hall. Do you know where that is?"

"Yes," I say, even though I don't.

"Okay, we'll see you then."

I hang up, wondering why the college president wants to meet with me. Is it because I'm here on scholarship? A scholarship that I didn't even ask for?

I whip the fridge door open in search of something sweet, something to help tame this bitter mood, almost expecting to find an arsenal of Diet Cokes and chocolate bars—snackables à la Drea, my roommate and best friend from prep school. But instead everything inside is labeled: juice boxes, yogurt containers, eggs, pints of strawberry milk, chocolate pudding packs. They've all got Janie's name magic-marked across, marking her edible territory. I slam the door closed and bury my face in my hands, feeling completely lost and more out of place than ever before.

My insides are shaking. I grab the phone again, eager to talk to my mother. She's only a couple hours away. Maybe she can come and get me. Maybe we can go to dinner tonight and I can tell her that I've made a huge mistake by coming here. I dial the number; I even get to the second-to-last digit, but then I hang up, knowing how disappointed she'd be, how she wouldn't understand.

Not the way Jacob would.

I grab my spell box from underneath my bed and take out a thick red candle. I consecrate it with lemongrass oil, running my finger down the length and around the circumference. "As above," I whisper, touching the top end of the candle. "So below," I say, touching the bottom.

The oil smells like him, like all the times I'd press my nose into the collar of his shirt, like every time he'd wrap his arms around me and whisper into my ear, saying that he never wanted to let me go.

I'd do almost anything to sense him right now, to feel him beside me. Those first nights following the accident, I'd have these vivid dreams about him, about us—doing spells together, holding each other, and the sticky, sweet smell of our love. I'd close my eyes and picture him—his dark, wavy hair, his strong jawline, and those piercing slate-blue eyes. It was like we were still connected in some way.

Now I barely dream at all.

I look at my reflection in the dresser mirror across from my bed, noting how different I look now that he's gone, like a paler, lifeless version of my old self. I've been wearing my dulled brown hair pulled back in an elastic band for the past four months. My eyes look tired, too. There are pockets of fatigue beneath them. Even my cheeks look like hollow bags, like someone's plucked out the roses.

I look away and grab a razor blade from my bag. Starting at the top of the candle, I carve Jacob's name down the side, tiny bits of dark ruby wax flaking toward the floor. I rotate the candle three times counterclockwise and then carve the word DREAM down the other side, opposite his name. I close my eyes, concentrating on the lemongrass scent, imagining it opening up my senses and increasing my psychic awareness. I've done numerous dream spells like this before but, since Jacob's disappearance, not one of them has worked.

"I pray this day with thoughts so deep," I whisper, "that memories of you will visit my sleep. From now until forever be, I will keep your lighted flame with me. Blessed be the way." I set the candle down on my pearl-plated dish and light the wick, watching the flame a few moments, imagining Jacob's spirit within it.

I position the lit candle on my night table, away from any debris, and check the clock. It's almost noon; I still have a couple hours before Holistic Health. I glance at my bottle of tranquilizers, deciding against taking one. Instead I curl back into my pillows, hoping to dream, hoping that Jacob will find his way to me again.

Shell

Shell runs as fast as he can through the forest, the sound of police sirens in the near distance. He almost hopes they'll find him. The old man from the cottage is following close behind him, baseball bat in hand.

Shell aims his flashlight beam as he works his way through the woods, swiping branches and brush from in front of his face.

"I'll get you," the old man calls after him. "I know these woods better than anyone."

It couldn't be any darker or colder. There are patches of ice and snow underfoot. Shell does his best to avoid slipping, but he's only wearing a pair of rubber-soled sneakers and he's already had to catch himself twice.

His eyes are full of tears from the cold, making everything blurry, making him lose his confidence even more. He thought he could get away; he thought, considering the old man's age, it would be easy to outrun him, but he can hear the snapping of twigs just behind him—the old man is getting closer.

"Might as well stop now," the old man shouts.

But he can't stop. If he stops, the old man will probably kill him. Nobody besides Clay, Lily, and some of the other campers even knows he's here. Would they come forward to report his disappearance? Probably not, since that might give them away as well. It's not like they haven't stolen from private properties before.

Shell continues to run at full speed for several seconds. It's then that he notices the trampling of feet behind him has stopped, as well as the snapping of twigs. He stops too, shining his flashlight around the area, searching for the old man. Did he turn back? Did he fall? Maybe he's hurt.

Shell presses his eyes shut, wondering what to do, if maybe he should try and find the old man. At the same moment, something falls on his head, making him jump and let out a gasp. The object slips down past his shoulder and he's able to catch it—a stick. He breathes a sigh of relief, deciding that he needs to get out of here, that the old man can fend for himself. He turns to leave, but slips on a patch of ice and lands hard against his backside. His ankle throbs—a gnawing ache that shoots up his calf.

"I know you're alone," a voice whispers from somewhere behind him.

He turns to look, shining his flashlight in that direction, but there's nothing there—just a narrow, snow-covered pathway with brush all around it. Shell manages to get himself back up and hobbles away as best he can, searching for an end somewhere—a way out.

He struggles for several minutes through the woods and thinks he spots something up ahead of him—a cottage maybe. He heads for it, hoping that someone lives there, hoping that they have a phone.

"I know you're alone," the voice repeats in his ear.

Shell turns around. The old man is there. He clamps his hands around Shell's neck, nearly cutting off his breath.

Shell chokes out a scream.

It's his own voice that wakes him up from the nightmare.

Clay is sitting there, at Shell's bedside, looking down at him.

"What happened?" Shell asks, all out of breath. His ankle is throbbing.

"Time for breakfast," Clay grins. He gets up and exits the room, leaving Shell even more confused than ever.

Shell

At breakfast, Shell makes an effort to shake the lingering chill of his nightmare, but it felt so real that it's got him all jangled up inside. He may have been able to escape the old man after his failed mission last night, but he can't escape the sound of his voice; it plays in his mind's ear over and over again—the old man wailing out in pain.

Shell looks down at his plateful of rice, knowing that he won't be able to digest it. Instead, he pushes the mound of stickiness around with a fork and pretends to eat, so as not to appear ungrateful for the food.

Lily is sitting across from him; Clay, beside her; the elders and small children, at both ends of the long and splintery table; and Brick and Daisy are seated on each side of him.

Things are just as they should be, and yet everything feels so different.

Maizey, one of the children, whines that her rice is already cold, that she'd prefer jam and toast, but she's silenced almost immediately by Rain, her mother, with a sharp reprimand and an evil eye.

Shell wonders how many of the campers know that he didn't go through with looting the old man's place last night. He looks up, trying to gain eye contact with Clay or Lily, but neither will even look at him. Breakfasts are usually quiet at the camp, but he doesn't remember one as silent and oppressive as this. The sound of forks scraping on plates sends nerves down his back. Why did Clay come to his room before breakfast? Why did he want him here?

Once Clay found out that Shell had returned from the old couple's place without so much as a single piece of hockable silver, he was less than civil. He punched the steering wheel a bunch of times, telling Shell that he'd failed his friends and family and that he wasn't worthy of his keep. Is that what this silent treatment is about?

Shell continues to slide the rice around on his plate, trying to sneak peeks at Lily, but she continues to ignore him. Instead she nudges him a couple times under the table with the toe of her boot, both startling and reassuring him.

He looks over at her, admiring her long and twisty golden hair and the way her cheeks dimple when she chews. He wonders if she too might be disappointed with him. He's sure the others are. Aside from Clay's appearance in his room this morning, no one has so much as looked at him. There are twenty-two people living under these roofs, and yet not one of them will give him any inkling as to what happened last night after he went to bed. Had Clay called a meeting behind his back?

Lily whispers something in Clay's ear and the two laugh in unison. "It'll be our little secret," Clay says to her.

"May I be excused?" Shell asks.

Clay turns to him, finally. "We need to have a meeting. All of us." He looks around the table with his steel-gray eyes, nabbing the attention of most of the campers, save for a couple of the younger children. Shell figures that Clay can't be more than seventeen at most, and yet he seems to yield almost as much power as one of the elders . . . even Mason himself.

"When?"

"When I say so," Clay snaps. He tucks a lock of his floppy, dark hair behind his ear.

"We'll meet now," Mason says.

Mason is nearly sixty years old but with the health and strength of a man half his age. He's lived at the camp longer than anyone—when it was only an abandoned shack and there was only him and Rosa, his wife, who passed away shortly after they got set up. It was he who built these rustic cabins, with the help of a few passersby—wanderers, he calls them—in search of a more peaceful and self-fulfilling life.

He paid them with room, board, and his teachings, and soon the wanderers turned into full-on campers. "Nobody leaves the camp," Mason often says. "Nobody ever wants to. And nobody ever should."

Brick once told Shell that campers *have* left the camp and returned back to the pains of normal society. He's also told Shell that no one—not even Clay—is allowed to talk about it.

Shell wonders if it's because of tasks like last night's that made those campers want to leave.

Lily sneaks a smile at Shell as Clay stands to begin the meeting.

"We need to discuss the events of last night," Clay begins.

His voice is loud and bellowing, making up in projection what he lacks in height and visible strength.

"One of our campers was asked to perform a task," Clay continues. "He was asked to break into one of the cottages in the town and take whatever valuables he could find—anything he wanted."

Several of the elders gasp in response. Mason wraps his arm extra tight around Rain and then strokes the length of her inky black hair. She and Mason have been together for at least a few months now, despite their obvious age difference. Though she's considered an elder because she's an adult, Shell figures she can't be more than twenty or twenty-one at most, just a few years older than him.

"As we all know," Clay continues, "taking without first considering the worth an item has to its owner is called stealing. This camper was asked to steal as much and whatever he could so that we, as loving campers, may go on in our peaceful ways . . . so that we may continue in our loving mission, living without the evils of man."

Several of the campers, including Lily and Brick, shake their heads in disapproval.

"We don't need the evils of television," Clay insists. "We don't need the evils of cell phones . . . of computers . . . of microwaves."

"No way," several of the campers mutter under their breath.

"We listen to each other," Clay says. "We talk. We're each other's source of fulfillment, discussing subjects face-to-face. We don't need plastic man-made objects to talk—objects that transmit cancerous airwaves. We don't need beeping boxes that heat our food in unnatural ways, zapping away all of the nutrients. We cook over a fire. We plan meals with each other in mind. We love. We share. We live in peace."

"Yes," several of them cheer. Lily bows her head in thankfulness.

"So," Clay continues, "when we asked this camper to perform an act against peace—to thoughtlessly *steal* from another—he showed fear . . . he showed reluctance. He didn't want to do it. But, at the same time, he didn't want to disappoint us."

Shell grows more and more confused by the moment. Lily peeks up at him and smiles, reaching across the table to grasp his hand.

"Shell," Clay says, raising his glass of water. "You came to us just four months ago. The mission we sent you on last night was a test—to test your loyalty, but just as important, to test your character. I am proud today to say that you passed that test. You went on that mission to please your fellow campers, but at the same time, you stuck to your moral convictions."

The rest of the campers raise their glasses in unison. "To Shell," they say.

"We're happy and proud to call you our brother." Clay sips from his glass and the rest follow, filling Shell with an enormous sense of relief and acceptance.

"I don't know what to say," Shell says, taking a giant breath. He shakes his head, trying to formulate the words—the gratitude. If it weren't for these campers, he doesn't know where he'd be right now. They're his family. They gave him a home and saved his life. If it wasn't for them, he probably would have starved to death on the streets.

Lily leans over the table and kisses Shell's cheek. "You're so brave," she whispers. "It was so hard to keep that from you all morning and last night."

Brick shakes Shell's hand. "I'm so glad you came to our camp. You've become a good friend to me."

"And so have you," Shell says, shaking Brick's hand with a firm grip, sensing that Brick has more to say.

A moment later, Shell is interrupted as the rest of the campers line up to show Shell their approval as well. A couple of the elder women weep over the emotion of it all, including Rain, who huddles in closer to Mason.

"We're proud of you," Mason says.

Shell stands in respect to shake Mason's hand. "Thank you for everything," he says.

Mason smiles and nods, the glint in his pale blue eyes just a little bit brighter than usual. He scratches at his facial scruff, at the tuft of silvery hair to match the longish mane he's got tied back with an elastic band. The happy couple leaves, enabling the remaining campers to relax a bit. Bottles of cider and containers of fruit cookies are brought out from the pantry. There's cheering and kissing and hugging—everyone taking part in the celebration.

"I love you," Lily says. She wraps her arms around Shell and kisses him full on the lips. But the moment is spoiled by his surprise—she *loves* him? He embraces her nonetheless, grateful for the affection, and glances over her shoulder at Clay, whose eyes appear to burn into the image of the two of them together like that.

stacey

I must have taken a wrong turn on my way to my Holistic Health class. It appears as though I'm in the basement of the science wing, where they do all the lab stuff. I take another turn, down a long, dark hallway—the walls and floor all concrete—and pull my schedule from my pocket. It clearly says that my Holistic Health class is in Room 111, which is why I elected to come down here, but there's no sign of anything— no doors or windows and not a living creature to speak of. It's almost as if I'm between two buildings, in an underground tunnel maybe.

I walk quickly, the clunk of my shoes making an echoing sound. I'm hoping to get to the other wing before I'm late for class, but it seems the farther I get, the darker the tunnel becomes.

"Hello?" I call out, my voice echoing. I stop a moment, my heart pumping hard, and turn to look behind me. But it's just as dark; I can barely see my hand in front of my face.

I turn back around. There's a light of some sort at the very end of the tunnel—a bright, blazing whiteness that glows, like fireworks.

"Stacey," whispers a female voice.

I move toward the light, toward her voice, squinting to try and see something, to try and make out any movement. A chill runs over my shoulders. I wrap my sweatshirt tightly around me, noticing how I can't stop shaking, how everything smells like citrus.

"Stacey," she whispers again.

"Who are you?" I ask.

Her shadow passes before the light, causing a flickering. "Come this way or you will pay."

I move closer, wondering if she's on the other side now, hoping it might be the way out.

"Come this way or you will pay," she repeats.

She has a child's voice, but I don't recognize it. "Who are you?" I demand, confident that it isn't Maura.

She appears before the light once more and I'm able to see her silhouette. She has long, flowing hair that blows back with the intensity of the glow. It appears as though she's draped in a gown of some sort, and she's carrying something—maybe a stick or a wand. It has long, star-like spikes that spout from the tip.

"I'm not coming any farther unless you tell me who you are," I shout.

She reaches for something in her pocket. I think it's a ball. She sets it on the ground and I hear it roll toward me— a low, pattering sound against the ground. As it gets closer, I notice that it's making a trail of liquid. I reach down to stop the ball from rolling, but just as I do, it sinks into the rising stream, as though it's sprung a leak.

"Why the frown? Scared to drown?"

"No!" I shriek from the mere toxicity of the word *drown*.

I go to step out of the water, but it's all around me now, up to my ankles and getting deeper by the moment. I reach down into the water again, in search of the ball, hoping that if I pull it out, the water will stop. I think I feel it; there's a round, rubbery object by my left calf. I go to pull it upward, but something grabs my wrists. I hear myself scream out. Water flows in harder, up to my knees now. Using all the strength in my legs, I pull upward. There's a pair of the palest hands wrapped around my wrists. It's the girl. She's strong, almost stronger than me, and she wants to pull me under.

"No!" I scream out. My breath quickens. My legs shake. I twist and turn my wrists, trying to pry her away. I kick around under the water, but the weight of the rippling stream makes it difficult.

Taking a giant breath, I anchor my weight into my feet and thrust my arms upward. The girl's grip on my wrists breaks and I see the water wave, a giant ripple that crashes against my thighs. There's a glow of light that swims its way up the stream, beneath the water, back toward the source of light at the end of the tunnel.

"Who are you?" I shout out.

It's silent for several seconds, but then I hear her breathe; it's all around me. "I may look like a little girl to you, but I'm really a mother of a girl so blue. She needs your help, that's no lie. And if you don't, that boy will die."

"Die?" I ask. "Who?"

"Dead, dead, dead, dead, dead," she sings.

I wake up with a gasp. The phone is ringing. Amber is sitting beside me in bed. And I'm still breathing hard.

"Stacey," Amber says, squeezing my hand. "Are you okay?"

I shake my head, trying to get a grip.

"Don't freakin' tell me," Amber says. "Another nightmare?"

I nod.

"Holy freaking funk." She pulls at her cherry-red pigtails in frustration. "Not again." The phone is still ringing. Amber grabs it. "Hello?" She looks at me and shakes her head. "She can't make it to the phone right now—she's got a raging hangover." Amber holds the phone away from her ear and gags a few times to make the excuse sound legit. "Not pretty," she explains to the caller. "Can I take a message? I'll have her call you when she's done dry-heaving." Amber winks at me, grabbing Janie's grocery-labeling marker from atop the fridge. She writes the message across her palm, grimacing the whole time.

"I can't believe you just did that," I say, once she's hung up.

"You have bigger flounder to fry, sweet pea."

"Why? What's up?"

"President's office, that's what."

"Oh my god." I look at the clock—it's after four. "I missed the meeting."

"What meeting?"

"It doesn't even matter." I take a deep breath, noticing how my legs still feel like they're shaking.

"What doesn't?" She plops back down beside me. "Stacey, what's going on?"

"I don't know. All I know is that I'm having nightmares again."

"Yeah, but no visible spew." Amber takes a moment to inspect me. "No blood, no urine, no bodily excrement to speak of. A good sign, no?"

In the past several years, Amber's seen me have several bouts of nightmares—recurring dreams that turned out to be premonitions warning me that something horrible was going to happen. Each time my body would have a physical side effect—impromptu bedwetting one time; projectile vomiting the next; nosebleeds, nine months later. Years before I'd met her, when my nightmares first started, they were accompanied by horrible crippling headaches. Eventually I realized that each reaction was my body's way of forcing me to deal with my premonitions and, at the same time, lead me to the answers—to what I needed to do to stop the impending danger.

"Maybe it was just a random nightmare," I say. "Maybe it wasn't a premonition at all." But why am I still shaking? And why do I feel so cold?

"Yeah. I mean, unless there's a present in your pants that you're not telling me about—" she slides a few inches away on the bed—"I wouldn't worry about it."

"You're so gross."

"*Me*? You're the one with the present."

"There *is* no present," I snap, shifting a bit in my seat, just to be sure. "But I don't know. It felt like a premonition. It was like she wanted me to join her, to be with her."

"Who?"

I shake my head and swallow hard, pulling the bed covers around my shoulders to temper the chill. "She sounded young, like eight or nine, but then she said she was a mother of a girl so blue, a girl who needs help . . . or else some boy will die."

"Slow down," Amber says. "You dreamt about *blue people*? Are you sure they weren't green and driving a flying saucer?"

"Be serious," I say.

"I'm trying."

I sigh. "I know; it doesn't make sense and it certainly doesn't help that she was speaking in rhyme."

"Rhyme? Are you sure you didn't maybe just take some of Janie's funny dust before bed?"

"You know me better than that," I say, thinking about my bottle of tranquilizers.

"I'm kidding, of course," Amber says. "Did it sound at all like—"

"Maura?" I ask.

Amber nods.

I shake my head and look away.

Maura was the little girl I used to baby-sit five years ago. I ignored the premonitions I was having about her, telling myself that they were insignificant, that they were just a bad bout of dreams. The next thing I knew, Maura was missing; she'd been abducted, the victim of a pedophile. Shortly after, her body was found in an old, abandoned shed in the woods.

Three years later, I was having nightmares about Drea. I dreamt that she was going to be killed by a mysterious stalker. In the end, I was able to save Drea, but I wasn't able to save Veronica Leeman, a classmate who got herself mixed up in the stalking. I found her body on the floor of our French classroom. She'd been hit over her head; there was a pool of blood surrounding her neck and shoulders. Sometimes when I close my eyes, I can still see her looking up at me, her piercing emerald-green eyes disappointed that I didn't get there in time.

This past summer I lost Jacob, my one and only soul mate. I was so preoccupied trying to save Clara, a girl I'd just met, that I couldn't save *him*. Shortly after I arrived at the cottage on Cape Cod, I started having nightmares about

Clara—that she was going to drown, that her body would be washed up on the beach. I kept getting this tightness in my chest, nearly cutting off my breath. I chocked the feeling up to stress—to the pressure of trying to save Clara's life. But I knew there was something more. I just wasn't able to figure it out. I didn't spend enough time listening to my body and what it was trying to tell me.

And now Jacob's gone.

I close my eyes, remembering the stream of water running through my nightmare, wondering what it's supposed to symbolize. And then it hits me.

"Stacey?" Amber asks. She rubs my back, the way Drea used to. "Are you okay?"

I nod and wipe at my eyes, my heart rapping hard inside my chest. "It's Jacob."

"What's Jacob?"

"My nightmares . . . the water . . ."

"What water?"

"There was water in my dream. Maybe it's supposed to represent the ocean. Maybe there's something Jacob wants me to know."

"Stacey," Amber says, taking my hands. "Listen to yourself. I mean, I know you've been through a lot, but you're starting to sound like a loon."

"You don't understand," I say, snatching my hands away. "I haven't dreamt in *months*."

"*And?*"

"And, now that I am, maybe I'll dream about Jacob."

"I think you're overanalyzing this," Amber says. "You know as well as I do that not all dreams are premonitions. I mean, I have nightmares all the time—about getting warts on my ass, about going to class dressed in my mother's granny-panties—but it's not like those things would *ever* happen."

"I can't believe you're saying this—after everything I've been through. My dreams are *real.*"

"I didn't say they weren't."

"Then what? If there's a chance that I can be with Jacob again—even in my dreams—I'll take it. Can't you understand that?"

"Sure, but don't you think if this were truly about Jacob, the dreams would be all squishy and romantic? Not about some pale-ass death-girl who chants in twisted rhyme about some blue girl. I mean, I hate to sound like a mega-beeatch or anything, but just because you dream about water, it doesn't mean that you're dreaming about Jacob."

I take a giant breath. "It's not *just* about the water," I say. "What about the boy?"

"What boy?"

"I told you." I sigh. "The boy who might die if I don't help the girl-so-blue. What if that boy is Jacob?"

"Stacey, honey—Jacob's already dead. I know you don't want to hear that or deal with it or whatever, but he is."

"Believe whatever you want," I snap, "but I think the mere fact that I'm dreaming again is a good thing . . . a hopeful thing."

"I guess," Amber says, propping herself up on her elbows, looking at me like I'm a giant puzzle.

I reach into the fridge for something cold, wet, and fizzy, forgetting for a second that its contents are labeled and spoken for. I slam the door shut and collapse back in bed, trying to put Amber's doubt out of my head, trying instead to trust my instincts.

stacey

Amber makes a deal with me: if I agree to go straighten things out with Mr. President, she'll agree to treat me to a chocodile sundae at Ice Cream Coma downtown—a fair deal, especially considering that the tuna sandwich Amber brought back for me from the cafeteria last night is now warm and fuzzy. Not to mention that I really would like to get all this president business straightened out. Suddenly the idea of going back home, having to face a much-disappointed mother who never even had the opportunity to go to college, let alone to do so on a free ride, isn't so appealing.

I phone the president's secretary back and she gets all snippy with me, telling me that Dr. Wallace waited over a half-hour for my arrival before heading off to a meeting, for which he ended up late—on my account, of course. I try to slip in an apology, but she's talking so fast, going through his jam-packed schedule, reiterating how busy Dr. Wallace is, how he doesn't have time to wait around and meet with tardy students. Finally she finds me another open slot, apparently squeezing me in before his meeting with the college provost.

"Can you be here in an hour?" she asks.

I grunt out an affirmative, hang up, and then dial in to get my phone messages. I have four of them—one from my mother, one from Drea, another from Chad, and one from the Student Activities Director, announcing the week's worth of on-campus festivities. I delete Mr. Student Activities' voice right away and focus on the others. Drea and I have been best friends since our freshman year of high school. She and Chad, her on-again-now-off-again boyfriend, my *ex*-boyfriend, went off to Payton College this past September, over four hundred miles away. They both want me to call them back, but it doesn't sound like it's anything big. Ever since Jacob's disappearance, they've made it a habit to call me every couple days to see how I'm doing—to be sure I'm still breathing, more likely. My mother wants me to call her back as well. Unfortunately, they'll all have to wait.

I head over to the main campus to search for his office. Standing in front of the student center, facing the tall iron clock, as Amber suggested, I take a deep breath and look down at my campus map. The place is absolutely huge, like Hillcrest Prep times twenty. There are buildings scattered all about—ivy-covered brick ones, a couple bulky glass ones, tall ones, short ones, and a bunch of cobblestone revivals in between. Amber's marked a giant red *X* over the quad area, and drawn a winding line that leads me to Ketcher Hall. It appears as though my most direct route involves walking up three brick pathways, crossing one duck pond, going across one footbridge, and cutting through two playing fields. I sigh at just the thought of it. If I start now, I should be able to get there in just under an hour and, hopefully, I won't turn into a Popsicle along the way—it's got to be at least ten below with the wind.

"Are you lost?" I look up from the map. There's a guy standing there. He's dressed from hat to hiking boot in Gap-like attire—weathered baseball cap, artfully faded teal-blue sweatshirt under an equally faded charcoal pea coat, and khaki cargo pants.

"What?" I ask, even though I clearly heard him.

"You look a little lost. Are you a freshman?" He adjusts his cap, his short, gelled-up brown hair sticking out just a bit on the sides.

"Is it that obvious?"

He smiles, his muddy-brown eyes squinting ever so slightly. "Don't worry. It'll be our little secret."

"Well, I hate secrets."

"Then I'll tell everyone I know." He turns, looking around until he spots someone familiar. "Hey, Nelson," he calls out. "I found myself a lost freshman."

"That's nice," Nelson shouts back.

"I should probably go," I say, suddenly feeling a bit awkward.

"Wait," he says. "What are you looking for?"

"Ketcher Hall."

"Sure." He explains the route, using my map, adding only that I should watch my step while walking across the duck pond because the bridge is sometimes slippery with ice. "I'd take you over to Ketcher myself, but I'm already late for a meeting," he says.

"I'll be fine. You've been a big help." I go to turn away, but he stops me with a touch to my forearm.

"I don't even know your name," he says.

I pull away, feeling even more uncomfortable. "Stacey."

"Well, it's great to meet you, Stacey. I'm Tim." He extends his hand for a shake, a broad smile across his face. "Maybe I'll see you around some time."

I fake a slight smile and turn on my heel, grateful to get away. It's not that I think he had any weird motives; it's just . . . I don't know. I don't want anyone to get the wrong idea about me. Not that he would. I mean, let's face it—I look like Morticia Addams without her makeup.

After just twenty minutes or so of walking, I spot Ketcher Hall just up ahead. I eke the heavy wooden doors open and ascend a shiny mahogany staircase, the smell of old pine mixed in mahogany wood all around me. I arrive in a large, open waiting area and Ms. McNeal, a stout, gray-haired woman wearing a tan corduroy dress, tells me to sit a moment while she checks to see if the president is ready to see me. The place is oppressively dark, lit only with soft yellow lamps. There's classical music playing in the background and thick, velvety curtains that line the windows and block out the light. I pick a spot on a shiny leather couch with tarnished-gold studded trim, noticing how the floor creaks beneath my step.

There's another girl here as well, maybe fourteen or fifteen years old at most. She's dressed in dark layers—a mixture of smoky gray and navy blue. Her long blond hair hangs in her face, her eyes barely peeking out from the bangs. She's sitting on the floor in the corner of the room with books propped up all around her—to block what's she's doing maybe. She catches me looking at her and narrows her eyes at me.

"Stacey?" Ms. McNeal calls out from her desk. "Dr. Wallace will see you now."

I feel my eyebrows furrow slightly. "She was here before me," I say, gesturing to the girl.

"Don't worry about her," Ms. McNeal says. "She's fine."

The girl gives me a dirty look. She drags her barricade of books inward, like this is grammar school and she's a seven-year-old. It almost tempts me to go over there and sneak a peek at what she's doing. Ms. McNeal opens Dr. Wallace's office door wide and clears her throat, perhaps trying to get me to hurry up.

I move into his office and Ms. McNeal closes the door behind me, leaving Dr. Wallace and me alone. He looks much different than I imagined, not the white-haired, wool-suited, bifocal-wearing college president that I was expecting. Except for the giant giraffe tie he's sporting, he looks almost normal—medium height, salt-and-peppery dark hair, and black wire-rimmed glasses.

"Stacey," he says, standing up from his desk. He drops the Magic 8 Ball he's holding and extends his hand for a shake. "I'm Dr. Wallace. It's nice to finally meet you."

"Sorry about earlier," I say, noticing how big his office is.

"Not to worry," he says, still shaking my hand. "You're here now; that's what's important."

I nod, trying my best to smile.

"I've heard a lot about you, Stacey Brown."

"You have?"

"Please, sit down," he says, ignoring the question. He finally pulls his hand away and gestures to the buttery leather chairs in front of his desk.

"So," I whisper, practically scrunching down in the seat. The man is openly staring at me—almost as if he's trying to size me up, not in a skeevy way but in a "I want to know what she's about" kind of way.

"Yes," he says, snapping to attention. He leans forward in his chair. "How are you enjoying the campus? Did you get all the classes you wanted?"

I nod, wondering what I'm doing here, why he cares about my schedule. "Do you meet with all the scholarship students?"

Instead of responding, he continues to stare at me, turning my insides to nervous mush.

"I won't miss any more classes," I say, out of nervousness. "My mother really wants me to do this—to be here, I mean."

"You want that too, I hope."

I look toward his Magic 8 Ball, wondering what it says, if there's any prophetic message about my dismal future here. "I guess," I say, finally.

"Not so sure?"

I shrug and look away, feeling suddenly like I'm back in Dr. Atwood's office, being asked to dump all my emotional baggage.

"Well, I know that *I* want you here," Wallace offers. "That's why you got the scholarship."

"Excuse me?" I ask, looking back at him.

He peels open the folder on his desk and begins reading off a list: "Stacey Brown, Hillcrest Prep grad; overall GPA by the end of her senior year at Hillcrest . . . barely a 2.0. No extra-curriculars to speak of; no hardship case; no declared major; and lukewarm recommendations from her teachers."

Huh?

"But," he continues, "despite all that, this same Stacey Brown gets into Beacon University, one of the most competitive universities on the East Coast, along with her good friend Amber, also an underachiever. She gets a full scholarship—both room and board with zero required work-study—and all she has to do is maintain a minimum grade point average of 2.7 or better. Come on," he says, pushing back in his chair, the wheels squeaking slightly, "even my full-ride football players have to maintain GPAs higher than that."

"What are you trying to say?" I ask. "Has there been some mistake?"

"Mistake—no. But it does sound a little unfair, now, doesn't it?"

"I didn't *ask* for any scholarship," I say, hearing the agitation in my voice.

"Don't get me wrong," he says. "I meant it when I said that I want you here. I think you're quite extraordinary; that's *why* you got the scholarship." He closes up my folder and leans forward again to stare at me. "But do I need to remind you that your scholarship is one that needs to be renewed every year . . . pending presidential approval?"

It's then that it hits me—he obviously wants something from me. He's obviously heard about my involvement in the events that occurred at Hillcrest these past couple years.

"It would be a shame to lose such a scholarship—such an opportunity—over something small," he says. "Wouldn't you agree?"

"Small?"

"You believe in helping others, don't you, Stacey?"

I feel my body stiffen in the seat.

Wallace wheels his chair around and points to the wall behind him, where he's got a bunch of framed diplomas hanging—from places like Columbia and Stanford. But then I notice another one—a diploma from Hillcrest, very much like the one I have.

"So you're a Hillcrest grad as well," I say.

He nods. "I've been a devoted and supportive alumnus since graduation, nearly thirty years ago now. Since then, I've kept a hand dipped into the goings-on there, volunteering on various committees."

"So you've probably heard about all the stuff that's happened there."

"One girl, murdered; another, kidnapped and almost killed; one boy arrested and placed in a juvenile detention center for involuntary manslaughter; one man put away for attempted murder; a club dedicated to resurrecting the dead . . ."

I swallow hard, wondering where he's going with all this.

"Rumor has it," he continues, "that you were able to predict it all. Is that true?"

I shrug and look away, wanting more than anything to crawl out of here.

"I think it is," he whispers. "A sixth sense—isn't that what they call it?"

"What do you want?"

"Your help."

"I'm sorry, but I can't even help myself."

"You're my last hope."

"I'm sorry," I repeat. I stand and turn to leave.

"Stacey—wait," he says. "Please, sit down and hear me out."

"I have to go," I say, heading for the door.

"Not yet," he says. "Not until I tell you about my daughter. She's in trouble—and I think you might be able to help her."

I pause just inches from the door and turn back around.

"Did you see that girl out there in the waiting room on your way in?" He's standing now as well. His demeanor has changed—less confident, more desperate. He moves from behind his desk, taking off his glasses and tossing them down atop his ink blotter. "That's my daughter. She has nightmares, too."

Dr. Wallace is clearly upset; his eyes look red and his face is getting more flushed by the moment.

"She's been having them for the past year now," he continues. "At first we thought they were nothing—a reaction maybe to her mother's death. My wife passed away not long ago."

"I'm sorry," I whisper.

He nods and turns away, toward the wall of diplomas, to hide his emotion. "But the nightmares only seem to be getting worse, not better. She says she's dreaming about some camp . . . people working through the night, living backwardly, and stealing. She claims that some boy is going to be murdered . . . and then there's something about a lily."

"Lilies?" My heart speeds up, thinking how I used to dream about lilies, too; how my grandmother taught me that lilies mean death.

"Well, just *one* lily, I think," Dr. Wallace explains. "I think it might be someone's name, but I'm not sure. It's so hard to keep track of it all. The nightmares have really changed her. It's like her body's still there, but her eyes . . . it's as if they're vacant."

I open my mouth to say something, but I really don't know what—what he wants from me, what words will make it all better. I wish I could tell him that the nightmares will go away one day, but I know firsthand that isn't true.

"I'm sorry," he says, turning back to me. "I've been out of line."

"It's okay."

"So will you help me?"

"Help you?"

"We've been to several doctors—psychiatrists, neurologists, acupuncturists, you name it."

"And?"

"And they want to put her away." He pauses to take a breath. "They think institutionalizing her is the best answer."

"I'm sorry to hear that, but what does it have to do with me?"

"You could work with her as a peer. You've been through this."

"I have a lot on my plate right now."

"I don't know what else to do," he says. "I'm afraid I'm going to lose her completely. I think she's starting to believe the doctors when they say she's sick."

"I have to go," I say, feeling a tightening sensation in my chest.

"Stacey—please," he insists. "You're my last hope."

Shell

After the celebration, everyone in the community sixteen years old and older disperses to go about their daily chores, while the younger children scamper off to the elder cabin for their daily lessons. Both Shell and Brick have the grueling task of chopping wood for the evening's fire. Despite his sore and calloused hands, Shell happily works his way through the pile of wood, the image of Lily alive in his mind.

Did she really mean it when she told him she loved him? There's a part of him that hopes she did. But how could she? Even though they've known each other for several months now, until these past couple weeks, she hasn't paid him much attention.

"That was a great celebration," Brick says.

Shell nods in agreement, his mind wandering a moment to the old couple's cottage, the one he almost raided.

"You did good," Brick continues. "Everyone's really proud of you."

"Thanks," Shell says, remembering the pocket watch he found and the message inside—*To Candace, forever, with love*. He wonders why it upset him so. But maybe the pocket watch isn't the problem at all. He's heard before that people who find themselves victimized often try to tell their perpetrators bits of personal information or show them personal objects so the perpetrator sees them as a real person, making it difficult to commit the crime. Maybe the pocket watch just made the old couple a little too real.

"Most of us wouldn't have been brave enough to follow our convictions," Brick says. "Most of us would have done what we were told."

"*Most of us?*" Shell repeats. "So some of the campers *do* disobey?"

"Only sometimes," Brick says, pausing a moment from chopping. His wavy, blond hair flies back with the wind.

"Have *you* stolen before?"

"It's only stealing if you don't first consider the worth an object has to its owner; that's what Mason says. For example, some people have three or four TVs in their house, but do they really need *all* of them? Probably not. But something personal, something like an heirloom . . . well, that's probably priceless to its owner. It would be stealing to take something like that. Get it?"

Shell shrugs, still a bit confused.

"Mason says that it's human nature to want to give," Brick continues. "The problem is, some people don't *know* they want to give. We help those people; they give to us when we take their extra stuff—their needless possessions. They help us continue in our mission of peace."

Shell nods, mulling over the explanation but still not completely clear about it. After all, who's to say what's needless?

"Everyone was happy that you followed your heart," Brick says, his icy blue eyes tearing up from the cold. "Heart is essential for peace . . . so is bravery. Mason says that all the time, too."

"Mason says a lot, I guess," Shell says, suddenly at a loss for words.

"He thinks that we work well together," Brick says, the tiny gap between his two front teeth just visible in his smile. "He's going to pair us up for chores as often as he can."

Shell smiles back. Brick has become his confidant these past several months, offering tips and assisting with tasks.

"How about a break?" Brick suggests.

Shell nods, more than ready to rest his hands. A couple of his knuckles have started to crack and bleed from the cold.

The two sit down on a log, breaking out their day's snack food—homemade granola bars and Thermoses full of hot tea. They sit in silence for several moments and Shell takes a moment to observe their camp. There are eight cabins total: one for Mason and Rain; one for the children and their parents or assigned caregivers; one for the leaders just under Mason (campers like Clay); one for the elder women, sometimes used as an infirmary; one for the remaining females (campers like Lily and Daisy); another for the remaining males (campers like himself and Brick); and still another with a large kitchen and recreation area. There's also one designated bathroom cabin where people shower and bathe.

The backdrop to the camp is the ocean. There's also an expansive forest that extends to the right, just beyond their chopping station. After his first few weeks here, Brick told Shell that Mason inherited the land from Rosa, his late wife. Apparently the land had been in her family for generations and, when she died, Mason got to keep it all. Shell pauses a moment at the chainlink fence that surrounds the camp and the barbed wire that winds around it at the very top. He's wanted to ask Brick about it for a while now, but he's still not sure how much he can trust him.

"Look," Brick says, interrupting Shell's thoughts. He points up at the sky. Despite the early hour, the moon has made its appearance, just above the barren trees. A pale grayish sliver, approaching first quarter. "It's waxing," Brick says. "A good time to wish for something."

"And what should we wish for?" Shell asks.

"What else but peace?" Brick says.

"Peace," Shell repeats in agreement.

"Peace will set us free." Brick picks up a couple rocks from the ground, a stark white one with a flat surface and the other with a pointed end. Using the point, he scratches across the surface of the flat white rock, creating a five-pointed star surrounded by a circle. "It's a pentacle," Brick says. "Each point represents something different—earth, air, fire, water, and spirit. The circle is for the spirit's endless love." He flips the rock and draws another star, taking his time with each point. "See," Brick says, "when you draw it like this, from left to right, it empowers you to make something happen—to bring about change . . . *good* change."

"Are you a witch?" Shell asks, trying to remember where he's seen the symbol before, wondering where he's heard about pentacle invocation.

Brick nods. "Don't tell anyone, though. I'm not sure how the elders would like it. Rain caught me doing a soap spell once with tea leaves and a hand-rolled candle. She flipped out and went to Mason. Some people are afraid of what they don't know, you know. They don't understand how peaceful Wicca really is."

Shell agrees. He picks up a couple rocks and does the same, drawing a pentacle across the surface and silently praying for peace.

Shell

In the kitchen, the female campers prepare the evening meal—chicken drumsticks, pickled beets, and mashed potatoes. There are candles and lanterns placed on the table and countertops for extra light, and the fireplace is blazing for added warmth. Shell stands in front of it, rubbing his palms together, feeling the heat of the fire against his face.

"Hungry?" Daisy asks him.

Shell nods, his stomach growling from the mere smell of the cooking. He glances over at the stove where Daisy checks the doneness of a potato with her fork. Though the cabins themselves are pretty primitive, they do have some amenities, like heat and electricity supplied by a generator, and a well for water. Still, they conserve whenever they can so as not to be wasteful.

Shell jumps suddenly, feeling a tap on his shoulder. He whirls around to find Clay right behind him.

"Sorry," Clay says. "I didn't mean to startle you. Do you have a second? We need to talk."

Shell nods, following Clay into the living room area, just behind the kitchen. Clay takes a seat on the thick, velvety plum-purple carpet Rain brought back from the trading field last month; it's a perfectly good oriental piece with barely any wear and no stains to speak of. She apparently traded it for a pair of aquamarine earrings and a handmade rolling pin that Mason crafted himself.

"We're going out tonight," Clay says.

"Where?" Shell asks.

Instead of answering, Clay gestures for Shell to have a seat. Shell surveys the room for his options—a patched-up beanbag chair, an iron park bench, and on the rug opposite Clay. He opts for the bench, figuring that, from the graveness of Clay's present demeanor, he could use the extra stability.

"The only reason I'm telling you ahead of time is because I don't want you to become alarmed right in the midst of things and upset the other campers; I need them on my side tonight."

"How would I upset them?" Shell asks. He reaches into his pocket to hold the rock he scratched earlier, the one with the pentacle. He grips it hard, soaking up the natural energy, willing inner peace.

"You're still fairly new here," Clay explains. "You're still learning about our community . . . growing into our world of peace." He pauses a moment to admire the crackling of the fire and the orange glow of the logs.

"I'm learning every day," Shell says, hoping to reassure Clay of whatever reservations he may have about him.

"Of course you are." Clay turns back to smile at him. "And you're doing a good job of it. It's just, even though you've only been here a handful of months, I've noticed that you carry a lot of influence here. Campers are drawn to you. Take Lily, for instance."

Shell clamps the rock even harder, having feared this very moment. "What about her?"

"I'm curious about your intentions for her."

"I like Lily," Shell says, swallowing hard.

"A lot?"

"Is that a problem?"

"If it's the truth, it isn't," Clay says. "You should never be afraid of the truth."

"It is the truth," Shell says.

Clay nods, a dead stare to his eyes. "That's what I thought." He clears his throat and looks away. "I just wanted to be sure. And I wanted to tell you about tonight. Lily will be there and I know she's fond of you. I'd hate for you to influence her in a way that might keep us from our peaceful mission. Understand?"

"I'm not sure," Shell says, shaking his head, completely confused. "Would you prefer it if I didn't go?"

"Of course not. You of all people *need* to be there. How else will you learn our peaceful ways?" Clay stands, looking back at Shell. "You're going to do very well here. I'm sure of it."

•   •   •

Late that night, Clay, Lily, Brick, Shell, and Daisy cram themselves into the community car, a creamy beige Grand Marquis with scratches all over the hood and a Cape Cod bumper sticker on the rear with a giant smiling crab. Dressed in dark clothing, from knitted hats to winter gloves and boots, the group is well equipped with duffel bags, flashlights, and tools for breaking and entering.

Clay is driving. He waves to the campers on patrol duty—those who've been assigned to stay up and watch over the camp tonight—and then pulls out into the driveway.

"Is the camp patrolled every night?" Shell asks Brick, wondering if they're carrying weapons.

Brick nods. "Just in case."

"In case *what*?" Shell whispers.

But Brick doesn't answer Shell's question. He just continues to eyeball Clay in the rearview mirror.

Frustrated by the silence and a bit uncomfortable with the tense energy in the car, Shell stares out the window the whole way, trying his best to relax, wondering what the patrolling is all about. How would anyone even find their place? And what would they possibly want to take from it? It's not as though they're rich with possessions.

They pass by the honey farm where the owners—an old German couple, according to Brick—raise bees and sell candles. Shell memorizes street signs they pass, trying to get a firmer idea of where he is. It's a good ten minutes before he's able to see much more than barren trees and vacant streets.

"There's the Bargo Tower," Brick says, pointing out the window.

They come to a stop light at the end of the street. There's a tall brick tower standing high atop a hill, just to the right of them. Shell has to scrunch down in his seat and look up to appreciate its height.

"You can see the whole cape from the top," Brick says.

Shell nods, making the mental note, noticing the Brutus town sign that sits at the base of the hill.

They drive for another half hour at least, passing through two more towns, and finally cruising through a residential area. Clay slows the car and clicks off the headlights. "The family who lives at this house is away all week," he says, steering the car down a long, narrow road. He orders the campers to open their doors slightly, so as not attract attention or make any noise, and then he pulls up in front of a medium-sized cottage set a good distance away from the other houses on the street.

"How do you know?" Shell asks, noticing how the interior car light fails to go on despite the open doors—as though someone removed the bulb.

"I've been watching it." Clay points toward the front of the house. "Check it out—shades drawn down, curtains closed, lights turned off, and a collection of rolled-up newspapers strewn about the stairs. They haven't been around since Monday."

"Let's go!" Daisy cheers, pulling her ski mask down over her face.

The tension suddenly melted, the others follow suit with their masks—all except Shell.

"Come on," Lily coaxes him. "It'll be fun. We're giving this family an opportunity to share with us. It's beautiful, don't you think?"

Shell wants to believe her, but it still doesn't make sense to him. Maybe this family doesn't have the resources to give. Maybe they just barely make ends meet.

"Look at the exterior of the house," Clay says, regarding Shell. "It's mint. The walkway and driveway have been plowed. No paint chipping or peeling to speak of. No rot. Holiday wreath on the door. These people have it good."

But how can Clay tell all that in the darkness? There's a solitary street lamp, but it's several houses away.

"I don't think I want to go," Shell says, finally, reminded of his first break-in at the old couple's house—the fear he felt in the pit of his stomach. "Is it okay if I wait here?"

"No," Clay snaps. "It *isn't* okay."

"It was okay before," Shell ventures, more confused.

"*Before*, you were willing to try. You went into the house. It wasn't a blind decision. Now, you're refusing to participate before even stepping a foot inside. How are you going to learn our peaceful ways if you block yourself off from what we're trying to teach you?"

Shell looks to Brick for reassurance. "You can stick with me," Brick says.

"And me!" Lily beams. She rests her head on his shoulder and bats her eyes up at him from behind the mask.

"Okay," Shell says, comforted by the feel of Lily's head against his shoulder. "I'll go."

"That's all we ask." Clay smiles, clicking the ignition off, and reminds everybody to leave the car doors slightly ajar.

They sneak around the side of the house to the back, where it's even darker. Using his flashlight, Clay looks around the door for a key, checking under the doormat and running his fingers atop the door ledge.

"Found it," Daisy whispers, holding the key out for show. Apparently it'd been hidden in the planter at the foot of the stairs.

Clay plucks it out of her hand, unlocks the door, and the group enters, locking the door back up behind them. "Okay," Clay says. "You know the rules—be quick, be selective, and leave things as you found them. Sometimes these people are so prepared to give, they don't even notice when something's missing."

While Daisy and Lily scamper off down the hall and Clay remains in the kitchen area, Shell sticks close to Brick. They begin in the family room. Brick unzips his duffel bag and disconnects the family's DVD player, as though he's an old pro. "You don't have to take anything if you don't feel comfortable," Brick whispers. "I'll just say you helped me with this stuff." He checks the drawers, loading his bag with a handful of DVDs, a remote control, and a portable CD player.

A few moments later, Lily enters the room, duffel bag already full. "Come on," she whispers to Shell, dropping her bag, taking his hand, and leading him down the hallway, into what appears to be the master bedroom. She pulls him into a walk-in closet, clicks on the light, and closes the door. "They must be super rich," she says, "like movie stars." She pulls off her ski mask and grabs a mink stole from the hanger. She slips it around her shoulders, adding a matching mink hat and a beaded bag with rhinestone detail to enhance the look. "How do I look?"

Shell has to admit that she couldn't look more beautiful. It isn't the clothes per se; it's the way she wears them and how happy she is.

Lily snags a man's scarf from a hanger, a charcoal-gray one with black stitching. She pulls off Shell's ski mask, drapes the scarf around his neck and pulls him close, staring into his silvery blue eyes and running her fingers through his short dark hair. "I meant what I said before, you know," she says. "I love you . . . with all my heart." With that, she kisses him—a long, soft kiss that reminds him of warm honey. She smells like honey, too, like cinnamon French toast and hot maple syrup. Shell wonders when was the last time he's tasted something so wonderful.

"We're leaving," Daisy says, knocking on the door.

Lily breaks the embrace and her smile wilts. "I shouldn't take this stuff, should I?" she says, referring to the clothing. "It would be vain to keep such beautiful things, and I don't have the heart to sell them."

"I guess," Shell says.

"But maybe they wouldn't notice . . . "

"How about you just take one thing," Shell suggests, wanting more than anything to see her happy again, to see that glow about her.

Lily smiles and kisses him once more. "You're such a beautiful soul," she says, "like no one I've ever met." She carefully returns the stole and purse to their hangers, but saves the hat for herself, stuffing it into her pocket. "I want you to have this as well," she says, snagging the wool scarf from around his neck. She crams it into his pocket and the two exit the closet, joining the others out in the kitchen, holding hands and blushing with happiness.

stacey

After my meeting with President Wallace, I come straight back to the dorm and grab my bowlful of lavender pellets. I rub the individual bits between the tips of my fingers, the sweet herbal scent rising up, helping to calm me a little.

But it isn't enough. I unclasp the amulet necklace from around my neck. It's a tiny emerald-green bottle made out of sea glass and threaded through a silver chain. My mother bought it for me on my last birthday. I pop its tiny cork and spill a few droplets of lavender oil onto my finger. I dab at the pulse points on my neck, willing the homey scent to ground me even a little.

Both Amber and Janie have left notes for me. Janie is at a faith club meeting and Amber went to boy shop. I crumple the notes up, imagining Amber traipsing around from floor to floor, sporting a push-up bra and some skimpy form of faux animal skin to cover her fanny, searching for some serious male attention.

And why not? Isn't that what college is supposed to be about? Having fun, meeting new people, hooking up with random hotties, and partying from late Thursday night until early Sunday morning?

But instead I'm here. I pop one of my tranquilizers and lay back in bed, wanting more than anything to fall asleep, to dream about water again—to see if Jacob will make an appearance in my dreams.

I spend the next few days in bed, getting up only to raid the candy and soda machines in the dorm room lobby, to go to the bathroom, pop more pills, and defend myself from Amber's wrath. But I don't dream—not even a little.

"You smell!" Amber shouts on day four of my bed binge. "When was the last time you bathed?"

I respond by pulling a stick of rosewood incense from my drawer. I light it, waving the smoke toward her side of the room. "Better?"

"Janie doesn't even want to sleep here," she says. "Your stench is funking up her brain even more. She says she's been getting headaches all week because of you."

I roll over in bed, my back facing her, and tug the blankets up over my head.

"Don't think you're gonna skip your classes again," she says, tug-of-war-pulling the covers from me. "It's 9 AM—don't you have a class at 10?"

I shrug.

"Perfect. Just enough time to get that bubble butt of yours out of bed, into the shower, and into some clean clothes. You can snatch one of Janie's Gogurts on the way out; we'll tell her one of the dorm rats ate it."

"Maybe tomorrow." I sigh. "I want to sleep."

"Are you kidding? You've been coma-queen for days."

"Leave me alone," I say.

"You really want to go back home?" she asks, winning the tug-of-war fight over my covers. "Because that's exactly what's going to happen."

I reach for the bottle of tranquilizers stashed under my pillow, noticing that I've taken them all, that the bottle is empty. A whole month's worth used up in a handful of days. I won't be able to call in a new prescription for another couple of weeks.

"Well?" she asks.

"I already have a mother, thanks."

"Have you talked to her lately? Does she know you're funking up your chances here, that you're going to flunk out of college without having ever made it to class? I mean, you're starting to make *me* look good." Amber comes and sits on the corner of my bed. "Is that why the president wanted to see you the other day?"

I shake my head and move to sit up. "He wants me to help his daughter."

"What's wrong with her?"

I let out a sigh and tell her about his manipulative little plan—how he plotted to get me here and that's why I got the scholarship. "I should have known something was up," I say. "Nobody with high school grades like mine gets into a place like this."

"I did," Amber perks.

I bite the inside of my cheek, stopping myself from mentioning that Dr. Wallace brought her name up in our conversation, that he implied he knew we were good friends, and *that's* why she got in.

"So what's the story with his daughter?"

"Apparently she's having nightmares."

"Nightmares like yours—dead bodies, pools of blood, little girls chanting in freakish rhyme . . . ?"

I nod.

"Sucks for her," Amber says. She leans over to reach for the mini-fridge, opening the door wide to survey all of Janie's prized goodies. She thieves a Popsicle from the freezer section and tears off the paper, popping the icy end into her mouth and sucking at the bright cherry redness. "So what are you going to do about it?"

"What do you mean?"

"I mean, are you going to help her?"

I snatch the covers from the foot of the bed and drag them back up to my chin. "I can barely even get out of bed."

"Can barely or *won't ever?"*

"What's that supposed to mean?" I snap.

"Don't get me wrong." She points the Popsicle for emphasis. "I mean, I love you like a sister, and I know this is going to sound much bitchier than I mean it to, but you're even more deflated now than you were this summer—like Spidey over there the morning after a good night." She gestures to the blow-up doll on her bed and then holds her Popsicle out to me for a lick. "Sugar high?"

"No, thanks," I say, noticing how her teeth and tongue have turned fireball red.

"Why don't you give Dr. Atwood a call?" she suggests. "Aren't you supposed to be continuing your therapy?"

"Maybe I don't feel like listening to the tone of her disappointed voice."

Amber sighs. "She's not the only one who's disappointed, you know."

"What do you mean?"

She shrugs.

"Spill it," I insist.

"It's just . . . you used to be my rock, Stacey, my hero—the bravest person I knew. It didn't matter what was going on in your life or how stressed out you got . . . you still saved the day. I mean, I know you have a lot to deal with right now and I know it takes time, it's just . . . instead of moving forward even a little, I feel like you're slipping back."

"Well, I'm sorry," I say, feeling my teeth clench, "but guess what? I'm not some superhero; I'm a real person with real emotions and real feelings." I take a deep breath, trying to melt away some of the tension in my chest.

"That's not what I mean."

"Oh, no?" I ask. "Don't you understand? Jacob is missing—"

"Not this again!" she snaps. "He's gone, Stacey—*gone* . . . as in *dead*. When is it going to click?"

I shake my head, fighting the urge to cover my ears.

"But you're still here," she continues. "And so am I. And I want to help you; I want you to get through this."

"I really don't feel like talking right now," I say, looking away.

"I'm sorry. I just want you to get better."

"No," I snap, turning back to face her. "I'm the one who's sorry. I'm sorry that I came here. I'm sorry that I can't be a hero for you, a success story for Dr. Atwood, a perfect daughter for my mother, or now, a *savior* for President Wallace's daughter."

"Stacey—"

"Just leave me alone." I lay back down in bed, drawing the covers over my face to block her out. All I need right now is to fall back asleep—to try, once again, to find Jacob in my dreams.

stacey

I toss and turn in bed after Amber leaves, trying to fall back asleep, but I can't. I just can't stop thinking about everything she said—that she once thought of me as her hero, the bravest person she knew, and that I've suddenly been plucked from that position, whether I like it or not.

I sit up in bed, wishing I had one of my tranquilizer friends to help me get over this hump, but I don't. And so I decide to do the one thing I have yet to embark upon since first setting foot on this campus . . . the bravest thing I can think of.

I go to class.

According to my schedule, I have forty-five minutes until Life Science. I fish a clean sweatshirt and pair of jeans from my unpacked suitcase and rush down the hallway for a shower and tooth-brushing, almost plowing down a girl who fits the description of Sage, Janie's old roommate, along the way—a walking cliché of black clothes, black hair, pasty white skin highlighted by layers upon layers of charcoal-colored eye makeup, and lots of silver jewelry. Her stereotypical appearance makes me wonder if she's one of those Wiccan wannabes, the kind who knows nearly nil about the Craft but decides it would be cool to practice it anyway. It also makes me wonder if there's some truth to all those rumors.

Less than forty minutes later, I fly through the doors of the Stratcher Science Building. The classroom is packed—at least thirty students flipping back and forth through notebooks, pointing at diagrams in their textbooks, and quizzing each other with flashcards. I take one of the only two available desks toward the back of the classroom.

"What's with the study frenzy?" I ask the girl sitting beside me.

"Are you kidding?" She raises her barbell-pierced eyebrow for emphasis. "Today's the quiz."

Quiz? "But this is only the third time this class has met."

"It's on the syllabus."

Great. I chew at my lower lip, fighting the urge to bury my face in my hands.

Barbell-girl must notice my lip-sweat. She lets out an evil little smirk, raising her barbell up even higher.

"What's it on?" I ask.

She flashes me an index card, where's she got the words Unit Membrane written across the top. There's a couple rows of circles with squiggly lines sandwiched between them, and what looks like a sideways cheeseburger in the middle.

"What is that?" I feel my mouth drop open.

"Didn't you read the section on lipids and proteins? He's also going to include all the nuclear envelope stuff."

Huh? I swallow hard, feeling a sudden heaviness in my chest.

I peer up at the professor as he extracts his books and notes from a weather-beaten leather briefcase, wondering if he'll be understanding about my recent rash of school skipping. He looks kind of young—maybe late twenties at most—so I'm thinking he's one of those graduate student assistants you hear about. The kind that often sits in for the real professor and does all the correcting—all in exchange for a break in tuition and a reference on his résumé.

I approach his desk. "Excuse me . . . are you Professor Rosin's assistant?"

He pauses from unpacking to look up at me, his tiny blue eyes almost lost behind a pair of square black glasses. "No." He cracks his jaw and glances down at his watch. "Next question?"

"Professor Rosin?" I ask, positive that my lip is sweating now for sure.

"Muller," he corrects, resuming his unpacking. "Dr. Wayne Muller—at least, last I checked."

"Right." I glance down at my schedule, noticing that Professor Rosin is the name of my English professor. "Well, um, my name is Stacey Brown. I was sick earlier this week . . . that's why I wasn't here."

Instead of responding, Dr. Muller turns away to write something on the board.

"I understand there's a quiz today," I continue, my voice squeaking slightly out of nervousness.

"You understand correctly, Ms. Brown," he says, scribbling the day's assignment on the board.

"Well, I was just wondering if maybe I could make the quiz up at another time . . . since I was absent. I mean, I don't even have the syllabus."

He turns around to face me, a small menacing smile stretched across his pasty white lips. "This isn't high school, Ms. Brown. Sink or swim." He pulls an extra syllabus from his bag and thrusts it at me.

Huh?

"No life rafts in here." Muller turns his back on me once again, solidifying the obvious—that I'm absolutely screwed and that I absolutely hate him.

A couple minutes later, he passes out the quiz—one long list of words I've never seen before: *chromatin*, *nucleoplasm*, *nucleolus* . . . I glance over at barbell girl, who's obviously whipping right through—it appears as though she's already on the second side.

I sign my name and hand in my automatic F, feeling my cheeks get hot as I walk out of the room.

The remainder of my day's classes are equally as miserable. There was a short personal essay due in my English class—another big fat zero—and I obviously didn't outline the first two chapters for my Intro to Holistic Health class, nor did I single-space-type-out the answers to the chapter review questions at the back of the book.

I take a deep breath, feeling my chest tighten up once again. Apparently a lot of the professors at this college abide by the sink or swim philosophy—a philosophy in which I have obviously sunk.

stacey

I beeline it back to the dorm, almost making it without having to actually talk to anyone. But then I hear my name called out, about halfway up the dormitory steps. I turn and spot him—some guy standing amongst a throng of girls, a giant grin across his face.

"You almost knocked me down," he says, taking a step away from them.

I look at him, feeling my face scrunch up, wondering who in god's name he is.

"Tim," he says, reminding me.

"Right," I say, finally putting the pieces in place—the guy from the other day, the Gap attire, the medium brown gelled-up hair, the way he pointed out the directions to Ketcher Hall using my map.

"Where are you headed?" he asks.

"My room," I say, thinking how it must be obvious.

"How about some food first?"

"*Food*?" I repeat, like it's as foreign of a word as *chromatin* or *nucleoplasm*. I glance toward the pack of girls he was standing with, wondering if he's suddenly forgotten about them. One of them folds her arms in my direction, a huge scowl across her makeup-adorned face.

"Yeah," Tim continues. "Food." He smiles wider, adjusting his cap. "Don't you eat? I have an in with the cafeteria lady—she always saves the fresh stuff for me."

"Sure," I say.

"Great!"

"No. I mean, no."

His face twists up in confusion.

"I mean, sure . . . yeah . . . I eat—all the time, actually. Just not now. I have some serious catching up to do."

"Not on an empty stomach."

"A girl can live on snack food alone."

"Sounds like you speak from experience."

"Ring Dings and Cheez Doodles—basic staples of prep school."

"What kind of a healthy diet is that?" he asks.

"The only kind I have time for—if I want to stay in college for longer than a week, that is."

"Well, then, can I raincheck you? Maybe we could get dinner some time? I wasn't going to mention this," he pauses to glance over both shoulders, "but I also have an in with Pizza Prison across the street. What do you say to Double-Bubble Criminal Crust and Garlic-Cheesy Bankrobber Bread?"

"Excuse me?" I laugh.

"I take it you haven't been there yet."

I shake my head.

"So what do you say?"

I pause a moment to look at him—the way he's beaming at me, how his soft brown eyes crinkle up when he smiles, and how he's doing this cute little back and forth shuffle with his feet. "I have a boyfriend," I say, finally.

"Oh," he says, taking a step back. "Sorry, I didn't mean to—"

"No," I say. "It's fine. I just gotta go."

I turn on my heel and walk away, just like that—feeling like a complete and utter jerk. It's just . . . I don't know—too weird, too uncomfortable . . . too familiar. And I'm nowhere near ready for familiar yet.

I climb the three floors to our room, passing by that Sage girl yet again. She's carrying a basket of laundry. A silver pentacle dangles from a wiry rope chain around her neck, reminding me what I stand for—how it would be stupid for me to prejudge her based on clothes or rumors.

"Hi," I venture.

She does a double take at me, as though surprised that I'm actually speaking to her. She nods me a quick hello and then continues on her way.

When I get to my room, I grab my bathing essentials—including a bottle of eucalyptus oil to help cure myself of this funk, and some apple cider vinegar for its ability to cleanse the mind—and head down the hall to the bathroom. My grandmother, who taught me most of what I know about the art of kitchen witchery, always stressed the importance of properly cleansing the body in preparation for a spell. The spell I want to do this afternoon involves restoration; I need to start rebuilding the fragments of my life.

After a walloping thirty-five minutes spent standing under the bliss of steamy water mixed in eucalyptus and apple cider fumes, I slip into my study uniform (my favorite pair of flannel pajamas) and head back to the room. Janie's there; she's sitting on her swirly pink bed linens, painting her toenails a coordinating shade of strawberry.

"Hi," I say.

She forces a smile, her mood much less sticker-worthy than our last conversation. "Some girl named Drea called for you."

"Thanks," I say, reaching for the phone, feeling a sting of guilt that I didn't try calling her sooner.

"She said she was going out," Janie tells me. "She'll call you when she gets in."

I bite my bottom lip and return the phone to the desk, a bit disappointed—a bit lonely maybe. "How was your faith club meeting?"

She shrugs. "Okay, I guess."

"What do you guys talk about anyway?"

"All kinds of stuff. Stuff we're dealing with, stuff we're going through, parents, pressures . . . God."

"You know, witches believe in God, too."

Janie sighs, like she doesn't want to get into it. "Amber and I were really worried about you," she says, changing the subject.

"I know. I'm sorry. I just have a lot to deal with right now."

"Amber told me." She dabs one of her toenail screw-ups with a cotton ball of nail polish remover.

"About Jacob?"

She pauses from dabbing to look at me. "Is that okay?"

I nod and look away—into my stash of spell supplies.

"Well, if you ever need to talk about it, I'm a great listener. My friends tell me so all the time."

More nodding, imagining myself opening up to Miss Sticker Album herself. I glance above her head at the collage she's made—a zillion magazine cutouts of cats, with a bright pink sign that says "Cat-cha Later." But then I feel a pang of guilt. She's obviously just trying to be nice.

"So glad to see you bathed," she adds, with a smile. "It was starting to smell like sweaty socks in here."

Maybe *nice* isn't the right word. I muster a smirk, remembering how Amber said my stench was making Janie's head ache. Maybe I should burn a little fish oil—give her head something to *really* ache about. I take a deep breath, reminding myself about the rule of three—how whatever I send out into the universe will come back to me three times. The last thing I need to deal with right now is a whopper of a headache on top of everything else.

I remove some spell supplies from my suitcase—including a plastic food tray, a box of self-hardening clay, a pen and paper, a sponge, and a jar of moon-bathed rainwater—and position the family scrapbook on the floor by my side. Big and bulky, with yellowing pages and hardened candle wax droplets in the corners, the scrapbook has been passed down in my family for generations. It was given to me by my grandmother just before she passed away. It's basically this big jumble of stuff—spells, home remedies, favorite lines of poetry, and passed-down holiday recipes—all written by people in my family before me, those who, like me, had the gift of insight.

I flip the book open to a spell written by Kayleigh, my great-great grandmother's first cousin, and then I set the tray down, spreading the supplies on it, and remove the wad of clay from the box.

"Is that some art project?" Janie asks.

"Not exactly."

"Wait," Janie says, capping her bottle of nail polish. "You're not doing that witch stuff in *here*, are you? I mean, it's bad enough that you do it at all."

"I practice magic," I say, lighting a stick of incense and setting it down in its holder. "The *real* kind, not the *Charmed* kind."

"What's that supposed to mean?"

"It means that I use my magic in a positive way—to gain insight, to help others. No one gets hurt and I don't desecrate gravesites—that includes stealing their plot flowers."

She folds her arms and looks away, like the mere image of me and my spells will turn her to stone. "I just don't believe in that stuff."

"Well, whether you believe it or not, it exists."

"No, I mean, it's *against* my beliefs."

"Look." I sigh. "I'd do my spell outside, but it's thirty below—at least it feels that way—and there's really no place else." I run my makeshift pottery tools—a plastic fork, a wooden spoon, and one-half of a broken CD cover—through the incense smoke to charge them. Then I pluck my crystal cluster rock from my night table and grip it in my palm.

"I live here, too, you know," she snaps.

"Janie," I say, "it's not what you're thinking. You'd be surprised; we probably have a lot more in common than you think, belief-wise."

"I doubt it." She averts her gaze and fishes though her smiling-watermelon-sticker-covered purse for a cell phone. "I'm leaving," she huffs. She dials her way out of the room, slamming the door shut behind her.

A major plus, especially since negativity like that is bound to screw up my spell. I let out a cleansing breath before taking the smoking incense and rotating it three times over my spread of supplies, in an effort to clear the air and create a sacred space. The puffy gray smoke hovers over the area, filling the room with a lemongrass scent, reminding me right away of Jacob. I gaze down at the crystal in my hand, remembering how he gave it to me for protection—how he promised me we'd always be together. And yet I feel so all alone.

I glance over at the scrapbook, noting how Kayleigh suggests picturing your problem like the mound of clay and working it down pancake-thin, until you have complete control over it. I place the crystal to the side and dip my sponge in the rainwater, wetting the clay block down until it's fully saturated. The moistness helps to soften the clay, enabling me to round out the edges and work at the center. After several minutes spent pushing and kneading, the cool gray mass is supple under my touch and I'm able to flatten it out.

Except I know full well it's going to take a lot more than breaking down a wad of clay to solve my problem. I close my eyes, feeling the hot-wax tears drip down the creases of my face and spatter my pancake of clay. I honestly don't know if I'll ever be able to get on with my life. But, like Amber said, I owe it to myself to try. I need to rebuild the walls of my world before the foundation cracks and there's nothing left.

With a deep, inhaling breath, I gather a wad of clay and roll it out between both palms to create a coil. I add it to the foundation and create more coils, building up the walls to create a bowl-like structure. "Save these walls from warp and wilt," I whisper. "With newfound strength, my world rebuilt. I know not how I shall be strong, but I must remember my life goes on. Blessed be the way."

I run the incense smoke over the bowl, concentrating on the idea of rebuilding my life. Then I grab the pen and paper and write my question across it: WHAT DO I NEED TO DO TO GET ON WITH MY LIFE? I fold the paper up and place it into the bowl, hoping that my dream tonight will bring me the answer.

Shell

Shell wakes up with a gasp and sits up in bed, his heart pounding hard. Brick and the others are still asleep. He looks at the clock—5 AM; he still has another hour before he has to get up. But how is he supposed to fall back asleep when he can't stop shaking?

He grabs a pen and a piece of paper from the space on the floor beside his bed and writes the words "To Candace, forever, with love," just as it was inscribed in the pocket watch at the old couple's place. He looks down at the words, wondering why he dreamt about them, why they plague him so. He could hear the words chanting in his head, getting louder and louder by the moment, until he couldn't take it anymore and forced himself to wake up.

Does he know Candace somehow—from some place he's not remembering?

He shakes his head, frustrated by his lack of memory but, at the same time, grateful for it. Aside from his life at the camp during the past few months, he has no recollection of anything. Mason said it's because his past was so horrific that his brain is trying to protect him by blocking out the events, vaguely mentioning a life on the streets, complete with a near-fatal illness, some time spent in jail, and constant begging for food and money. Mason's also assured him that it's better he can't remember these things, that such horrific details might stunt his brain even more.

But now he wants to know.

He grabs another piece of paper and writes a question mark across it, wondering about his mind, if one day it might deteriorate completely. He folds the two pieces up and slips them under his pillow, beside the rock with the pentacle on it, silently praying for recollection.

· · ·

Less than an hour later, Shell wakes up—this time, energized by his dream.

He dreamt about Lily.

It felt good to see her so happy last night, to feel her body close to his, and to touch her like that. It almost made the whole idea of what they were doing—according to Clay, Mason, and the rest, not stealing from others, but providing well-off people the opportunity to give when they probably otherwise wouldn't—less harsh . . . more acceptable.

Almost.

The glint in Lily's eyes when she wrapped the mink stole around her and set the hat high atop her head made his heart stir. Shell wonders if the owners truly appreciate such items as much as Lily did. He closes his eyes, remembering their kiss, his lips tingling from the mere thought of it.

"Breakfast is early this morning," Brick mumbles groggily, pulling himself out of bed. "We should probably hurry up."

Brick's bed is directly across from Shell's. It's a pretty large room, large enough to fit six beds, two dressers, and one closet. There's also some storage space in an adjoining room but, since campers in general don't have need for the excessive materials of man, the extra space isn't really used.

Shell and Brick share the cabin with three other boys: Teal, Oak, and Horizon. The three of them, all a few years younger than Brick, around thirteen years old, are pretty much inseparable. Shell imagines he must be at least four or five years older than the boys, around seventeen or eighteen, from what he can tell of his reflection. When they found him on the streets, he didn't have an ID, and age seems less and less important at the camp.

Shell nods to Brick in acknowledgement. He knows he should probably get going. Today is trading day and Mason likes to leave right on time. While Brick grabs some fresh clothes and toiletries and heads out to the bathroom to shower, and Teal, Oak, and Horizon remain in bed, relishing the last few minutes of sleep, Shell grabs the folded pieces of paper from under his pillow, his head fuzzing over with questions. He knows that he did a spell last night, but he has no idea why. How does he even know about magic?

He presses his eyes shut, concentrating on the pieces of paper, pressing them into his palms to feel the grains. And then he remembers something else from his dream, something on Lily's neck. It was a mole or beauty mark of some sort in the shape of an X.

Shell

Several of the campers—including Shell, Brick, Lily, Clay, and Daisy—pile into the back seat of the camp car, while Mason and Rain take the front. Mason is driving. They're headed to the trading field. Every month or so, like-minded peace groups come together to trade their food, wares, and services. It's like a giant flea market except there's no money involved, since money is considered to be one of man's greatest sins—the source of greed, only to be used when absolutely necessary.

"That was quite a night we all had," Lily giggles, looking over at Shell.

Shell smiles slightly, catching the attention of Clay, and looks away.

"It was a *great* night," Clay clarifies. "Quick, easy . . . we all came together as a group."

"Let's not forget Shell," Lily chirps.

"Of course," Clay agrees. "Shell showed bravery and openness. We should all be as courageous."

"Indeed," Mason says, nodding to Shell in the rearview mirror. "I heard all about the night's success."

Lily giggles again, causing Mason's brow to rumple in confusion. Shell glances at her, wondering about his dream, if beneath her knitted scarf there really is a mark on her neck in the form of an *X*.

He, too, is wearing a scarf. Underneath his coat, Shell wears the wool scarf Lily made him take last night. He smiles at her, wondering if she can sense that he wears it, but then wondering why she would.

"Will you be trading the platinum necklace?" Brick asks Clay. "I can't imagine what someone would give for it."

"What necklace?" Clay asks.

"The platinum heart one from last night," Brick explains. "The one in the velvet case . . . in the woman's jewelry box."

"I didn't take it," Clay says. "It had the woman's initials engraved on the charm—much harder to trade that way . . . I also thought it might be sentimental."

Mason watches Clay from the rearview mirror, taking everything in. "A good decision," he says, finally, reaching across the seat to clasp Rain's hand. "Taking without first considering the sentimental value an object has to its owner is defeating the purpose of what we're trying to do."

"Which is giving people the opportunity to give," Daisy chimes in. She rests her head on Brick's shoulder, her orangy corkscrew ringlets hanging slightly in her face.

"Very good," Mason tells her.

They drive the rest of the way in silence, Shell feeling quite relieved that he didn't take the pocket watch from the old couple's place, since it too is undoubtedly sentimental. But he's still not completely clear on the camp's whole taking philosophy. What gives *them* the right to decide the worth of somebody else's possessions? It just doesn't make sense to him.

He lets out a sigh and looks out the window as they pass by the Bargo Tower. They enter a town called Dalmouth, which already seems more up-and-coming than Brutus. Shell continues to take note of his surroundings. There's a windmill in the center of Dalmouth, as well as a strip of shops—Beach Blanket Bagel; Cape Chowdah; Fricken Frappe, an ice cream place; and Tidewater Treats, a candy store. The streets are all paved with brick instead of asphalt. The town's quaintness leaves him with a nostalgic feeling, like maybe he's been here before.

They drive for several more minutes, well past the center, where it's starting to look more vacant. There's a long stretch of open fields on both sides of them—conservation land, maybe. They turn down a few more streets, finally reaching the trading field, which is almost filled up.

There are four long rows of traders. They've spread cardboard and blankets over the frozen ground to display their trinkets and announce their services.

Shell and the campers work on setting up their space. Lily is trading her services of hair braiding and neck massaging, while Mason and Rain trade jewelry trinkets acquired from their nightly taking quests, and Daisy trades sweaters, coats, and any leftover household items that couldn't be hawked in a pawn shop.

Brick and Shell have been assigned to walk the rows, scoping out the trades so they can report back to the group about the deals of the day. Clay follows several yards behind them, well out of earshot.

"What's he doing?" Shell asks Brick.

Brick shrugs. "Mason probably ordered him to keep an eye on us. So we don't get into trouble."

"What kind of trouble?"

"I don't know." He shrugs again. "So we don't run off or do anything weird, probably."

Shell looks back in Clay's direction. It appears as though Clay has slowed his pace a bit, giving them space.

"Just ignore him," Brick says. "That's what I try to do."

Shell nods, taking the advice. They turn down one of the longer rows, impressed the array of tradeables. This is Shell's second time at a trading field, Brick's umpteenth, and both marvel at the abundance of choices—palm and card readings, offers for manicures and hair dyeing, handmade quilts, wooden bowls, exotic seashells, and food staples of all types.

They pass by a group of young girls attaching sparkly white angel wings to each other's backs. "Are your wings broken?" one of the girls calls out to Shell.

Shell stops a moment, then approaches her, noticing how each set of wings is unique, all set apart by their shape—some pointed, some bubbly, others wavy, a few with diamond-shaped cutouts. "I don't think so," he says, finally. He looks back at Clay, who watches them from a few tables away.

"May I?" She whirls him around to inspect his back, running her hand across his shoulders. "What happened to you?" she asks, turning him back around.

Shell's face drops, confused.

"Your wings aren't just broken." She gasps. "They've collapsed." The other girls shake their heads with compassion. "Sometimes wings can break like that," she continues, "but it's usually only after something terrible happens—a lost love, a near death, a sudden illness—were you sick?"

"I believe so," Shell says.

The girl nods, unsurprised. "Well, you're still going to need some temporary wings until yours heal over. I think I have a pair that will be perfect." She turns to fish through a trunk behind her, pulling forth a simple, straight-lined, no-frills pair from the bottom of the heap. "These will be perfect," she says, holding them up to Shell. "And what have *you* got to trade?"

"Maybe I'll come back later," Shell says, looking to Brick for backup, though Brick remains expressionless.

"Well, don't wait *too* long," the girl says. "It's dangerous out there without your wings."

Shell nods and he and Brick leave, Clay following several paces behind.

"Are you sure you don't want a pair?" Brick asks.

"Are you serious?" He checks Brick's expression to see if he's joking, but he remains as straight-faced as ever.

"Why not?" Brick explains. "Maybe she can see something about your past. Don't you believe some people have a sixth sense?"

Shell bites his bottom lip, knowing that he must believe it. Why else, in the car earlier, would he wonder if Lily could sense he was wearing the woolen scarf under his coat? "Can *you* sense things?"

Brick shrugs. "I try to."

"What do you mean?"

Brick glances back to check for Clay, who's suddenly stopped. He's talking to some people at one of the tables.

"Can you keep a secret?" Brick asks.

Shell nods.

"On the way over here," he whispers, "when Clay said he didn't take that platinum necklace, I sensed he was lying."

"Seriously?"

"Forget it," Brick says. "I've spoken out of line. Please . . . forgive me."

"Sure," Shell says, his mind scrambling with questions.

"I've been working on developing my senses," Brick continues, "through meditation and spells and stuff. But sometimes it backfires and I just imagine things. I shouldn't have said anything. Clay's a good person. Please, don't repeat any of this. Do you promise?"

Shell nods, growing more confused by the moment. They continue their walk back toward the group's trading spot, farther away from Clay, who's still talking away at the cheese-trading table.

When they get just a few yards shy of their group, Shell pulls Brick aside. "Do you really think there's a chance that girl might have been sensing something about my past?"

"Maybe," Brick says. "If your past is as awful as Mason says . . . maybe she picked up on it. Sometimes I feel like people can sense stuff about me, too."

"Like who?"

"I don't know, but I feel like I have a guardian angel out there somewhere."

Shell nods, somehow knowing exactly what Brick means. He looks back in the direction of the angel-wing booth, suddenly more than eager to go back and talk to that girl, to ask her about his past. But he can't seem to spot her *or* her booth now amidst all the other traders, and how could he explain it to Clay? He continues to look anxiously about, in all directions, finally catching the eyes of Lily, Daisy, and Mason. They wave him and Brick over to the camp's trading spot—precisely where they belong.

stacey

I roll over in bed, reaching for the crystal cluster rock beneath my pillow. A few seconds later, the phone rings. Since I can't sleep anyway, I snatch the receiver from my night table, hoping that it's Drea on the other end. "Hello?"

"Stacey?" asks a female voice.

"Yes. Who's this?" I sit up in bed and click on the reading lamp, noticing that I'm alone, that Amber and Janie's beds are empty. The window on Janie's side of the room is open partway, causing the window shade to knock against the ledge.

"Hello?" I repeat, still waiting for an answer. I can hear her breathe on the other end of the line. I sit up farther in bed and glance at the clock—it's 3 AM. "Who is this?" I repeat.

The shade continues to knock against the ledge, the frigid January air pushing its way into the room, giving me chills.

"I know you're alone," she whispers.

"Janie?" I ask, wondering if this is her, if she's playing some sort of prank because she was so ticked earlier about my restoration clay spell.

"You *are* alone, aren't you, Stacey?"

I scan the room, confident that the only view in is through the window—when the wind pushes the shade away.

"I'm waiting . . . " she says.

"Tell me who this is, or I'm hanging up."

"You wouldn't do that," she whispers.

But that's exactly what I do. I slam the receiver down on its cradle, my heart pumping hard. I take a deep breath and chew at my bottom lip, wondering where Amber is, looking toward her bed for a note.

A few seconds later, the phone rings again.

I ignore it as best I can and climb out of bed to check the door. It's locked. I turn toward the window. The shade flaps into the room, making me jump. I take small steps toward it, wondering if someone's out there, if they can see me.

With trembling fingers, I reach for the window to pull it down, but it seems to be stuck. Using both hands, I anchor myself in place and press downward as hard as I can. Still, it won't budge. So I try the window shade. I try yanking it down even farther, but the shade slips from my fingertips and rolls up to the top, revealing a girl's face. She stares right back at me.

I gasp and jump back before realizing that the reflection is mine.

"I know you're alone," a male voice whispers from just behind me.

I steel myself in place, my heart pounding hard. I strain my eyes, trying to see something else in the reflection, but there's only me. After several seconds, I peek over my shoulder into the room. No one's there. But the closet door is open a crack.

The phone continues to ring. I pick up the receiver and hold it up to my ear, wondering if the voice was just my imagination, if maybe I'm just overtired. Surely the closet door could have been open like that all along.

But I'm almost positive that it wasn't.

"I know you're alone," the male voice whispers from the receiver.

"Who is this?" I demand.

No one answers.

I drop the receiver and move back to the door to leave. I unlock it and go to turn the knob. No go. I pull at the knob and try kicking at the door crack, but it's no use.

Someone's locked me in from the outside.

I grab the dangling receiver and go to call campus police. I press at the numbers but nothing happens. I can't get a dial tone—it's just dead on the other end. I hang up and move to the window, hoping I can crawl out, but there's not enough space. My arms shake, trying to pry the window open wider. But it's stuck in place.

I whirl around, hearing a whimper escape out my mouth. The closet door appears to be open even wider now. Slowly, I approach it, grabbing the tweezers off Amber's dresser and gripping them for protection.

In one quick motion, I wrap my hand around the knob and whip the door open. There, scribbled in red across the wall, are the words I KNOW YOU'RE ALONE. There are splotches of blood all around it, trailing down the wall. My jaw quivers. My breath stops. I feel myself taking steps backwards, my hand clamped over my mouth.

The phone rings again a second later, making me jump. I move quickly to my night table to answer it. "Hello?"

"Stacey Brown?" says a female voice.

"Who's this?"

"This is Ms. McNeal from President Wallace's office."

"You need to help me," I say. "Please—I need help—"

"No," she says. "You need *to help.*"

"What?"

"Porsha needs your help," she explains.

"Who?"

"Porsha, President Wallace's daughter. Her mother wanted me to call you—to tell you that Porsha needs help . . . or else that boy will die."

"What boy?"

"Do you have your crystal?" she asks, ignoring the question.

"What?"

"Your crystal cluster rock . . . the one Jacob gave you for protection."

I open my mouth to speak, but nothing comes out. At the same moment, I feel it—someone's breath on my neck.

"I know you're alone," the male voice whispers into my ear.

I drop the phone and shake my head, my heart beating faster. I turn to look. At the same moment, a hand reaches around my neck, cutting off my breath. The fingernails cut into my throat.

I go to step back, to kick at his shin, but he grabs tighter, cutting off my breath.

A moment later I hear a door slam shut—hard. The sound wakes me up out of sound sleep.

I sit up in bed with a gasp.

Amber is there, at the door. "Hey, you," she says, dropping her bag to the floor. "Hungry for dinner? I hear it's burrito night in the caf."

But I'm still shaking.

"What's up with you?" she asks. "You look like you swallowed a cockroach—maybe you've already *been* to burrito night."

"I have to go," I say, finally. I scramble from under my covers, pausing a moment to look at the clay bowl by my bed. I take and unfold the piece of paper inside, my question staring at me—WHAT DO I NEED TO DO TO GET ON WITH MY LIFE? At least now I have an answer.

stacey

I throw my coat on over my pajamas, pull on my boots, and slip my crystal cluster rock into my pocket.

"Time out," Amber says, still standing at the door of our room. "What are you doing? Where are you going?"

"I have to go out," I say, scrambling for a rubber band to tie my hair back.

The images of my nightmare are still alive in my head, causing my pulse to race, my heart to beat fast.

"*Where are you going?*" Amber repeats.

"I had another nightmare."

"About what?"

"Jacob."

"What *about* him?"

"It's a long story," I say, snatching a rubber band off the dresser, "but I have to get to the president's office before he leaves for the day." I glance at the clock—it's just after four.

"Why? What's going on?"

"I have to help Porsha."

"Who?"

"She's obviously the girl-so-blue from my nightmare, the one I'm supposed to help or the boy will die."

"*What?*"

"I'll explain later." I pocket my keys and my campus ID card. "I'll call you if I'm going to be out late."

"Wait," Amber says, holding her head. "What does that have to do with Jacob?"

"I don't know, but I have to find out."

"You're not making any sense."

"I know." I give her a quick hug. "I'll call you if I'm going to be late."

"Stacey," she shouts. "*You're in your pjs.*"

"So?"

"Well, can I at least lend you a boa or something?" She nabs a big frilly pink one from beside her bed.

"It might be a little much," I say, eyeing her bright red Mary Jane Doc Martens. But, with her matching fuzzy headband and puffy winter vest, she *does* look pretty cute.

Amber tosses me one of Janie's Snapples from her fridge and stuffs my pockets full of tissues and Jujyfruits, mothering me a little more—but in a good way, a way that feels comforting.

She tells me we need to have a long talk later and then I head out, rushing my way across campus, dodging ice patches and snowdrifts the whole way. The entire campus is lit up since the sun starts going down around four. I finally make it to Ketcher Hall and bound up the stairs, two at a time, to find Ms. McNeal still sitting at her desk.

"I need to talk to Dr. Wallace," I say, all out of breath.

"I'm sorry, but that isn't possible," she says, her squinty eyes narrowing on me, on my flannel pjs sticking out from my coat maybe.

"Please," I say. "It's really important. Don't you remember me? I was here the other day . . . Stacey Brown. Dr. Wallace wanted to meet with me . . ."

"I can leave him a message that you stopped by."

"Please," I insist, motioning to his office door and taking a step in that direction. "It'll only take a couple minutes."

"He isn't here," Ms. McNeal says, standing up, as though to stop me. "He had a late afternoon meeting and he isn't coming back to his office. He's a very busy man."

I feel my chin shake. I grab the crystal cluster rock in my pocket for strength and inspiration, wondering what I should do. "Do you know Jacob?" I blurt, flashing back to my nightmare, knowing even before the words come out how stupid the question sounds.

"Jacob *who*?"

"Forget it," I say, taking a step back, burying my face in my hands.

"Is there something I can do?" Ms. McNeal asks. "Would you like to talk to one of the counselors? You could use my phone to set something up. I'm sure they'd be willing to meet with you tonight, if you'd like."

I shake my head, thinking how the last thing I need right now is to talk to a useless counselor.

"Well, can I get you a glass of water?"

"Is there any way you can call Dr. Wallace at home?" I ask, ignoring her offer. "I know he'd want to talk to me."

Ms. McNeal takes a step back, as though suddenly creepified by my presence. "I think maybe you should be going now," she says. "I'll tell him that you stopped by."

I shake my head, feeling a storm of tears form behind my eyes. I move toward the door and, just as I do, she walks right in.

Porsha.

"Is my father here?" she asks Ms. McNeal.

She's dressed, once again, in dark layers—charcoal gray mixed with navy blue and black. The tips of her long blond hair are tinted a deep olive color. They hang in her face, practically covering her eyes.

"Porsha?" I ask, my heart beating fast.

She stares back at me, the corners of her eyes crinkling up in confusion.

"Porsha, dear, why don't you take a seat at my desk." Ms. McNeal ushers Porsha in that direction.

My heart beats fast, knowing that I've gotten her name right—that my nightmare predicted correctly. "Your father wanted us to meet," I say. "I'm Stacey. Did he tell you about me?"

Porsha shakes her head. "I don't want to talk to her," she whispers to Ms. McNeal. She's biting away at the tips of her fingers, looking around the room—from the wall, to the ceiling, to the floor, and then to me, perhaps waiting for me to leave.

"I think you should leave now, Ms. Brown," Ms. McNeal says. *"Now!"*

"I'm sorry," I say, keeping focused on Porsha. "I only stopped by because your father told me about you . . . about what you've been experiencing. He thinks I can help you."

"I don't want to talk to her," Porsha tells Ms. McNeal again. She shuffles a bit from side to side, as though anxious.

"Do I need to call campus security?" Ms. McNeal asks. She picks up the phone, awaiting my next move.

"I know about your nightmares," I say, ignoring the threat. "I know what it's like to dream about the dead. I dream about it, too."

Porsha breaks her eyelock on the ceiling to study me. Her eyes are red with dark circles under them, like she hasn't slept in days, like maybe she's been forcing herself to stay awake at night—to avoid her nightmares.

Just like I used to do.

"I don't dream about the dead," she says, finally. "I *am* dead—*dead, dead, dead, dead, dead,*" she sings, just like the little girl in my nightmare.

The whimsical tone of her voice saying that word sends shivers down my back.

Porsha ends her song abruptly and screams, *"I don't want to talk to her!"* Then she plucks a pencil from Ms. McNeal's desk and plunges it deep into her palm, stabbing the tip into her flesh, over and over again, until the pencil snaps in her hands.

Ms. McNeal tries to restrain her, to take the pencil away and get her to sit down, but Porsha is slapping the wall with her palm now, leaving splotches of blood, shouting over and over again how she doesn't want to talk to me.

I leave, slamming the door shut behind me so she hears my exit. Maybe all those doctors are right. Maybe she *should* be put away. Maybe she *is* crazy. I take a deep breath to shake off her chill, knowing that the *real* crazy part in all of this is that I know where she's coming from; I know what it's like to feel just inches away from insanity. And I know firsthand what it's like to feel dead.

stacey

When I get back to the room, no one's there. I curl up on my bed and silently count to ten, still picturing the bloodstains on the wall from Porsha's palm—just like in my nightmare.

The phone rings a couple seconds later, but I just let it. My heart is racing. My head won't stop spinning. I just can't shake this feeling—like something inside me is about to burst open, like every nerve in my body is about to erupt.

When the phone finally stops ringing, I roll over in bed and grab the receiver to call my mother. But before I can even get the words out—how I feel like I'm cracking, how I don't know if I'm going to make it here—she just starts gushing. She rambles on for five full minutes about how proud she is of me, how she's been bragging to anyone who'll listen that I got into Beacon-fancy-schmancy-University on a full scholarship.

And how I'm *her* hero, too.

I take a deep breath, feeling my eyes fill up. I gather a wad of comforter in my palm and assure my mother that everything's going great . . . better than I ever thought it could. And then I end the conversation by telling her that Amber and I are heading off to a party tonight, and that college is much more social than I ever expected.

Instead of lecturing me on how I'm here to study and not to party, on how I have a certain GPA to keep up, and how drinking and driving can—quote unquote—*kill a friendship*—all things she'd normally say BJD (before Jacob's disappearance)—she tells me to have a good time and to call her in a couple days.

I hang up, feeling a stabbing pain in my chest. I take another couple deep breaths and grab my bowl of lavender pellets. I rake my fingers through them, waiting for my nerves to stop rattling, but I just can't focus. I consider calling Amber on her cell phone, but I honestly don't feel like disappointing her even more than I already have. Instead I call Drea. Her roommate picks up. She tells me that Drea and Chad went out for the evening and that she doesn't expect them back for at least a couple hours.

I hang up, wondering if they're back together *yet again*, and reach into my night table for my bottle of pills. I already know that it's empty. What I don't know is how I'm going to fall asleep tonight without a little help. Will a dream spell alone be strong enough?

I grab the phone again and my address book and look up Dr. Atwood's cell number; she gave it to me in case of emergency.

I dial quickly, my heart tripping over from the mere anticipation of her response. Instead I get her voicemail.

"Hi, Dr. Atwood," I stammer into the receiver. "It's me . . . Stacey. I was wondering if maybe you could call me back as soon as you get this. There's something I'd like to ask you. Could you call me back? Thanks."

I clunk the receiver back down on its cradle, feeling even worse than just seconds before. A couple minutes later, the phone rings.

"Hello?" I answer.

"Hi, Stacey, it's Dr. Atwood."

I let out a breath of relief. "Thanks so much for calling me back."

"Sure," she says. "Are you okay?"

"Yeah. I just wanted to talk to you."

"How is your first week of college going?"

"Great," I say. "I mean, hard, but I'm enjoying it."

"Really." She sounds surprised.

"Well, it's hard," I repeat, my voice cracking over the words. "But I'm working hard, too—meeting people . . . studying."

"That's good," she says, reservation high in her voice. "Have you met with Dr. Sonja?"

"Who?"

"The therapist I recommended out there."

"Not yet," I say, practically biting through my lip. "I'm going to call her Monday, though. I just kind of wanted to settle in first."

"Well, I guess that sounds reasonable," she says. "But you *should* give her a call to set something up. She's expecting it."

"I know. I will." More lip-biting.

"You mentioned there was something you wanted to ask me."

"Yeah," I say, switching the receiver to my other ear out of nervousness. "I need more tranquilizers."

"What happened to the ones I prescribed you?"

I proceed to give her this lame little story about how I lost the bottle of meds in transit here, that I could have sworn I packed them in one of my suitcases. I tell her how I've even had my mother searching around at home, but that nobody, not even my roommates, has been able to locate them.

"I suppose I could do that." She sighs. "But this is the only time. You need to meet with Dr. Sonja, okay?"

"Sure," I say. "Monday morning. I promise, I'll call her."

Dr. Atwood tells me she'll call the prescription in tonight and that it will be ready by tomorrow morning. I hesitate, almost wanting her to call it in to one of those twenty-four-hour pharmacies, but I decide not to press my luck. I hang up the phone and turn over in bed, noticing Amber. She's standing in the doorway with her arms folded.

I freeze, my hand still curled around the receiver. "How long have you been standing there?"

"Long enough."

"What do you mean?"

"What's going on with you?"

I shrug.

"I mean, what's going on with your nightmares? You ran out of here like someone was holding a tweezer to your ass—and not in a good way."

I take a deep breath, relieved that she didn't hear my conversation with Dr. Atwood. "You really want to know?"

"Well, *yeah*." She rolls her eyes. "That's kind of why I asked."

"The little girl in my nightmare is Porsha's mother, President Wallace's deceased wife."

"Wait, didn't you say the girl in your nightmare was, like, eight or nine? How is that possible?"

"I can't explain it; I mean, I don't know why she's appearing in my dreams so young. But if I don't help her daughter, some boy will die."

"And you think that boy is Jacob."

"I don't know."

"This is all so freakazoid," Amber says.

"Which part?"

"All of it. I mean, President Wallace asked you to help Porsha out. Now you've got his dead wife on your ass. Talk about pressure."

"So you believe me?"

"That you're having nightmares about President Wallace's dead old lady in little girl form? Yes."

"And that the boy could be Jacob?"

Amber looks toward her collection of boas, avoiding the question.

"They never found his body," I remind her.

"I know."

"Then what?"

"How come you never dream about *fun* dead people? You know, like Elvis?"

"This is serious."

"Who's joking?" She sighs. "You need some fun."

"I need some *sleep*."

"No way," she balks. "This is your first weekend in college. I refuse to let you spend it in bed . . . alone, that is."

"Don't you understand . . . some boy's life is at stake!"

"Probably not tonight," she says, tossing me a leopard-print baby tee from her pile of clothes. "You're coming to a party. You need a change of scenery."

"I'm not going anywhere," I argue.

"You totally are," she says. "I've met the cutest guys this week—one of whom you've already met."

"*Who?*" I ask.

"Tim, that's who. You've made quite the impression on him."

"Excuse me?"

"He says you're just his type—sexy yet standoffish, serious yet seductive."

"Excuse me?" I repeat.

"His words, not mine. Apparently, he likes a challenge. I told him he's got his work cut out."

"How do you even know him?"

"When I told him I was rooming with Stacey-my-best-friend-from-prep-school, he got all quizzy, making sure *you* were *you*, the Stacey he'd already met."

"Yeah, but where did you meet?"

"The lobby. He's friends with some girls who live here. Small world, eh?"

"*Too* small," I say, hiking the covers up over my head.

"No way," Amber says, tearing the covers back down. "Tim's invited us to an off-campus kegger. So hurry up— get that pajama ass of yours into some chicness. Do you wanna try some of my new No Screw With You?"

"Bug spray?" I ask, eyeing the slender bottle in her hand.

"My new eyeliner," she explains. "It's guaranteed not to fade or bleed—no screwing around with this baby. Maybe it'll make your eyes look a little less *Night of the Living Dead*."

"Thanks for the sweet offer," I say, "but I need sleep."

"Are you kidding? You've slept more than my dead Aunt Paula. You need to get out of this room before Janie gets back and stickers you to death." Amber hurls a pair of faux-fur shorts at me, followed by her brand-new, straight-out-of-the-box knee-length sheepskin boots. "Get dressed!" she demands. "I'm getting you lucky tonight—whether you like it or not."

stacey

Despite Amber's hemming and hawing about going to the party with her and Tim the flirt, I end up convincing her that I need to spend some serious time studying if I want to stay here beyond two weeks.

She really can't argue, which is why she finally leaves, pouting her way out the door. The only problem: I'm anything but tired. I decide to nab myself a shower, hoping the steamy water coupled with droplets of chamomile and lavender oil will help relax me.

And it does. I step out of the shower stall and wrap myself up in my terry robe, feeling much more centered . . . more balanced, like I might actually be able to fall asleep. But no sooner do I get back to the room than my nerves start rattling again.

There's a "do not disturb" sign hanging on the doorknob —a picture of a giant set of curly lashed eyes, one of them winking at me. I know it's not Amber's—she definitely would have showed me something like this. I rap lightly a couple times on the door, but there's no response. Maybe it's just a joke. "Hello?" I call. "Amber?"

A moment later, I see that Sage girl exit her room. She's got a backpack slung over her shoulder, like she's going off to study or going out to do a spell maybe. She's dressed in a long velvety black dress with a purple corduroy coat that has one of those big and fluffy faux-fur collars à la Amber. She peers over her shoulder, catching me looking in her direction, and waves. I wave back, but it's too late; she's already turned away, down the exit stairwell.

And I'm still standing here in my robe. I let out a sigh, fish my key out of my basket full of bathing stuff, and open the door only to find Janie. In bed. With her boy toy.

She's straddling him, wearing a sorry excuse for a bra (two tiny swatches of fabric joined together with a string) and a pair of matching stringy undies. The guy is barely clothed as well—just a pair of boxers and lots of glossy sweat.

My mouth drops open just as Miss Smiley Sticker herself pauses a moment from licking down the length of his face.

"I'm so sorry," I blurt, my eyes practically popping out of my head.

"Didn't you see the sign?" she shouts. "We're a little busy in here."

"I'm sorry," I repeat. "I was in the shower."

"Come back in a couple minutes," her boyfriend tells me.

Janie frowns at him. "Make that *an hour.*"

While they resume their activity, I avert my eyes, grab my book bag, pluck some clothes from the foot of my bed—including Amber's knee-high sheepskin boots—and head back to the bathroom to change. The worse part in this whole scenario—aside from the fact that Little Miss Sticker is getting stuck in *our* room, making me have to evacuate the premises—is that not only do I have to go to the library for real now (since that's the only place I can think of to go), but I also have to wear the ridiculous outfit Amber picked out for me, baby tee and all. I cannot *believe* these are the clothes I picked up. Thank god I also managed to scoop up my sweatshirt with the broken zipper.

So while Amber spends her Friday evening at some off-campus kegger, I spend mine dressed like a prostitute in a study carrel, raving it up with subjects like lipids, proteins, and narrative essays. The one saving grace—my holistic health class. I know I'm technically already failing it, but I'm thinking it's going to be one of my better courses since I already know a lot of this stuff. I mean, it's actually *interesting* —Ayurvedic principles of earth, fire, water, air, and space;

Tibetan herbal teas laced with yak butter; and Chinese healing rituals.

It's actually quite motivational, which is why I end up pulling an all-nighter. *That* and because when I call the room to check if Janie and her boy toy are finally done, she tells me that they aren't, but I'm welcome to sleep in our room anyway since it's "really no big deal."

Needless to say, it's a less-than-tempting offer—one I don't even need to think twice about. So Saturday morning, in lieu of heading straight back to the room for a shower and some sleep, I forget that I'm still dressed like a prostitute and hop on the bus that will take me into town to pick up my prescription.

When I get back to the room, Janie's in bed—alone, this time. So is Amber. I pop a pill, change into my flannel pj's, and set my dream box down on the pillow beside me. It's a small wooden box I bought at a flea market last year. Made of smooth golden pinewood with a chrome hinge and a matching clasp, I open it up so that it can catch my dreams. Jacob taught me all about dream boxes. He'd been keeping one since his freshman year of high school and found that when left open before bed, it enabled one to remember what they dreamed about, so they didn't end up forgetting as soon as they woke up.

Concentrating on Jacob—on the time we painted henna on each other; on the night we did the spell to banish secrets, and how he held me right after; how we physically declared our love for one another—I lie back in bed and close my eyes, the blissful memories lulling me to sleep.

I wake up with a start, several hours later. There's a knocking at the door. I look down at my dream box. It's still open, still sitting beside me on the pillow. But I don't remember a thing.

I take a deep breath, wondering who's at our door. Amber and Janie are still in their beds, seemingly unaffected by the banging. So maybe I should ignore it, too. I roll over in bed, dragging a pillow over my ear to block out the noise.

That's when I hear Amber moan her annoyance. She gets up and staggers over to the door. "It's only ten-freaking-thirty in the morning," she whines. "Unless you're packing a serious bag of Skittles and looking for a good time, I don't want any." The next thing I know, the door creaks open and I hear Amber shout, "Tell me I'm having a nightmare!"

I roll back over to face the door just as PJ, Amber's ex, busts his way in. "Hey there, sweet thing," he says, kissing both her cheeks, French style. "Guess who arrived to light up your life? And *don't* say Debby Boone."

"*Who*?" Amber asks.

"Leave it to you not to know a real musical *artiste* when you hear one. Now, I don't have Skittles, but I'm *always* looking for a good time. Will peanut M&M's suffice?" He flashes the yellow package inside his pocket. "Saved all the green ones for you, Trisket."

"What are you doing here?" she asks, her mouth hanging open in a gawk.

Except for his hair color, which he tends to change at least twice a semester and which, at present, oddly appears to be a mainstream shade of honey brown (to contrast his usual shades of plum purple and melon orange), he looks exactly the same—tall, thin, with dark gray eyes and short, spiky hair.

"And you thought you could slip your little self away from me so easily."

"PJ!" I say, leaping out of bed. I wrap my arms around him, even surprising myself. I mean, PJ and I have never been close; it's just, after everything, it's refreshing to see a familiar face—especially one that knows what I'm going through, who was there when I lost Jacob.

"Hey there, Miss B," he says, hugging me back. "I meant to call you once or a hundred times, but you know how it goes for a swanker like me—"

"Too busy harassing girls?" Amber asks.

"No way, my jealous jar of jelly. The only girl I'd ever think of harassing is *you*." He winks at her and then focuses back on me. "So how are you feeling?" Instead of answering, I squeeze him tighter. "Better watch out, teacup," he says to Amber, "you might have a little competition on your hands."

"It's good to see you," I say, breaking the embrace.

"*Au natural*, my little witchy one."

"What's going on?" Janie asks, sitting up in bed.

"Chips ahoy," PJ says, stepping over a pile of clothes to greet her. He extends his hand for a shake, but ends up kissing the back of her hand instead, his lips landing on a sticker of a happy bunch of grapes. "I'm PJ; maybe you've heard of me?"

"Yeah," Janie says. "You must be Amber's ex-boyfriend."

"So she *has* talked about me." PJ taps a finger over his lips in thought.

"Just a little," Janie says, picking a matching grape sticker off her face.

"Do tell. I suppose she told you all about our fits of passion, how she couldn't keep her hands off me . . . the little schoolboy outfits she had me wear. Such a kinkoid, that one." He growls.

"Maybe in your dreams," Amber says.

"As a matter of fact, I have been known to wake up in the middle of the night—sweaty, jammers torn askew, screaming out your name . . . feisty little one." He winks at her.

"*Help!*" Amber moans.

"Don't let her negativity fool you," he continues to Janie. "She's just bitter because I broke it off with her. See that Spider-Man doll over there? She closes her eyes at night and imagines it's me."

"Oh my god, you're *so* cute," Janie says, hopping up and down on her bed.

"Finally, a lady with taste," he says.

"Do you go here?" Janie asks.

PJ turns to Amber. "I do *now*."

"Um . . . *what*?" Amber's mouth hangs open.

PJ's completely beaming now. "Guess who Beacon University's newest transfer student happens to be?"

"Tell me you didn't."

"Gotta love a straight-A first semester at community college, late registration here, and a hefty donation from Dad to sweeten the deal."

"Oh my god," Amber says, taking a seat on her bed. "This isn't happening. Tell me this isn't happening."

"*Au contraire*, my thorny little bush." PJ pounces down next to her, planting not one, not two, but *three* mushy kisses on her cheek. "Believe it or not, there is a splash of bad news amidst all this loveliness."

"There's *more*?" Amber groans.

"I'm homeless."

"How's that possible?" I ask.

"The dorms are all filled, that's how. I'm staying at the Shady 8 Motel and Smoke Shop down the road. So," he swivels back toward Amber, "unless you're craving something a little bad-girl-and-broomsticks-with-soundproof-padding-stapled-to-the-back-of-the-bed, we'll have to conduct our love-fests here."

Amber pulls Spider-Man over her as a shield, flopping backward in bed, though it's doubtful that even Spidey can save her. It looks like PJ is here to stay, which, from the way things currently stand, is more than I can say about myself.

stacey

PJ gives us all his contact info—including his motel room address and phone number, his cell phone number, and his new campus e-mail address. He makes us promise to call him later. We agree; it's either that or he won't leave.

Amber is beyond stressed. She's resorted to pulling a Drea—gnawing away at a chocolate bar in an effort to eat her funk. "He's going to hang all over me," she whines. "It's going to be just like high school—him hanging around all the time, making it look like we're a couple, ruining my game."

I bite my tongue, fighting the urge to remind her how jealous she got this past summer when PJ showed interest in someone else.

"He's such a cutie," Janie says. "I can't believe you don't like him."

"Coming from someone who was shacked up with an egghead last night," Amber says, "that doesn't mean a whole heck of a lot."

"I take it you walked in on them, too?" I ask.

"Unfortunately," Amber says with a shudder. "G-strings and smelly fruit stickers—I'm still trying to block it out."

"It's not like we did anything wrong," Janie whines. "We didn't go all the way, if that's what you're thinking. I *do* have my limits."

"And what's your limit?" Amber asks. "Getting jiggy in front of the entire floor, as opposed to just your roommates?"

"Don't talk about me that way." Janie folds her arms and crosses her legs, bobbing her Strawberry Shortcake slipper back and forth. "For your information, I'm saving myself for marriage."

"Are you sure?" Amber asks, arching her eyebrows. "Because it didn't look like you were saving that much."

"You're one to talk," Janie says. "You and that blow-up toy of yours."

"His name happens to be Spider-Man and, from the looks of things last night, he's probably a lot more useful in the sack than that egghead of *yours*."

"Excuse me," I say, interrupting them, "but speaking as someone who didn't get *any* sleep last night, shouldn't we discuss more important matters?"

"Totally," Amber says, arching her eyebrows up and down. "Let's hear it—the who, the where, and the how many times."

"Sorry to disappoint." I sigh. "But I spent the night at the library."

"Do tell," Amber says. "The stacks can be *so* hot."

"I studied."

"Ho hum." She passes me her chocolate bar for a bite. "You know that Tim guy really likes you."

"He's a flirt," I explain. "It's his job to like everybody."

"Puh-leeze," Amber says, rolling her eyes. "The poor boy salivates at the mere sound of your name."

"I doubt it."

"You know what's weird, though?" she says, ignoring me. "He thinks *you* have a boyfriend." She gives me a pointed look.

I shrug and look away.

"Don't worry," she continues. "I set him straight. You're welcome, by the way."

"Thanks a lot." I sigh again. "Can we talk about the sleeping arrangements now?"

"Now *that's* more like it," Amber says, rubbing her palms together.

"That's not what I mean." I turn to Janie. "It's not fair that I have to spend the entire night at the library," I say.

"No one said you had to," Janie says. "You were welcome to come back here."

"With you and Boy Toy playing tongue hockey? No, thank you."

"I live here, too," Janie says. "It's not exactly fair that I get stuck living with a Satan worshipper."

"*Please,*" I say, holding my hand up to shut her off.

"*You* please," she says. "All that witchcraft stuff you do . . . who knows what you might do to me?"

"Yeah," Amber says, narrowing her eyes on Janie. "It might not be safe for you. Have you considered finding another room? Maybe Egghead has some space . . . "

"Witchcraft has nothing to do with Satan," I say, interrupting them.

"Yeah, that's what Sage said, too," Janie snaps. "But then she tried stealing from a gravesite."

"You have no idea what you're even talking about," I continue. "Wicca is a peaceful religion; it has nothing to do with breaking into cemeteries or putting evil hexes on people."

"It's against my religion."

"Is it also against your religion to educate yourself a little?"

"I'm in college, aren't I?"

"All I'm saying is that if you opened your mind even a smidge, you'd see . . . there's probably a lot we agree on."

"Why don't we just agree to disagree," she says.

"Fine," I say, completely frustrated with her narrow little mind. "Let's get down to some rule-making."

"Great," Janie says. "If I'm with a boy, I'll put the sign on the door."

"And how often do you plan to do that?" I ask.

"I don't know." Janie shrugs. "Not *that* much. Maybe three or four times a week."

Amber's mouth falls open. "Freak!"

"What?" Janie asks, pasting a twinkling star sticker to her chin. "It's not like you guys can't do the same. It's not like *I* don't have to live with a witch." She glances a moment at the side of my bed—at my chunky cluster rock, my bowl full of lavender pellets, and the clay bowl from my restoration spell.

"Egghead has stamina," Amber continues.

"For your information, his name happens to be Hayden, and he's very sweet—we sing in the church choir together."

"Jesus would be so pleased." Amber rolls her eyes.

We argue for several more minutes about our sleeping arrangements and my spell schedule. Basically, Janie has kindly agreed to continue living with me, but she doesn't want to see any of my spells. In exchange, she's agreed to cut her Egghead time down to one or two rendezvous per week, taking advantage of his room as well, and to give Amber and me a little heads-up time so we can plan accordingly. Meanwhile, we're all going to post our weekly schedules.

"Wait," Janie interrupts. "All of this can't kick in until tomorrow. I already told Hayden that we could be here tonight. It's only because his roommate's planned something special with his girlfriend—they're going to be using his room."

"Fine," I say, figuring I'll be spending the rest of the day in bed, catching up on sleep. "I should probably study anyway."

"Well, it isn't fine with me," Amber balks. "I'm going to a party tonight, but there's only so long you can chow down at Denny's afterwards. I'll probably be back by three."

"We should be done by then," Janie chirps.

Perfect.

"Oh, and one last thing," Janie continues. "I think you and Amber should get your own fridge. I'm tired of you stealing all my stuff. Don't think I haven't noticed."

Amber stifles a laugh and looks away.

"Deal," I say.

The basic rules in place, I check my phone messages. Both Drea and my mother called me back last night. Instead of returning their calls right away, I slip back down into the sheets and cradle my dream box, eager to dream about Jacob.

Shell

Before they leave the trading field, Shell tells Mason, Clay, and the others that he thinks he dropped his glove in front of the cheese traders and would like to go back and have a peek. Mason agrees, a bit distracted as he and the others pack up the car.

Both gloves jammed into the waist of his pants, Shell glances in Brick's direction, sensing that Brick knows he's lying. He can see it on his face—the way Brick's eyebrows furrow up for just a second.

Shell heads down the row where the girl was passing out angel wings. He finds the booth a little too easily. There's nothing else around it now, just open fields for as far as he can see.

The girl is standing there, beaming at him. "Back so soon?" she asks.

Shell looks around him, wondering where all the other traders went. He looks back toward where his fellow campers were loading up the car—but they're gone now, too.

"What are you waiting for?" She grabs the angel wings she picked out for him earlier and props them up on the table. "Try them on."

Still confused over everyone's sudden disappearance, Shell studies her a moment. She even looks like an angel—pale peachy skin, light silvery eyes, pinkish lips, and corn-silk-blond hair that hangs down the back of her long and shimmering gown.

"What's your name?" Shell asks.

"Angel," she says.

Shell holds back a laugh.

"What's so funny? At least I *know* my name."

"What's that supposed to mean?"

"What's *your* name?" she asks.

"Shell."

"What's your *real* name?"

Shell looks away, avoiding the question. He doesn't re-member his real name. So, like many of the campers who elect to change their name when they become members of the community—sort of like starting over fresh—Shell was renamed by Mason.

"I'm waiting . . ." she sings, adjusting the makeshift halo she's got wired over her head—a glittery cardboard ring attached to a stick that she's got clipped to the back of her dress. It wavers back and forth as she moves, like antennae.

Shell focuses on her necklace a moment. "Where did you get that?" he asks. It's a tiny emerald-green bottle that's been threaded through a silver chain.

"My mother gave it to me. It was made from sea glass." She grips the tiny cork, spilling a droplet of oil onto her finger. "Lavender oil," she says. "Would you like a sniff?"

Shell nods, knowing that he's seen a necklace like that before. It looks so familiar.

"I'll bet it does," she says, as though reading his mind. She dabs the oil at both sides of her neck, a smirk across her face.

"What are you talking about?"

Angel smiles wider. "Come closer," she says, opening the collar of her dress. "Sometimes scents can help us remember things from the past."

Shell leans forward, but he doesn't smell a thing. Instead he notices the dark brown X on her neck, right over her collarbone, about the size of his thumbprint.

"Is that a tattoo?" he asks.

Angel runs her fingers over the X and nods. "It's the rune for partnership. You have one as well, don't you?"

"A tattoo?"

"No." She sighs. "A partner."

Shell nods, thinking of Lily.

"Not *her*," Angel squawks, still reading his mind. "Your *real* partner. The one with the X on her neck."

"Excuse me?"

"You're onto something with the whole *To Candace, forever, with love* thing . . . the inscription on that old couple's pocket watch . . . I know how much it puzzles you."

"What does it mean?"

"Are you kidding me?" Angel says, rolling her eyes. "Am I supposed to do *all* the work? A little brain power of your own, please."

"Sorry."

"Whatever. Let's just get back to your partner. Do you know who I'm talking about . . . the one who's got your wings all broken up . . . ?" She gestures toward his back, toward his invisible broken wings.

Shell shakes his head, thoroughly perplexed.

"Figures," she says with another sigh. "Here." She thrusts the pair of cardboard wings at him. "Put these on before you completely tick me off."

"How do you know so much about me?"

"I'm your guardian angel," she says. "It's my *job*."

Shell's face scrunches, even more confused. "I'm not dead."

"Hold that thought," she whispers.

And, with that, Angel kisses his cheek and disappears, right along with his wings.

Shell

Shell wakes up a couple seconds later. Breathing hard, he rubs at his eyes and shakes his head, trying to get a grip. He looks over at Brick, still fast asleep in his bed, and then at the younger boys in their bunks across the room. He's thankful that he didn't wake them, but how is he supposed to fall back asleep now?

Instead of even trying, Shell crawls out of bed, grabs his coat, gloves, and hat, and heads outside. Using the waxing moon as his light, he walks past the chopping station, past the woods, and takes the trail that leads to the beach. There's a dock out there, a fishing boat attached. Clay, Mason, and some of the elders often take the boat out—either for food or on one of the taking missions.

Shell takes a seat on the dock, looking toward the boat, wondering where Clay and Mason keep the ignition key. He dangles his feet toward the sea, suddenly feeling a bit scared, a bit uneasy, but he doesn't know why. What's bothering him? Is it the night . . . sneaking out and the fear of getting caught? Is it the dream he just had?

He breathes the salt air in, trying to figure it out, wondering if Angel is really the name of the girl at the trading field and if, in some way, she really was able to sense stuff about him. He cradles the pentacle rock in his coat pocket, imagining it as a giant crystal cluster that has the power to protect. Maybe if he'd had that sort of protection out on the streets, he wouldn't be missing whole chunks of his life. He takes a deep breath in, watching the dark, murky sea as it splashes up on the dock legs, making him feel a little nauseated.

Why does he feel this way? Why did the sea glass necklace in his dream—Angel's necklace—look so familiar to him? What did she mean when she said that he's on to something with that inscription in the old couple's pocket watch? Is it just his subconscious playing with him? Or is it something more?

A couple seconds later, he hears something—the squeak of rubber soles bearing down into the wet sand just behind him. Shell braces himself, wondering if he should hang off the dock, into the water, so as not to be seen. Mason has strict rules about not being out after curfew. What if someone noticed that his bed was empty?

He squints hard, trying to make out a figure. A moment later, a bright light shines in his eyes.

"Who's there?" Shell calls out.

"'Tis I." Brick laughs, angling his flashlight beam so that it lights up his face. "Did I scare you?"

Shell lets out a sigh of relief. "What are you doing here?"

Brick joins Shell on the dock. "I could ask you the same. Aren't you freezing out here?"

Shell nods and follows Brick to the beach, where the group often has campfires. Brick starts the flame, extracting a small pouch from his pocket. "Dried dandelions," he says, passing the pouch to Shell. "Have you ever used them before?"

Shell opens the pouch and holds it in the flashlight beam. He looks down at the bits of green, yellow, and brown, and then brings it to his nose for a sniff. The familiar sour scent of dried grass wafts up in his face. "For conjuring spirits, right?"

"I'm impressed," Brick says. "You've obviously tried it before."

Shell nods, confident that he has indeed tried it, but not remembering where.

Brick takes the pouch back, spilling the contents out over the fire. "So who shall we conjure up? Abraham Lincoln? Ghandi? Or maybe somebody more accessible . . . somebody we know . . . "

Shell thinks about it a moment. Does he know anyone who's passed on?

"How about Rosa," Brick suggests. "Mason's first wife. Mason said she died because she was raised in a material world; her family had lots of radiation-bearing gadgets like TVs, computers, microwave ovens . . . he says she became sick because of it."

"Do you really believe that?"

Brick shrugs. "I believe Mason believes it. He often says how proud she'd be of our community, of what we're doing here. Maybe if we contacted her, she could tell us secrets about—"

"My uncle," Shell says, interrupting.

"What uncle?"

Shell shakes his head, his heart beating fast now. "I think I may have had an uncle who died."

"You're remembering stuff from your past?"

Shell nods, sure that he remembers going to a funeral—the procession of cars, the sea of long black coats, the flickering candles in a musk-scented church. "It just kind of came back to me . . . with the scent of the dandelions," he says, remembering how, in his dream, Angel told him that scents can sometimes help people remember the past.

"It must be a powerful batch," Brick says, enticing the fire by picking at it with a stick. "Can you picture what he looked like?"

Shell closes his eyes, trying his hardest to concentrate on a face, but all he remembers is that the casket was closed, like a giant, empty box.

"Hello?" Brick says, snapping his fingers.

"I don't remember," Shell whispers, opening his eyes.

"Well, it's still good news. I mean, maybe your brain will eventually let you remember good things."

Shell hopes that's so. But then why did Mason tell him that nothing in his past was good?

"I want to talk to that girl again," Shell says. "The one from the trading field."

"With the wings?"

Shell nods.

"Told you, you should have tried on a pair."

Shell shrugs. "When's the next trading day?"

"Not for another month," Brick says, tossing the stick into the fire. A series of embers fly up into the wind.

"I need to find her."

Brick chews at his lower lip. "We're supposed to be going into town tomorrow. Mason wants us to shop for supplies."

"And?"

"And, who knows . . . maybe she'll be there. If it's meant to be . . . Don't you believe in fate?"

"I believe we make our own fate." Shell scrunches his face at his own words, at his seeming confidence in them.

"It was fate that brought you to our camp," Brick says, swiping a piece of his long blondish hair from in front of his eye. "Did you make *that* happen?"

"I don't know how I got here. I just woke up one day and here I was."

"Precisely," Brick says. "Fate."

Shell thinks about it a moment and shakes his head. Whenever he asks about his arrival at the camp, he always gets the same version of the story—that Clay, Mason, and Rock found him on the streets, that he was starving and nearly beaten to death. He sits back on his heels, remembering the wounds that covered his body—the gash to the back of his head, where it's still tender, where his dark brown hair hasn't fully grown back yet. He remembers Sienna, one of the elder women, looking after him in the elder women's cabin.

"Whatever happened to Rock?" Shell asks.

"He isn't here anymore," Brick explains. "He left the camp shortly after your arrival. We're not really supposed to talk about him."

"Why not?"

"Just a rule," Brick says. "Mason doesn't like it when people leave the camp. I think he's afraid talking about it might encourage more people to go."

"Is that what the barbed wire fence is for?"

Brick shrugs. "Mason says the wire's to keep people out —strays, you know—people who don't belong, who don't understand our mission of peace."

Shell looks away, knowing that it's all a pile of crap. Why else would they need a chaperone to leave the camp premises? Why else would they not be allowed to stray too far into the woods? Shell wonders if he'll ever be able to leave and, if so, where he'd possibly go.

"Speaking of missing rocks," Brick says with a smirk, "did you hear about the stone jewelry that was taken from Rain's trading table today? She said it was a turquoise ring and a jade bracelet."

"Does she know who did it?"

Brick shrugs and looks away, grabbing another stick. "She thinks it was probably someone she traded with. Maybe they took more than their share when she wasn't looking."

"What do *you* think?" Shell asks, clearly sensing that Brick doesn't believe that's the truth.

Brick pauses from fire-poking to meet Shell's eye. "Maybe we shouldn't be talking about this."

"You think it was Clay, don't you?"

Brick shrugs.

"Do you still think he took that necklace?" Shell continues.

Brick squirms slightly. "Let's talk about something else."

"You can trust me. I won't say anything."

"That isn't the point."

"Then what *is*?" Shell demands. "It's not like we don't steal, too."

"We *don't* steal," Brick says firmly.

"Well, I don't know what else to call it." Shell sighs. "We break into people's houses and take their things behind their backs. How is that any different than Clay taking from Rain? Haven't *you* ever questioned it? Even once?"

Instead of answering, Brick resumes prodding the fire with the stick. "He has a gun, you know?" he says after several moments.

"Clay?"

Brick nods. "I'm pretty sure, but no one's supposed to know about it."

"How come *you* know?"

"I was there," he says, focusing back into the fire. "I think he took it on one of the taking missions. He acted like the sight of the gun made him sick but, when I checked the drawer on my way out, it was gone."

"Why do you think he'd need a gun?" Shell asks, growing more uneasy by the moment.

Brick shrugs. "For protection, probably."

"Protection from what?"

"For the taking missions, maybe. Or for trespassers who break into our camp . . . who want to violate our mission of peace."

"Do you really believe all that?"

Brick doesn't answer. Instead, he sits back and wipes at his brow, at the tears of sweat that roll down his face in spite of the chilly morning air. "You won't tell anyone about this, will you?" he asks, finally.

Shell shakes his head, not exactly sure what he's agreeing to. "As long as you don't tell anyone that I'm starting to remember pieces of my past."

"But that's *good* news. Why don't you want anyone to know?"

"For the same reason you don't want me to say anything about Clay."

Brick smiles slightly, and the two sit in silence for several minutes, watching the fire as it snaps up into the wind.

"We're a lot alike, I think," Brick says, venturing to look up at Shell.

Shell nods. He couldn't agree more.

stacey

I'm walking down a long, dark tunnel toward a bright and shimmering light. There's a rhythmic sound all around me, like a beating heart. Is it mine? I place my hand over my chest, but I can't tell. The nerves in my body tremble. My fingers shake. There's a splashing sound at my feet. I look down, realizing that the sound is coming from me, that I'm walking knee-deep in water. There are hands sticking up through the surface of the stream—long, pale, and twisted fingers that reach out to touch me, to pull me under. I do my best to walk a straight path to avoid them, but it's hard.

"Long time no see, Miss Stacey B," says a female voice, the same childlike voice from before. "I'm the girl who'll set you free."

"How?" I hear myself shout out. "Who are you?"

Her shadow scampers through the light; I see her dress skirt out behind her. "Don't you remember, cutie pie? About the boy who's going to die." At that, a hand wraps around my leg and tries to pull me forward, into the water. I hold myself back, struggling to keep my balance, trying to kick the hand away, using the heel of my other foot.

"Dead, dead, dead, dead, dead!" she sings. Her silhouette appears in the light. She has long, straight hair that goes past her waist. The rest of her is draped in the dress, big and flowing, like maybe she's playing dress-up. There's a ball in her hand. She bends down to roll it at me. The ball travels along the surface of the stream before it gets eaten up.

I continue to kick at the hand, but it won't let go. It grips tighter, cutting at my circulation. My leg throbs. My foot turns numb.

"My daughter has a burning arm, you see. A bright red heart and the letter *T*. You need to help her, it's what you're meant for. 'Cause if you don't, Jacob will be no more."

Jacob? My eyes widen. "Is he here?"

She reaches into her other pocket, pulling out what I know is my chunky crystal rock. She holds it up, the light casting through the chips and indentures making it glow. "Dive right in, Miss Stacy B, if it's Jacob you've come to see."

With that, the girl dives into the water. I follow, allowing the hand to pull me under.

. . .

I spend that night studying in the library, trying to catch up on my work, motivated by the dream—by the promise of Jacob. I play the words from the dream over and over again in my mind—*a bright red heart and the letter T*—wondering what they mean, what the letter T stands for. I brainstorm ways to connect it to Jacob, but nothing seems to work— not his middle name (Cameron), not his astrological sign (Capricorn), not his hometown (Vail), and not his favorite food (brownies). For just a second, I feel my heart thump, remembering that he owned a dog for part of his child- hood, but that the dog ran away. I rack my brain, trying to remember the dog's name. But when it hits me, my heart goes flat again. His name was Sleepy, named after one of the Seven Dwarves. How ironic, I think, since sleepy is ex- actly what I'm feeling.

I take a deep breath, reminding myself that I have other work to do. I plug my way through chapter summaries and lists of words, knowing that I *need* to do well, that I *need* to stay here. If helping out the president's daughter means seeing Jacob in my dreams, if the two things are somehow linked, then that's what I have to do.

When Sunday morning hits, I can't wait to get back to the room to sleep. I plow through the door, eager to jump into bed, but Amber completely startles me.

"Yowch!" she screams. She's standing at her dresser, still in her cheese-print pajamas, and it appears as though she's just slammed her finger in the drawer.

"Ohmigosh," Janie yelps, jumping up out of bed. "Are you all right?"

Amber gives her the wounded middle finger, the nail painted robin's-egg blue. "Does it look like I'm all right?"

I whip Janie's fridge open and pull out a jar of mayonnaise. "Here," I say, unscrewing the lid. "Stick your finger inside."

"Yuck!" Amber shouts.

"Just do it. It'll help stop the swelling."

Amber complies, plunking her finger down into the creamy whiteness.

"Isn't that better?" I ask.

"It feels like butt cream," she says, making a yuck-face.

"*You* would know," I tease. "Just hold it in place. The eggs in the mayo will help soothe it. Just like they soothed your burning face last summer, remember?"

"Don't expect me to use that now," Janie says, referring to the mayo. Her name is written in big black letters across the label.

Amber extracts her finger for a lick, totally rubbing it in. Meanwhile, I grab some dried mint leaves from inside my spell suitcase and sprinkle them into the jar.

"For flavor?" Amber asks, double-dunking her finger.

"For healing," I say. "Mint helps speed things up."

"Wait," Janie squeals, "is this more of your witch stuff?"

"Better look out." Amber looks up toward the ceiling. "I feel a lightning bolt about to strike."

"Not funny," I say, taking an egg from the fridge.

"Those are mine," Janie whines. "I didn't even get to hard-boil them yet."

"Why do you even have a dozen eggs, anyway?" Amber asks. "It's not like we have a stove in here, and you're not exactly the Easter Bunny."

"There's a stove over at the townhouses," Janie explains, "where Hayden lives. I like to boil them up for snacks."

"De-lish," Amber says, sticking her tongue out in sheer yuckification.

"We'll buy you a dozen," I say, placing the egg inside Amber's other hand. "Hold it as close to the wound as possible," I tell her, "and picture the cut leaving your finger and entering the egg."

"Does that really work?" Janie asks.

"It's what *I* use. My grandmother taught it to me."

"And *that's* witchcraft?" she asks.

"Pretty painless, huh?"

"More like pointless," she grumbles.

While Amber continues to treat her finger, I crawl into bed, neglecting even to change my clothes. The problem is I'm so hyped up, anticipating how my dream will continue —if I'll finally get to see Jacob this time—that it takes two full hours, one dream bag spell, and two attempted telephone calls before my mind and body can even think about snoozing.

After Amber and Janie head out for brunch, I do the spell and then call my mother and Drea back, neither of whom pick up. I leave messages for both and grab my bottle of tranquilizers. I chase a couple down with a steaming mug of Echinacea Green and then lay back on my pillow, finally feeling myself doze off.

I sleep for fourteen hours, but I don't dream at all. Not even a little.

I wake up Monday morning completely frustrated, but also somewhat relieved that the weekend is finally over. So, after making it to all my classes, I head straight to the president's office. Ms. McNeal is there, sitting at her computer, playing a round of Solitaire.

"Is Dr. Wallace in?" I ask her.

She turns from the computer screen and stiffens up right away. "He's been expecting you."

Her response takes me aback. She obviously told him everything that happened here Friday. Ms. McNeal goes into his office, shutting the door behind her. Several seconds later, she comes back out, leaving the door wide open for me. "Dr. Wallace will see you now."

I take a deep breath and head into his office, noticing right away that he isn't alone. Porsha's there as well. She's sitting on the floor in the corner of the room, books barricaded all around her like before. She peeks up at me for just a second, but then resumes her work like I'm not even here.

"Stacey," Dr. Wallace says, standing from his desk. "I'm glad to see you back."

"I want to talk to Porsha," I say.

He nods, taking a giant breath, as though relieved by my decision. "She'd like that. I spent the weekend telling her about you, about your experiences with premonitions—as least as much as I know."

I look at Porsha, wondering if she would indeed like that or if she'll end up pulling a tantrum like Friday. It appears as though she's drawing lines down the pages of a textbook. Her hand has been bandaged up—from the pencil stabs, I presume.

"This is a good thing," Dr. Wallace continues. The emotion is clearly visible on his face. He looks away, toward the windows, as though checking something outside—to hide what he's feeling maybe.

A few moments later, he excuses us from Porsha, leading me out of his office, down the hallway, and into a small conference room so that we can go over a few things in private.

He shuts the door behind us and tells me that if Porsha should try to hurt herself, I'm to tell him (and no one else, if I can help it) right away. He also gives me his beeper number, his cell phone number, and makes me promise not to tell anyone about our arrangement.

"You can use my office," he says. "I have to go out to a meeting now anyway."

"Fine," I say, motioning to the door, eager to get started.

"Wait," he says, before I can even turn the doorknob. "Be sure to keep track of any charges that are incurred during your time with Porsha."

"Charges?"

"If she takes anything of yours or ruins any of your belongings—inadvertently, of course."

I feel the surprise on my face, wondering if she'd ever try to hurt me like she hurts herself.

"Just don't let her get control of the conversation," he says. "She's good at that—at playing with people's psyches. She's been to so many psychotherapists that she's gotten quite adept at asking the right questions, if you know what I mean."

My surprise melts into confusion.

"You'll do fine," he says, but I don't know if he's trying to assure me or himself.

At that, he escorts me back to his office and checks Porsha's pockets and clothes, extracting a pack of cigarettes and a lighter from the waist of her skirt. "Where did you get these?" he demands.

Instead of answering, Porsha turns away to face the wall.

"She's not supposed to have these," Dr. Wallace tells me, stuffing the cigarettes and lighter into his coat pocket. "I'll want to hear from you later." He tells Porsha goodbye, blowing a kiss to the back of her head, and then leaves me with her—*alone*.

stacey

I ask Porsha if she'd like to have a seat in the sitting area toward the back of Dr. Wallace's office. There's a long glass coffee table surrounded by a couple creamy leather chairs and a short velvety couch.

But she doesn't answer me. She just resumes drawing lines down the pages of her book.

I approach her slowly, taking a seat on the floor in front of her. "What are you working on?"

She still doesn't answer me, so I take a few moments to inspect the books surrounding her. They've all been damaged—pen lines and blade incisions carved deep into the covers. "Do you want to tell me about your nightmares?" I ask.

More silence.

"Maybe you want me to leave," I say, with no real intention of going anywhere. Instead of answering, she scribbles something down the margin of her book page.

I angle myself to look. A gasp escapes my mouth before I can stop it.

"I know you're alone," it reads.

Just like my nightmare.

"How did you know?" I ask her, my heart beating fast.

She doesn't answer.

"That phrase was in my dream," I continue. "I hear that you have dreams, too . . . something about a camp . . . about a girl named Lily. Are those things true?"

She continues to ignore me.

"Are you the girl with the burning arm?" I ask.

Porsha looks up at me, finally. Her eyes are a silvery gray color, highlighted with thick dark rings—a mix of sleeplessness and eyeliner pencil, maybe.

I concentrate hard, trying to remember the little girl's voice in my nightmare. "Is one of your burns heart-shaped?"

Porsha doesn't answer. She stares at me, not blinking.

"There's another burn, too, isn't there?" I go on. "Is it shaped like a capital *T*?" I reach out to touch her arm, the one I suspect has the burn marks. "Will you tell me what 'I know you're alone' means?"

Porsha pulls away and shakes her head, her hair hanging down over the pages of her book, the tips still dyed a deep olive color. "Haven't you heard?" she whispers. "I'm crazy."

"That's not what your father thinks."

"Yes, it is," she says, the rims of her eyes all crusty and red. "Part of him thinks that you're crazy, too . . . and that he's crazy himself for putting us together."

"I don't think that's true."

"Who cares what you think?"

"Your mother does," I say. "She wants me to help you."

"My mother is dead."

"I know. I dream about her."

"That's bullshit."

"It's true," I whisper.

"Then prove it."

"How?"

"Tell me something only she and I would know."

I shake my head, picturing the little girl in my dreams, with her flowing hair and drapey dress, wondering why she appears to me as a child rather than an adult. "I can't."

"I didn't think so." She looks back down to resume her scribbling.

I take a deep breath. "What does the *T* on your arm stand for?"

"Toasty," she hisses, snapping her head back up to look at me.

"*Toasty*? Toasty *what*?"

"*Trouble*," she continues. "Tuna fish, tomato, tasty, tiny, terrific, tarantula, tricycle—"

"Porsha," I say, interrupting her list of T-words. "This is serious."

"*Dead, dead, dead, dead, dead*," she sings. She goes to draw on her bandaged hand, but I reach out to stop her.

"No!" she shouts, tugging her hand away, drawing a deep black pen line down my arm.

I pull away to inspect the damage. She managed to break the skin near my wrist.

"Go!" she shouts, the pen raised high above her head like a knife. "I don't want to talk to you."

I keep my eye on the pen and lower my voice to a whisper, refusing to give in to her so easily. "I'll go if you want," I say, "but first, listen to me." I take another deep breath, reminding myself of courage. "It's happened to me, too. I've dreamt about my best friend's death, about my own death, the death of a stranger, and of the little girl I used to babysit."

Porsha lowers the pen to her lap. "And, aside from you," she asks, "did any of them die?"

I nod.

"Why?" Her eyes are wide. "Was it because of you? Because you weren't able to save them in time?"

I bite my bottom lip and look away, trying to get a grip, wondering why I wasn't able to predict Jacob's accident, why I was able to save Clara—a virtual stranger—but not the person I loved most in this world. "I did my best," I whisper.

"But it wasn't good enough, was it?" She smiles slightly, inching her way closer to me, knocking down her barricade of books. "And now you have to live with it all."

"I've forgiven myself."

"Not completely," she says, still studying me.

"No," I say, swallowing hard, still trying to get a hold of myself. "Not completely. I did the best I could . . . predicting things, but I haven't been able to get over everything."

"Which one eats at you?"

"Look," I say, remembering Dr. Wallace's warning about not letting Porsha get control of the conversation, "we shouldn't be focusing on me. We should be talking about you, about your experience with nightmares."

"Was it your best friend that died? Or was it the little girl?"

"Stop," I say, inching back from her.

She locks eyes on me a moment. "It was the little girl, wasn't it, the one you baby-sat?"

I look away.

"But that's not the one that eats you," she continues, still staring. "It's not the one that's sucked all your blood . . . " She makes a slurping sound for effect.

"Porsha—"

"It was a lover, wasn't it? What was his name?"

"Let's talk about something else."

"*What was his name?*" she hisses.

"Jacob," I whisper.

"*Jacob,*" she repeats, overly enunciating the two syllables of his name. "You weren't able to predict *Jacob's* fate soon enough and now he's dead. *Dead, dead, dead, dead, dead*," she sings.

"I have to go," I say. I get up and head for the door.

"Go!" she shouts, standing now. "Or you'll be dead, too."

stacey

I'm still shaking after my meeting with Porsha. I glance down at my amethyst ring, the one my grandmother gave me, and remind myself that what I'm doing is important. Maybe if I had someone to talk to when I first started having nightmares, I wouldn't have been so afraid of them. Maybe I would have been able to deal with them better.

I whip the door of the library open, dreading the next couple hours. Tim has graciously volunteered to be my study buddy for Sociology. Turns out we're both in the exact same 300-person section. We've arranged to meet at the back of the reference room to study for a quiz. I probably wouldn't be so nervous if I could stop thinking about what Amber said—how she claimed to have "set him straight" about my dating situation.

Before I even reach the reference desk, it suddenly dawns on me that I was supposed to call Porsha's father—as if things could get worse. I turn on my heel to backtrack to the lobby pay phones, but then I spot Tim. He's all ready for our study session—books spread out on the table, two steaming coffees somewhat concealed behind his backpack, and a gleaming smile across his face. He waves me over.

"Hi," I say, forcing a smile and making my way over to join him.

He gestures to one of the coffees, pulling a bunch of creamers and sugar packets from his pocket. "I didn't know how you like it, but I assume caffeine is okay . . . since we're studying . . ."

"Thanks," I say. "It's perfect."

"*And*, since *I* can't drink coffee without sweets . . . " He points toward the floor, where he's got a wax-paper bag full of doughnuts hidden behind a stack of encyclopedias.

"Don't tell me," I say. "You have an in with the lady at Dunkies."

"Smart girl like you shouldn't be failing Sociology." He slides the chair out beside him for me to sit.

"I have to make a phone call first." I pull out my wallet and go fishing for my phone card.

"Use this," Tim says. He pulls his cell phone out of his bag and hands it to me.

"Thanks," I say, pausing at him, feeling a completely genuine smile sneak across my lips. "I've been meaning to get one of these."

"Welcome to the twenty-first century," he says, gesturing to his phone. "Complete with video games, wireless e-mail access, cool ring tones, and text messaging."

I let out a laugh and the reference lady gives me an evil look. "I'll be right back," I whisper. I move out into the lobby, plucking Dr. Wallace's contact info from the pocket of my jeans. I dial his cell phone number and he picks up right away.

"Dr. Wallace?"

"Stacey," he says, obviously recognizing my voice.

"I meant to call earlier—"

"How did it go today?" he asks, practically cutting me off. "Did she talk about her nightmares . . . about the camp?"

"We talked," I say, fishing for words.

"And?"

"Did *she* say how it went?" I ask.

"Not really."

I pause a moment, the anxiety mounting in the pit of my stomach.

"Stacey?"

"I'm still here."

"Do you have some time tomorrow?" he asks, dropping the question. "I'd like you to come to the house, though, if that's possible. She's home-schooling with her tutors most of the day."

"I guess. I could come over after my Sociology class."

Dr. Wallace is delighted. I can hear it in his voice. He offers to have the school van drive me to his house, located on the drag across the street from the main campus.

"I'll walk," I say.

"Very good. Tamara, our live-in helper, will be there if you need anything."

We say our goodbyes and I hang up shortly after, telling myself that this is a good thing, that if I ever want to see Jacob again—even if it's only in my dreams—this might be the only way.

When I get back to the table, Tim is munching a chocolate cruller. He's set one out on a napkin for me as well.

"Is everything okay?" he asks.

I nod, somewhat reluctantly, not exactly sure *how* I'm feeling. I take a seat beside him.

"Something's bothering you, isn't it?" he asks.

I shrug. "Don't worry about it. There's just a lot going on for me right now." I pull out my Sociology text.

"I think I know what it is."

I bite my bottom lip and look at him, knowing that he doesn't know—that he couldn't possibly—but not wanting to go into it either.

"It's about your boyfriend. Amber told me. I'm really sorry, Stacey. I can't imagine . . . "

"What did she say?"

"That you guys were in love—the real thing."

I nod and look away, fighting the urge to get all emotional in front of him. "She also must have told you that he's not around anymore."

Tim nods. "Don't worry about it. It's totally cool; we can just hang out . . . no strings." He slides my cruller closer toward me.

"You're really nice, you know that?"

"It's easy being nice to you." He smiles.

"Can I ask you a question?"

"Sure."

"Why do you even like me?"

"Are you serious?"

"Yeah, I mean, I haven't been the most friendly person to you—to anybody for that matter."

"I hadn't really noticed," he jokes.

"Come on." I roll my eyes at him. "I mean, I can't even imagine why you'd want to be in the same room with me, never mind help me study and buy me coffee."

"Okay, totally serious?"

I nod.

"You know how you just get a feeling about somebody, like you just know that you have to get to know that person better? It's sort of like that with you. I mean, maybe that sounds cheesy, but I like you. I can't help it—despite your sour grapes."

I nod and smile, taking a bite of cruller. Tim pauses a moment to glance at my mouth as I chew. The moment is completely sweet and awkward. I feel my cheeks heat up, my heart thump inside my chest.

Luckily, we have PJ to interrupt us.

"Hey there, sweet thang." He comes and kisses me on both cheeks.

"Hey," I say back, almost relieved by his presence.

"And who shall I say is calling?" he asks, gesturing to Tim.

I introduce Tim as my study partner, but PJ totally isn't buying it. He winks at me, grabbing the cruller from my napkin and inspecting it with a sniff. "Nothing like a long, dark study snack, is there?" He purposefully bites the tip, following up with a couple yummy-good groans. Completely humiliating.

Tim's pale peach complexion has turned just one shade lighter than five-alarm red.

"So," PJ continues. "I'm Shady-8ing it again tonight."

"What's that supposed to mean?" I ask.

"My humble abode, lest we forget. Last night I thought my walls were going to come caving in on me—total earthquake-material."

"Why don't you find an off-campus apartment?" I ask him.

"Like it's so simple, pimple," he says.

"You need a place to stay?" Tim asks.

"Do I detect a man with connections?"

"My roommate just moved off campus with his girlfriend. I can ask him if there are any units available where he's renting."

"Wait," PJ says. "Did someone take his pretty-boy place at your pad?"

"Not yet," Tim grimaces.

"Perfectamundo," PJ says. "When should I move in?"

"It isn't that easy," Tim says. "The Resident Life Office probably already has a replacement lined up."

"Details, schmetails," PJ says. "I'll take care of everything. I have my own connections, you see. Now, tell me, where is this cozy nest of ours?"

Tim reluctantly gives up the whereabouts of his on-campus townhouse, reiterating Resident Life's probable plans for placing someone in there, probably someone on the wait list for a room—someone exactly like PJ.

PJ bids me farewell by chomping down on my cruller, stuffing the entire thing in his mouth. "I'll see you later, roomie," PJ says to Tim, between chews. He flashes us the peace sign and heads on his way.

stacey

I head back to the dorm after my study session with Tim and notice Sage in the lobby. She sees me too, pausing a moment from her cans of Diet Pepsi and Pringles. She's sitting at one of the game tables, watching *Jeopardy* on the widescreen TV.

I wave and she waves back—the perfect opportunity to go and introduce myself. I approach her table and she nods me a hello, tilting her Pringles can in my direction as an offering.

"Thanks," I say, taking a chip. "I'm Stacey. We live on the same floor, I think."

"Yeah. I know." Her voice is barely more than a whisper. "Rumor has it you're a witch, too."

"So you *do* practice Wicca."

She nods, wisps of her inky dark hair hanging down the sides of her face from her frumpled ponytail. Her eyes are dark, caught between a shade of violet and blue, and she's got the longest, curliest eyelashes I've ever seen—like straight out of a CoverGirl package. She gestures to the seat across from her and I slide myself in, noticing the silver nose ring she's got threaded through her nostril and the matching silver bracelets that clink when she moves her hands.

"How long have you been practicing?" I ask, curious to hear someone else's experience. Aside from Jacob and my grandmother, I've never really met anyone else who practices Wicca.

Sage shrugs. "On and off for about a year."

"Are you a solitary witch?"

"A *what*?"

"I mean, where do you learn? Do you study with a group? Or on your own?"

More shrugging. "I just learn as I go. There are lots of New Age shops where I live. Have you checked out the Karmic Cauldron downtown?"

I shake my head.

"You should. It's this really cool shop with lots of candles and incense and stuff."

I nod, wondering if browsing in stores has been the primary source of her Wiccan education.

"Where did *you* learn?" she asks.

I tell her about watching my grandmother practice folk magic when I was younger, hovering over her in the garden and at her side in the kitchen when she'd whip up things like peppermint tea syrup for an upset stomach and jasmine incense for prophetic dreams.

"Cool," she says, leaning back in her seat and gazing up toward the TV screen. She smirks at something one of the contestants says and then focuses back on me. "I suppose you've heard some stuff about me."

I nod, somewhat reluctantly.

"It isn't true. At least not all of it."

I nod, almost relieved that she's bringing it up.

"Like the cemetery story," she says. "I mean, yeah, I got arrested, but it was only for breaking in, and I only took a couple of the flowers from one of the baskets, not the whole bunch. I was using them for a spell. I wanted to find out how the lady died."

"Did you know her?"

Sage shakes her head and lets out a laugh. "That was the whole point—to test myself. I wanted to see if I could find out how she died through one of my spells and then look her name up online to see if I was right."

I feel my face scrunch, somewhat appalled by her logic, by her obvious ignorance of a religion that she tries so hard to appear a part of.

"I also didn't cast a spell on that Sam guy," she continues. "The boy flunked out because he was a stoner, not because

I put a hex on him that made him go stupid. Not that I *wouldn't* have liked to have put a hex on him—that guy was a total jerk."

"You really don't know much about Wicca, do you?"

"What's that supposed to mean?"

"It means you don't even know what you're talking about. Don't you know about the rule of three?"

"*What?*" She's looking at me, mouth hanging open, like I'm speaking another language.

"Why do you call yourself a witch if you obviously know nothing about it?"

"Whatever," she says, rolling her eyes.

"I have to go." I get up from the table, completely disappointed by Sage and her warped idea of witchcraft.

When I get up to the room, Amber and Janie are there. They're sorting through heaps of dirty laundry piled high on their beds, Amber sporting a pair of cow-print footie pajamas and Janie in a nightgown with smiling fruit patterned all over it.

"We won the scavenger hunt!" Janie cheers.

"Huh?" I ask, still trying to get over Sage.

"Free washing and drying for a whole week," she explains. "Isn't that the greatest?" She holds out a celebratory bag of popped microwave popcorn to me. Her name is in huge black letters down the side.

"No, thanks," I say, wondering what she's even talking about—*what* scavenger hunt? "I'm full of cruller."

"Kinky," Amber says, arching her eyebrows. "Was it *yummy?*"

"Tim and I *studied*," I tell her.

"Figures." She rolls her eyes and gives me the middle finger, a pair of leopard-print undies dangling from the tip. "Check it out. No swelling. Who knew mayo and eggs could work such wonders?"

"PJ," I say. "I think mayo's one of his aphrodisiacs. Maybe you two have more in common than you think."

"PJ is *such* a cuteable," Janie says, folding up a pair of her bright pink pants.

"A *whatable*?" Amber asks.

"He's super cute," Janie clarifies. "I don't know why you don't snatch him up."

"Are we talking about the same boy here?" Amber asks.

"He obviously really likes you," I say. "I mean, to come all this way . . ."

"That was *his* decision," Amber says. "Plus, since when do you want me and PJ together?"

"It's your business," I say. "But if you seriously *do* like the boy, what are you waiting for? Life's too short."

"She's not even mentioning the latest," Janie says, gesturing to a giant pink gift bag sitting on the floor by Amber's feet. "PJ dropped it off here earlier."

"What is it?" I ask.

Amber opens it, pulling forth a Hello Kitty lunch box wrapped in pink and aqua tissue paper. "He said it was to replace the scratched-up one I've been using since high school."

"And don't forget to mention what's inside," Janie sings.

Amber pops the lunch box open and a bunch of strawberry-flavored taffy sticks and temporary tattoos fall out.

"That is so completely sweet," I say.

Amber smiles and shrugs—a telltale sign that she knows it's true.

While she and Janie resume their laundry detail, I gather up some spell supplies for my jaunt outside. It's well after ten, but I really want to do a spell tonight while the moon is still waxing, and I need to honor the roommate rules we've hammered out—or else I might end up having to Shady-8-Motel-it right along with PJ.

"Where do you think you're going?" Amber asks, pausing from her pile of leopard prints.

"Out for a spell," I say. "Literally." I gesture to my basketful of spell supplies.

"I kind of thought we might have a chat," she says.

"How about when I get back?"

Amber shrugs and looks away, clearly disappointed.

"I'll only be a little while," I tell her. "I'm just going out back. There are lights behind the dorm and it's quiet back there."

"What are you going to do?" Janie probes further.

"A spell," I reiterate, like it's not clear enough.

"Yeah, but what kind?"

"Nothing bad. No gravestones will be desecrated, I can promise you that."

Janie doesn't respond. She just continues to look at me and eye the supplies I've got stashed in my basket, including a sugar shaker, a bottle of olive oil, and a green bell pepper I bought at the corner grocery yesterday.

"Be careful out there," Amber perks up. "You just never know what hotties might be lurking in the bushes. I'd bring some protection if I were you. Want some?" She goes for her night table drawer.

"You're so disturbed," I tell her, adding a knitted blanket to my basketful of spell supplies.

I make my way down two flights of stairs and halfway through the dormitory lobby when I spot Tim at the front desk, chatting up the girl who's working behind it.

"Hey!" Tim shouts when he notices me. "You forgot your notebook." He waves it midair and I feel my insides bubble up. Maybe it's because of how cute he looks—his cheeks all red from outside—or maybe it's because the gesture is so completely sweet, like something Jacob would have done. I just can't seem to stop it—the smile that's creeping its way across my lips. I try to bite it down, but it just gets bigger.

"You came all the way over here for that?" I ask, joining him at the front desk.

He nods. "I didn't know if you might need it . . . if you might be doing more studying tonight."

"You could have called."

"I guess you're right," he says, his cheeks turning even redder, as though the thought never occurred to him.

"But thank you," I say, taking the notebook from him.

"Sure." He smiles at me and nods a few moments, as though searching for something else to say. I glance down at my basketful of spell supplies and look out toward the moon. "Where are you off to?" he asks, finally.

"Sort of a nature project."

"Seriously?" He eyes the knitted blanket.

"Sort of. I practice Wicca."

"Cool."

"Really? You know about Wicca?"

He shrugs. "There's a few people around here who practice it, I think." He smiles, his chocolate brown eyes crinkling up. "I should probably let you get going."

"I guess," I say, noticing how my heart is beating even faster now, how I can't stop smiling at him.

And how I don't want to leave.

Stacey

I find a spot behind the dorm, under the waxing moon as it approaches first quarter. I clear the area by swiping the snow away and then spread my knitted blanket down. It's freezing out here, but still, there's something about being outdoors in the quiet of night, under the moon, that makes me feel at peace.

I lay my spell supplies out over the blanket and collect a bunch of broken twigs from the ground, noticing the smell of pine trees all around me. I pause a moment to look up at the sky, at its plum-purple color and the spattering of stars across it. The waxing moon, almost at fullness, is right above me. I close my eyes, still picturing its brightness, wondering if somehow, somewhere, Jacob is looking at it, too. A few stray tears roll down my cheeks. I wipe them with my mitten, feeling a dark heaviness in my chest, wondering if the tears are from sadness or the chill.

I remove my mittens and dab my finger with a bit of the olive oil. I consecrate the pepper, rotating it three times in the moon's light before slicing off the top and pulling out the membranes. Jacob once explained to me that peppers are useful for magic. Not only do their seeds inspire growth but, when emptied, the pepper's cavity is able to store things.

Once fully consecrated, I place a few of the smaller twigs inside the body of the pepper and sprinkle some sugar on top. The twigs, having broken off from their source, are to symbolize rebirth, while the sugar is a symbol of my love. I add in droplets of olive oil for purity and stir it all up with my finger. "I love you now and I love you then," I whisper, "and in my dreams we'll meet again." I repeat the chant three times, packing the pepper up with snow, hoping I'll be able to help Porsha.

And that somehow she'll bring me closer to Jacob.

Using a metal spoon, I dig a hole through the snow and place the pepper inside. I take a deep breath, concentrating on the little girl in my nightmare, confident that she's Porsha's mother, in the form of a guardian angel maybe, looking out for her daughter.

I look up at the stars, trying to block out the fears that keep fleeting through my mind—that Jacob might be with Porsha's mother right now, that he might have seen Tim and me together.

And that he might have sensed what I felt in my heart just now when Tim returned my notebook.

More tears stream down my face. This time I let them, imagining Jacob wiping them away himself by kissing each one. I lean forward slightly on my knees, clasp the crystal cluster rock in my pocket, and close my eyes once more, feeling cold droplets kiss at my cheeks and forehead. A cool tingle lingers across my lips for several seconds.

"Jacob," I whisper, opening my eyes, noticing that it's snowing. I look up into the inky black canvas of sky, relishing the sparkling white snowflakes as they fall all around me like glitter. I take it as a sign that Jacob is watching over me, that the universe is trying to assure me that everything will be okay.

"Come to me like the waxing moon," I whisper, sprinkling the pepper membranes over my offering to the earth. "Grow in fullness and in bloom. With each and every dream at night, may you come to me so full and bright. Blessed be the way."

I bury the pepper, patting over the snow so everything is level. Then, with the tip of my finger, I draw a pentacle in the snow from left to right to invoke my dreams. I lean back on my heels and look up at the waxing moon, the snow cascading over me, landing on my tongue, on the tip of my nose, and over the crown of my head. I pray in my heart that somehow, somewhere, Jacob is doing the same.

Shell

Shell gets up early the following day, well before the morning bell sounds. He washes up, dresses quickly, and then makes his way out. It's snowing this morning—a light fluffy batch that floats down over him, chilling the back of his neck. Why didn't he wear his scarf?

Finally, he reaches the dining cabin, stomping his boots on the mat so as not to drag dampness across the hardwood floor. Sierra and several of the other campers are already up, tending to their early morning chores. While Sierra and Daisy prepare breakfast, Lily washes laundry in the pantry sink basin and Rain entertains a group of children in the adjoining living room, singing songs and telling stories.

"Hey, there," Lily says, a beaming smile across her face. She takes a step away from the sink basin, wiping her hands on the skirt of her apron. "What a pleasant surprise to see you up so early."

Shell looks toward her neck, wondering about the X, the rune for partnership, but knowing somehow that there isn't one there.

Sierra flashes Lily a stern look. "You're not finished with that yet," she snaps, as though the heaping sack of laundry isn't evidence enough. Lily frowns, but obediently turns back to resume washing.

"What gets you up at this early hour?" Sierra asks Shell. "Not feeling well?"

"I think I might be coming down with a cold," Shell says, hoping he won't be karmically penalized for the lie, wondering how he even knows about karma. "Would you mind if I grabbed a teabag from the cabinet?"

"Of course not," Sierra says, gesturing toward the cupboards. "Do you want me to prepare it for you?"

Shell declines the offer, knowing that he has other items to sneak. While Sierra turns her back to set the table, Shell grabs a teabag from the cupboard and quickly scans the spices in search of vanilla.

"Can I help you find something?" Sierra asks, after several moments.

"Just looking for chamomile."

"Top shelf to the right," she says, watching as he takes it.

A second later, Rain calls Sierra into the living room to give her a hand. Shell works quickly, grabbing a spoon from the drawer, a piece of cheesecloth from the countertop, and continuing to scour through the cupboards for the vanilla, knowing full well that Lily is undoubtedly watching him.

"Is everything okay?" Lily whispers.

Shell gives a slight nod, finally finding it—a tall glass jar of dried vanilla beans. He takes one, shoving it into his pocket along with the spoon and cheesecloth.

"Aren't you forgetting something?" Sierra asks, already back from the living room and startling him from behind.

Shell shakes his head, feeling his face grow warm.

"How do you expect to drink tea like *that*?" she says, gesturing to his hand, the teabag clutched in his palm.

Shell laughs in relief as Sierra takes the teabag from him, muttering something under her breath about men in the kitchen. She extracts a mug from the cupboard, fills it with steaming water from the kettle, and sets the tea at the table for Shell to enjoy.

"Thank you," he says, frowning at it, knowing that he doesn't have much time before the other campers awaken. He sips the tea down as quickly as possible, so as not to raise suspicion, and manages to save the teabag from his cup.

"I'll see you at breakfast," Lily says as he gets up, a curious look on her face.

Shell nods, hoping she doesn't suspect anything.

He takes the path that he normally uses into the woods—just past the area where he and Brick chop wood.

It's a winding dirt-covered trail that leads him to a spot that's somewhat secluded—behind one of the thicker trees but still within eyeshot of the camp cabins, in case he needs to dart off quickly. The wooded area that extends from the camp feels somewhat shallow now that all the leaves have dropped for winter. Still, it's dark, the sun just beginning to peek out through the towering trees and branches.

Shell sits on the stoop of a rock, spreading his spell supplies out in front of him. Using the back end of the spoon, he chisels into the dirt with all his might, working to break through the frozen ground. After several minutes, he's made a hole the size of a softball. He takes the vanilla bean and holds it up to the sun, noticing how the crisp brown peapod shape fits across the length of his palm. He does the same with the cheesecloth and teabag, hoping the sun's rays will consecrate his spell ingredients and make them pure. "To health," he says, tearing the teabag open and spreading the contents out over the cheesecloth. "And to mental clarity." He smothers the vanilla bean with the moist tea leaves, breathing in the flowery sweet scent of chamomile mixed in honey. He wraps it all up in the cheesecloth, concentrating on the idea of mental health, and then he looks up at the sun, just beyond the tree limbs, knowing in his heart that he indeed had an uncle who passed away.

"Uncle Kyle," he whispers, confident that that was his name. It's slowly coming back to him in bright and fleeting patches—his uncle's broad and beaming smile; his gray-blue eyes, just like his own; and the time his uncle taught him about vanilla beans—how they have the ability to support mental power and intuition.

Shell places the wrapped ingredients into the hole and buries it with the dirt, hoping that the vanilla coupled with the tea leaves' ability to heal will help him remember more.

Shell

Shell emerges from the woods and spots Brick right away.

"I've been looking all over for you," Brick says, pausing from sweeping snow from in front of their cabin.

"Is something wrong?" Shell asks, nervous that his early morning absence might have caused alarm among some campers. He glances around the camp but, aside from himself and Brick, it seems as though most of the campers are still inside their cabins, probably getting dressed and preparing for the day.

"No," Brick says, pulling Shell behind the cabin. "I wanted to tell you. I did a spell for you last night."

"What kind of spell?" The two sit down on a couple slabs of rock. "I was thinking a lot about our conversation last night," Brick continues. "I think it's good you're starting to remember stuff . . . and I won't tell anyone. I want to help you."

"How?"

"I did a channeling spell with pinecones and dried oak leaves. I want you to see that girl again . . . the one from the trading field."

Shell smiles at the gesture. "Thanks."

"Sure . . . I mean, anytime. I have a good feeling about this. I think you're right . . . about questioning stuff."

"You do?"

"I've wondered about stuff, too, but I've been good at putting it out of my mind, you know. It's easier that way— safer."

Shell knows all too well. It's been easy listening to Mason, making excuses for why he has no memory of the past.

"I mean, who wants to get more work?" Brick continues.

"Is that the punishment for having your own mind?"

"If you're lucky," Brick says. "Way before you came here, Mason twisted Daisy's arm so hard, he almost broke it."

"Why?"

"You'd never know it now, but she used to have a hard time on the taking missions. She wasn't taking enough . . .

thinking too much about the owners' feelings. She's gotten much better since then," Brick continues. "We all get better at it. We forget those first few times, you know; then it gets easier."

Shell nods. It's all becoming much clearer for him now—all the mind games . . . the brainwashing.

"I guess it beats living on the streets," Brick says.

"Is that where you're from, too?"

"Most of us." Brick nods. "I ran away a couple years ago. My parents split up and my mom got this drunk bastard of a boyfriend. He liked putting out his cigarette butts on my arm." Brick pushes up the sleeve of his coat, revealing a couple burn marks that never went away.

"So your mother might actually be out there looking for you?"

"Man, where are you from?" Brick laughs, pulling down his sleeve. "I used to leave home for weeks at a time, camping out at friends' places. My mother never cared. I don't think she even noticed. It's like that with a lot of us here . . . at least that's what they tell me."

"What about Lily?" Shell asks.

"She's a little different," Brick explains. "She's been here forever, practically. Her father brought her here when she was around five or six. He used to be one of the campers, but then he up and left one night. Teal's mother is Luna, one of the elders; and Oak's dad is Hawk."

"Wow," Shell says, absorbing it all. "You'd never even know it . . . that they're their parents."

"Mason says we're all family here—that we're all brothers and sisters, parents and children. He thinks we should all treat each other the same . . . not give familial preferences." He smiles. "I guess you pick up on all this stuff when you've been around for as long as I have."

"Don't you ever want to leave?"

"I would, but where else is there to go? Any ideas?"

Shell shrugs, wondering how hard it would be—to find their own place, get their own jobs, and buy their own food.

"Just promise me one thing," Brick continues.

"What's that?"

"Don't leave without me."

Shell nods and shakes Brick's hand. He plucks the pentacle rock from the pocket of his coat and flashes it at Brick. "I always suspected you were a rebel."

"That's right." Brick laughs. "If Mason decides to rename me, that's what I'll suggest."

"*Rebel*?" a voice repeats, startling them.

It's Clay.

He turns the corner, standing over the two of them, still huddled on their rock slabs.

"You've been listening this whole time?" Shell asks him.

"Do you have something to hide?" Clay asks.

"Not at all."

"What are you two doing here? Brick, why aren't you sweeping?"

"I had a problem," Brick blurts out. "I wanted to talk to Shell about it. I dragged him back here."

"What problem?" Clay asks, his dark gray eyes narrowing on them.

"Daisy's angry with me. I told her she had Ronald McDonald hair and she got upset."

"Why don't I believe you?"

Brick shrugs, swallowing hard.

"What's that?" Clay asks, pointing at the pentacle rock.

"It's mine," Brick says, snatching it out of Shell's hand. At the same moment, Mason makes his way across the yard toward them.

"Maybe Mason would like to see your rock," Clay says. "Maybe he'd like to hear that you're obviously practicing the magic arts again."

"Tell him, then," Brick says. "And then we can tell him about the platinum necklace you stole."

Shell's mouth drops open at Brick's sudden boldness. Does he realize what he's doing?

"You don't know what you're talking about," Clay says smoothly. "I never took that necklace."

"Then I never had a magic rock," Brick says, meeting Clay's eye.

Clay clenches his teeth at the response and looks away, toward Mason.

"I've been looking for you," Mason calls out.

"For me?" Clay asks.

"No, for Shell. The two of us have some talking to do," he says. "*Alone.*"

stacey

I come straight back to the room after my spell behind the dorm and, to my surprise, Amber is gone. Janie's still here. She's got her foot propped up on her bed, her back toward me.

"Where is she?" I ask Janie. "I thought she wanted to talk."

Janie stuffs something under her comforter and turns around to face me—her face all grimaced, like something's seriously wrong.

"What are you doing?" I ask.

She sighs, like there's no point in trying to hide it, and whips her comforter upward, revealing an egg and a fresh jar of mayonnaise. "I got a splinter," she says, sticking her foot out for show. There's a giant glob of mayo stuck to her heel.

"Did you get it out?" I ask, holding back a laugh.

She shakes her head, two sparkling pink mouse ears sprouting up from her headband. "I tried to tweeze it, but it's too deep."

I nod, thoroughly amused that she'd even think to resort to my evil egg remedy. "So where did Amber go?" I ask.

Janie hobbles to sit at the edge of her bed. "I don't know. She took her cell phone out to the hallway and started making all these phone calls."

"To who?"

"*Whom,* not who," Janie corrects. "And how am I supposed to know? She obviously didn't want me to hear."

"So much for our chat."

Janie shrugs, like she could care less. "Where did *you* go?" she asks.

"You *know* where," I say, returning my remaining spell supplies into the suitcase under my bed.

"So are you going to help me or do I have to beg?" she huffs.

"With what?" I grin.

"My splinter, what else?" She rolls her eyes.

I resist the temptation to tease, and grab a bowl that's big enough for her foot. I fill it with a mixture of olive oil, lemon juice, and honey, all regular spell staples that I keep on hand. "You wouldn't happen to have a piece of bacon fat in your fridge, would you?" I ask.

"Are you serious?" Her face twists up in disgust.

"It was worth a shot," I say. "Bacon fat is good for splinters, but so is this stuff." I direct her foot into the mixture. "This will help soften your skin so the splinter can slip out." I take the egg from her bed and crack it into another bowl, being careful to keep the shell as intact as possible. I apply the skin of the shell to her splinter. "It's best to use the insides of eggshells for splinters," I explain.

"Are you sure this will work?" she asks.

"Trust me," I say. "I know what I'm doing."

"Well, thanks. I tried calling Hayden for help, but he isn't around. I couldn't imagine trying to hobble over to the nurse's office by myself."

"Just hold the shell skin to the splinter." I hand it to her and then take a seat back on my bed, almost plopping down on my crystal cluster rock.

"What *is* that thing?" she asks, zooming in on the crystal.

"It's for protection." I hold it out to her for show. "See all the tiny fractures and cuts? They've all been healed over with chunks of itself, the jagged edges all smoothed and polished. It's sort of like self-healing, when you think about it."

Janie studies me for a few seconds, her eyes softening slightly. "You really miss him, don't you?"

The question completely takes me aback. Still, I nod, feeling my lower lip tremble slightly.

"Sorry," she says, pressing the eggshell against her heel. "I didn't mean to get you upset."

"It's okay."

"I hope you don't mind," she says, "but I saw what you wrote." Janie gestures to the clay bowl sitting at the side of my bed. The piece of paper—my question—is still sitting inside from the last time I opened it. "I thought it was a phone message," she explains. "I wasn't thinking and picked it up."

Coming from Little Miss Label Maker, it's an unlikely excuse, but I nod anyway since I really don't feel like getting into another argument right now.

"Do you always write down the stuff that you want?"

I shrug. "Sometimes I just meditate on it."

"Sort of like praying."

"It *is* prayer to me."

Janie lets out a tiny sigh. "I'm sorry if I've been all icky lately. There's just a lot I don't quite get."

"I'm not like Sage."

"I know that." She nods like she does know it.

"Then what?"

"I don't know." She shrugs. "I was just talking to the college chaplain about some things. We can talk about it sometime."

"I'd like that."

"Hey, look," she says, peeling the eggshell away. The splinter has worked its way out through the skin. Janie plucks it out completely, a huge, beaming smile across her face. "It totally worked. Thank you *so* much."

"You're welcome."

She dries her foot off with a Pink Panther towel, sticks a Barbie bandage to the wound, and then rewards me with her mouse-ear headband, pushing my hair back and slipping it in place.

"Thanks," I say, peeking up at the ears. They dangle just over my eyebrows.

"Next time you need to do a spell," she says, scooting into bed, "why don't you just do it here?"

"What about our agreement?"

She shrugs and pulls the covers up.

I wait several moments for her to say something else, but she doesn't. It's a huge milestone, I think, like maybe she's starting to figure it out—that my way of life has nothing to do with anything evil.

The phone rings a couple seconds later. "Hello?"

"Stacey, hi," my mother says. "How's it going?" she asks.

"Okay," I say, my voice cracking over the word.

"There's something going on, isn't there?"

"What do you mean?" I ask, almost thankful that she can read me so well—even through a phone.

"Are you having nightmares again?"

Instead of lying, I spend the next several minutes spilling my guts out. I tell her all about Porsha and how I need to help her, how the little girl in my nightmare said it was the key to seeing Jacob again.

"Jacob is *gone*, Stacey."

"He'll never be gone."

"You're not hearing me," she says.

"Yes, I am. You want me to forget him."

"No," she insists. "I know Jacob will always be with you, just like Grandma—in the magic you do, in your ability to love."

"There's more to it," I say. "I'm dreaming about him."

"What about?"

"He's going to appear in my dreams," I explain. "Soon. I just know it; I feel it. There's something he wants me to know."

"Are you sure?"

I nod, as though she can hear it, and peer over at Janie in bed, wondering if she's listening.

"I think you need to reflect on your intentions," my mother says after a pause.

"What do you mean?"

"Your intentions for helping Porsha. She obviously *needs* your help, but it sounds like you're helping her for selfish reasons, not because you truly care about her."

"I *do* care," I say.

"Really?"

I take a deep breath, knowing in my heart that she has a point. I mean, yes, I feel for Porsha, for what she's going through, and I *want* to help her. But I want to see Jacob again so much more.

My mother tells me she'll call me tomorrow and we say our goodbyes. Meanwhile, I change into my fleecy sweats and sink down into bed, knowing there's no *way* I'm going to fall asleep tonight. I mean, what if my mother is right? What if I am acting out of selfishness?

I glance over at Janie to make sure she isn't looking—she isn't—and pull open my night table drawer to snag a tranquilizer from my stash. I sift through bottles of lavender and tangerine oil, a eucalyptus-scented eye bag, and a couple packages of cinnamon incense cones, but for some reason I can't find my bottle of tranquilizers. I look under my pillow—empty. I jump out of bed, checking my coat pockets, my backpack, and my spell supply suitcase, but I can't find them anywhere.

"Janie?"

"What's wrong?" she asks.

"Did you go into my night table drawer?"

"No."

"Are you sure?" I ask, wondering if she did a bit more snooping than she's letting on.

"No way," she says.

"Did Amber?"

She thinks about it a moment, her roundish face puckering up. "I think so . . . to look for a pen, maybe."

I bite my bottom lip and peer over at Amber's corner of the room.

"Are you missing something?" she asks.

I shake my head. "Go back to sleep."

When she finally does, I check through Amber's stuff. I open her night table drawer, rifle through her dresser, her bed linens, and even check in all her shoes. I find several unmentionables, including a jar of banana-flavored body balm and a pink pleather thong with a matching whip.

But no pills.

I bite the inside of my cheek, wondering if I should call PJ at his motel room to see if that's where Amber went. It's obvious that Amber nabbed my bottle of pills, that that is why she wants to chat with me. She thinks I have a problem.

Even though I don't.

Stacey

She's just up ahead, but swimming at full speed. I paddle hard so as not to fall behind. It's dark down here at the bottom of the sea, but the soft, glowing light emanating from the girl's body, from her long and flowing gown, makes it easier to maneuver.

She swims past clusters of pink coral, schools of glittering fish, and treasure chests spilling over with bright yellow gold. She looks back at me, making sure I'm still following maybe, and tries to say something, but the words are just bubbles. It's bubbling all around me, making it possible to breathe underwater.

She rounds a corner by a lost life preserver bobbing at the ocean's floor. I pause at it, wondering if it's Jacob's, if she's taking me to see him.

There's a smallish structure up ahead of us, in the shape of a house. The girl enters in through the front window, but I stop at the front door. It comes up to my waist, like a child's playhouse or fort. The door edges open, inviting me in.

"It's dry in here. Take a seat and have no fear."

I bend down to enter. It's just a box inside, barely enough room for two people. The girl is sitting cross-legged in the sand.

I sit down across from her, noting how the house *is* completely dry, how it has a sort of submarine feel. You can see fish swimming by outside the windows.

"Are you ready to know the truth, or will I have to let you sleuth?" she asks.

She looks so much different up close—long wheat-blond hair that goes straight down her back; pale, grayish eyes; pointed chin; and a tiny curl of a mouth. She's like a younger version of Porsha.

"Are you Porsha's mother?" I ask.

"Close your eyes and I'll show you a surprise," she says.

I close my eyes and she takes my hands. Her fingers are cold; they quiver slightly in my grip.

"Okay," she says after several seconds. "I'm ready."

I peek my eyes open. Sitting before me is no longer a little girl. It's a grown woman. I gasp and try to pull my hands away, but she squeezes them, holding me in place. "Don't be afraid," she whispers.

I scoot back to give her room, noticing how much she's grown in the past few seconds. She's still wearing her long and flowing gown, only now it fits her, and, aside from the obvious age difference and growth spurt, she doesn't look so much different than her little-girl version.

"Are you Porsha's mother?" I repeat.

She nods. "You can be any age on the other side."

"The other side?"

"I haven't quite made it there yet." She tucks her feet up under her legs to avoid kicking me.

"Where is *there*?"

"That's up to you to decide," she says, angling her neck forward so her head doesn't bump against the ceiling. "I can't tell you what to believe."

I shake my head, growing more confused by the second.

"It's hard to explain," she continues. "Even though I haven't crossed over, I still have some of the other side's privileges—like changing my age at will."

"Will you ever go to the other side?" I ask, noticing how she's no longer speaking in rhyme.

"I hope so," she says. "With your help. You need to help my little girl."

"I'm trying."

"You need to try harder."

"She won't listen to me. She doesn't want to talk to me."

"You have to *make* her listen."

"How?"

Porsha's mother thinks about it a moment, tapping against her teeth with her fingernail. "Tell her the onyx bracelet is in her pillowcase."

"What onyx bracelet?"

"It was mine. A sterling silver chain with diamond-cut onyx chips. Porsha will know; she wears it sometimes to feel close to me. Last week, she misplaced it. Tell her it's in her pillowcase. She wore it to bed and it slipped off."

"That's amazing," I say, feeling a chill run down the back of my neck. "People who have passed on really can see us down on Earth?"

She nods. "Another privilege."

I bite my bottom lip, wondering about Jacob.

"So, let's get down to business," she says, extending her hand to me for a shake. "My name is Jessica."

"Jessica Wallace?" I ask, shaking her chilly hand.

She nods. "I was killed."

"How?"

"It was an accident. I don't blame anyone, especially her."

"Porsha?"

Jessica nods and looks away. "When you see her tomorrow, tell her that. Tell her that I shouldn't have gone out like that. I should have stayed around to talk. I knew she was hurting, but I wanted to punish her by leaving. I tried to communicate all of this to her on my own." She sighs. "But Porsha took it all the wrong way and thought I was trying to haunt her dreams . . . silly girl."

"Wait, what does all of this have to do with the night-mares she's having now?"

"The nightmares she's having now are different. She's dreaming about a boy. If she doesn't help him, he's going to die."

"Who *is* he?"

She shakes her head. "I've said enough for tonight."

"Please," I say. "Just tell me. Is it Jacob? I have to know."

"What do *you* think?"

"I don't know."

"Yes, you do. Follow your instincts. He's a lot closer than you think." Jessica draws the letter *T* in the sand.

"What does that mean?"

She draws an invoking pentacle over it. "I've said enough for tonight," she repeats, looking toward the window.

I follow her gaze, wondering if Jacob's out there some-where, swimming in this sea.

"Go now," she whispers. "Tell Porsha what I said."

"Tell me about Jacob first," I demand. "What does the letter *T* stand for?"

Jessica turns away and closes her eyes, tears rolling down her cheeks. "Please," she whispers.

I reach out to comfort her, to touch her forearm, but, this time, my hand passes right through her. "I'll do all I can," I say, finally.

And, with that, she disappears.

stacey

After class, I head straight over to President Wallace's for my meeting with Porsha. On the way there, I review all the details in my mind—everything that Porsha's mother said to me in my dream.

I'm still all jittery over it, not only because of her mother's obvious grief but also because it seems Porsha and I are more alike than I realized. She blames herself for the death of her mother, just like I used to blame myself for the deaths of Maura and Veronica.

And Jacob. I focus toward the president's house, trying to put him out of my mind, trying to remind myself that Porsha's mom told me that I need to trust my instincts, that he's closer than I think.

But what about the letter T?

I take a deep breath, grateful that I was even able to dream last night, since dreaming has been sort of sporadic for me lately. But so has sleeping—at least sleeping without having to take a pill or two.

And then it hits me. I didn't take a tranquilizer last night and I was able to dream. The same thing happened the other night, too—no tranq and I had a full-fledged nightmare. Is it possible that the tranquilizers are funking up my ability to dream?

Of *course* it is. A gush of excitement rushes over me, having figured it out—knowing that the key to helping Porsha's mother, to dreaming about Jacob, is to stop taking tranquilizers.

To stop taking them completely.

I swallow hard, trying to digest the revelation. I mean, I couldn't be happier about it, but, at the same time, it also scares me. It's just so easy popping a pill—the quickest route to Sleepy Land. And now I won't be able to.

I reach into the pocket of my coat for the crystal cluster rock and wrap my hand around it, reminding myself of strength. The college's presidential mansion is at least the distance of two full parking lots back from the street. With the snow and the wind and the mistake of wearing rubber-soled sneakers instead of boots, it takes me a lot longer to get there than I intended. I ring the doorbell, and a girl not much older than me, with bottle-blond hair tied back in a ponytail and silver hoop earrings the size of bracelets, answers the door.

"You must be Stacey," she says, flipping the gum in her mouth back and forth with her tongue. "We've been expecting you."

"Are you Tamara?" I ask, remembering how Dr. Wallace said they had a live-in helper—whatever *that* is.

She nods and takes my coat, stopping a moment to cringe at my snow-drenched shoes.

"I can take them off," I offer.

Tamara tells me she'll toss them in the dryer and see that I get a ride home, and then points me up the stairs to Porsha's room. "It's the third room on the right, love," she says, faking a British accent. "She's been expecting you. Just give me a shout if you need anything."

I make my way in that direction, marveling at the lavishness of the place—the creamy marble floors, the giant picture windows that look out at the yard, and the swirly peach-colored oriental carpets.

The door to Porsha's room is open a crack. I rap lightly against it. "Porsha?"

I hear her moving in the room—the creaking sound of her weight on the floorboards. A second later, the door slams shut.

"Porsha," I call, knocking louder now. I try the knob, but she's locked it. "You have to listen to me. I want to help you."

I wait several seconds for her response, but, unsurprisingly, there isn't one. "Listen to me," I say. "I have stuff to tell you about your mother. She wants me to tell you the bracelet is in your pillowcase. *Her* bracelet. Please," I plead. "Just check it out."

I shake my head, wondering if she's even listening to me, hoping more than anything that my dream predicted correctly—that there actually *is* an onyx bracelet, that Porsha misplaced it, and that it's sitting at the bottom of her pillowcase right now. I take a deep breath, wondering if maybe I should go back downstairs and ask Tamara if she has a key to Porsha's room.

I turn on my heel and begin down the stairs. A moment later, the door to Porsha's room creaks open and she steps out into the hallway, the sterling silver black onyx bracelet dangling from her clutch.

Stacey

My heart jolts, knowing that my nightmare predicted correctly. Porsha moves out of the doorway, silently inviting me into her room. I take a step inside. Aside from the cream-colored walls, it's hard to believe I'm in the same house. Her room is anything but mansion-like. There are heavy metal band posters covering the walls and ceiling. Naked Barbie dolls hang from telephone-wire nooses in front of the windows. The mattress is bare—no sheets to speak of—but she's got a skull and crossbones comforter that she's scribbled over with pen. There's a laptop sitting on the floor amidst everything, including a heap of clothes, and a plasma TV hanging purposefully crooked on the wall.

"How did you know?" she asks, standing just behind me now.

I turn around to face her, noticing how she's trying to put the bracelet on one-handed. "I've been dreaming about your mother," I say, taking a step closer. "Her name is Jessica, right?"

Porsha nods, running her finger over the bright black stones. "What did she say to you?"

"She said she doesn't blame you. She said she knew she shouldn't have left you that night. She did it because she was angry and wanted to hurt you. But it's not your fault."

Porsha turns away, her eyes filling up.

"What happened to her?" I ask.

"She went out for a jog," Porsha says, her voice all broken from being upset. "We'd gotten into this huge fight. She was mad because I was seeing this older guy."

"So what happened?"

"She got hit by a car. It was night and the lady said she couldn't see my mom because she was wearing dark clothes on her jog."

"And so you blame yourself because of the fight?"

Porsha shakes her head. "I blame myself because I knew she was going to die. I dreamt it. I saw the whole thing play out in my dream, but I didn't say anything because I was so mad. Nothing like that had ever happened to me before, you know?"

More tears fall down Porsha's cheeks. I wrap my arms around her, telling her that it's not her fault, reminding her that she isn't to blame, that her mother loves her and wants her to be happy. "She tried to tell you herself," I say. "Were you having dreams about her recently?"

Porsha wipes her eyes and moves to sit on her bed. "Yeah. About a month ago. I kept hearing her voice in my head. I'd wake up in a cold sweat, picturing her lying dead in that casket. The way they did her eyes up—with this bogus green eyeshadow—and what they made her wear—this horrible checked yellow dress."

"She was trying to communicate to you," I say, "to tell you not to blame yourself. It's sort of like what happened with me. I never knew that my premonitions about Maura would come true, but they did, and I've had to forgive myself."

"But Maura wasn't your mother," Porsha snaps. "I never got to apologize for our fight. I never got to tell her I loved her—not once."

I sit down beside her and she collapses against me. This time I don't say anything. I don't tell her that it will all be okay. And I don't try to compare my past experiences to hers. I just fasten the onyx bracelet around her wrist, pull her close, and silently acknowledge the obvious—that, regardless of the stakes, this is no longer about me.

stacey

Even though I have so much to ask Porsha—about her nightmares and the letter T, about the camp she's supposedly been dreaming about, and the boy in danger . . . if she knows who he is—I end up leaving once she's pulled herself together. It's not that I don't want to get down to business. It's just that I feel like we had a major breakthrough today and that, coupled with the message from her mother, is more than enough progress for one afternoon.

I open the door to our room. Sitting on her bed with her arms folded and her bright pink lipsticked lips pressed in a scowl is Amber. And she isn't alone.

Sitting beside her is PJ, his arms folded, legs crossed, and foot bobbing at me, all serious-like. And sitting across from them, on Janie's bed, are Drea and Chad.

Drea and *Chad*.

"Oh my god!" I yelp.

But instead of joining me in my enthusiasm, Drea gives me an awkward smile and then looks away, and Chad just sits there, studying me.

"What's wrong?" I ask, stopping short from giving them a hug.

"They came because I asked them to," Amber says. "We're intervening—just like they do on Dr. Phil." She reaches into her Hello Kitty lunchbox and pulls out my bottle of pills.

"Is it true?" Drea asks, looking up at me.

"Is *what* true?"

"Are you hooked on hooky?" PJ asks, bobbing his foot with extra vigor. "Popping the pill-age pleasure?"

"Excuse me?"

"You're off the hook," Amber explains. "We're worried about you. You've been messing up in class, comatosing for days in a row, downing downers by the fistful."

"Not anymore," I say.

"Are you kidding?" Amber asks. "Janie told me how you went all wiggy looking for something last night—your *pills,* no doubt—and then I saw my goodie drawer was broken into."

"Okay," I say. "I won't deny it. But the reason I've been taking the pills is because I wanted to sleep—to dream about Jacob. But the tranquilizers are actually *keeping* me from dreaming."

"So that means you're not going to take them anymore?" Chad asks. He's sitting a good distance from Drea on the bed, his posture turned away from her, set to just-friends mode.

"That's exactly what it means," I say.

"It isn't so simple, my little witchy one," PJ says. "I've known many a hooked-on-hookie in my day, and believe me, it isn't a day at the roller rink when they try to quit."

"I don't expect it to be a roller rink." I sigh. "But I can't afford to screw up. There are lives at stake here."

"Amber told us you're having nightmares again," Drea says, swiping a long golden Barbie-doll ringlet from her eye.

I nod, telling them all about Porsha and how she needs my help—how her experience with nightmares seems a lot like mine. I tell them how her mother's been communicating to me in my dreams, how she needs my help so she can rest in peace.

"So, let me get this straight," Chad says, running his fingers through his sandy blond locks. "This girl's dead mother is talking to you in your dreams . . . "

"It isn't like Stacey hasn't dreamt about the dead before." Drea rolls her eyes toward the ceiling.

"Pardon me for a little reality checking," Chad says.

"Care to check *my* reality?" PJ asks, elbowing Amber. Instead of zapping him with a dagger of a response, Amber lets out a schoolgirl giggle and elbows him back.

Where have *I* been?

"Look," I continue. "I know it sounds weird, but when doesn't it? I mean, this is my life."

"So that's it?" Chad asks. "You're going to help this girl and flunk out of school in the process?"

"Who's flunking out?"

"Um, you are," PJ says, raising his hand, at least four inches of bracelets sliding up toward his elbow. "I mean, even *I* wouldn't cheat off you."

"Okay, so maybe I didn't do so hot my first week of classes. But I'm doing much better now. I just got an A on my holistic health quiz. And I got B on my English paper. I mean, I'm studying now. I'm going to all my classes. I'm getting tutored."

"By a hunky junior, no less," Amber adds.

"Really?" Drea asks, sitting up in attention.

"Just some guy," I say.

"His name is Tim," Amber says. "And he's totally stoked on her—like birds to bees."

"Birds aren't attracted to bees, you nitwit," Drea says. "Didn't you learn anything in sex ed?"

"Wait," Chad says to me, interrupting them. "Don't you think it's a little soon to start dating someone new? I mean, it's only been a few months."

"Jealous much?" Drea snaps, inching even farther away from him on the bed. "Personally, I think it's fabulous."

"Better than fabulous," Amber says. "I mean, you should see this guy's butt. Total pinch material." She squishes the air to demonstrate.

"Care to practice on me?" PJ asks, pointing his butt in her direction. Amber smacks it instead and PJ lets out a meow.

"Can we get back to business?" Chad asks. "Does this Porsha girl even want your help?"

"I think so."

"Well, she's lucky to have you," Drea says.

"Thanks," I say. "But there's more. I think helping Porsha will help me learn about Jacob."

"*Learn* about him?" Drea asks.

"I think there's something he wants me to know. Porsha's mother said he's closer than I think."

"Porsha's *dead* mother, correct?" Chad says, arching his eyebrows.

"Laugh all you want," I say. "But maybe there's more to Jacob's accident than just him falling overboard. Maybe there's something he didn't get to tell me, something he wants me to know . . . just like Porsha's mother . . . like how she's trying to communicate with her daughter through me."

"Well," Amber says, "speaking as someone who dates inanimate objects on a regular basis, I'm totally behind you . . . so long as you quit the shit." She shakes the bottle of pills for emphasis.

"Of course we're behind you," Drea says, standing up from the bed. She comes and wraps her arms around me. "We just want you to be okay."

"Thank you so much for coming," I say, hugging her back. "And I *will* be okay." And maybe for the first time in my life, I think I'll be just fine.

stacey

After the third degree, we all head across the street to Pizza Prison before Drea and Chad have to make the long drive back to school. The whole place is set up like a jail—the floors and walls are nothing more than crude cement, the waitstaff is dressed in striped prison uniforms, and there are groupings of tables set up in cells, behind bars.

"This is my kind of place," Amber says, eyeing one of the servers passing by with a tray full of handcuffs.

The host leads us down a long corridor of prison cells already taken up, finally seating us at a table in one of the solo cells at the very end. He closes the bars behind us, locking us in, but leaves the key in the lock so we're not completely imprisoned.

"Is it me, or is this all a little too real?" Chad asks.

"Maybe that's why I'm feeling extra hot," Amber says, snuggling in close to PJ. "There's something about being caged that gets me all—"

"Thank you *very* much," I say, interrupting the thought.

"So what are we eating?" Drea asks, peeling her menu open.

A moment later, our cell unlocks. I look up. It's Tim, dressed in one of the prison uniforms.

"Hey, there!" He beams at me.

"Hey, roomie," PJ says. "My stuff's all moved in. Thanks again."

Tim flashes him a slight smile but then focuses back on me. "Did I mention I work here?"

I shake my head, feeling my face warm over.

"Good tips," he says, smiling even wider now.

"You must be Tim," Drea says, kicking me under the table.

Tim nods, furrowing his brow, probably wondering how Drea even knows about him.

"It's the butt," Amber whispers across the table. "I told you it was pinch-perfect."

I introduce everybody and Tim takes our order—Second-Degree Zucchini Sticks, Garlic-Cheesy Bankrobber Bread, and a large Handcuffed Pizza, as insisted upon by Amber.

"He's *so* cute," Drea says, once Tim leaves.

I shrug, knowing that it's true, that he *is* cute, not to mention unbelievably sweet and thoughtful. But I also can't help but feel incredibly guilty. I look at Chad and he's staring right at me. "What?" I ask.

He shakes his head, continuing to stare, like my voice of conscience.

"We're just friends," I tell him.

"Too bad!" Amber sighs.

"What's with *you* two?" Drea asks, noticing how Amber is practically sitting in PJ's lap now.

Amber shrugs, resting her head against PJ's shoulder.

"The poor girl was lost without me." PJ growls in Amber's ear and the two end up in a long and slurpy liplock.

"Okay, I think I've lost my appetite," Drea says, pushing her empty plate away.

Tim arrives shortly after with our garlic bread, but PJ and Amber are too occupied in the corner, rediscovering each other's tonsils, to stop for a bite of actual food. *So* embarrassing.

"Let me refill these for you," Tim says, grabbing our empty soda glasses.

"I'm all set," Chad says.

"You'll need a drink for the pizza," Drea tells him.

"If I do, then I'll just have some of yours."

"No, you won't."

"Okay, fine, I won't." He sighs.

"What is *wrong* with you?" She rolls her eyes toward the ceiling. "You've been acting all prep-school pissy since we got here."

"No, I haven't," he says.

"You *so* have." She folds her arms.

"I'm assuming *they're* all set with drinks." Tim gestures to Amber and PJ, breaking a bit of the tension.

"Drinks—yes," I say. "But maybe they could use a cell of their own."

"For a conjugal visit," he jokes.

Amber gives Tim the thumbs up, not breaking her lip-lock on PJ.

"*So* yuck," Drea says.

"Are we still on for our study session tomorrow night?" Tim asks me.

I nod. "At 8 o'clock, right?"

"I was thinking maybe we could go out after."

"*Out?*"

"Nothing big," he assures me. "Maybe just out for a burger. Studying gives me an appetite and I hate to eat alone."

Drea kicks me under the table, urging me on. But I thought Tim understood. I'm not really interested in starting anything right now. I glance over at Chad, who's giving me this look—this you-obviously-don't-love-Jacob-if-you-go-on-a-date-with-this-chump look.

"Maybe not," I say, suddenly feeling guilty.

"Are you kidding me?" Amber asks, ripping her lips from PJ's ear. "Of course she'll go."

"It's fine . . . really," Tim says, turning a bright shade of pink.

"That's right," Amber says. "It's totally fine. She'll be there . . . with spurs on."

"We'll talk about it tomorrow," I say, sensing his misery and sharing in it.

"Sure," he says. "It's cool." Tim turns on his heel and flees the cell faster than an escaped convict.

The pizza comes a few minutes later. There's a set of plastic handcuffs in the center as a decoration. PJ snaps them up, locking him and Amber together.

I manage to get a couple slices down, despite all the gurgling going on in my stomach. We eat pretty quickly, especially since, with Amber and PJ *preoccupado* in the corner of the cell and Drea and Chad stuck in one of their usual tiffs, there isn't much talking at the table. I give Tim an extra good tip and we leave—and not a moment too soon.

Before we make it out to the parking lot, however, Drea pulls me to the side. "I want to talk to you a minute before Chad and I head back."

"Sure," I say, glad that we won't be letting things just end like this.

Drea asks Chad for the keys to his Jeep and, while the others wait inside the restaurant, we sit out in the parking lot with the heat in the Jeep turned up to full blast.

"Thanks again for coming all this way," I say. "It's too bad you can't stay overnight."

"Not possible." Drea sighs. "I have an exam first thing in the morning."

"I've really missed you," I say.

"Me, too." She smiles. "It's not the same rooming with someone who can't whip up PMS sachets on a moment's notice."

"Not to mention spells for zapping zits."

"Or spells for getting your ex-boyfriend to notice you exist."

"I don't think there's any question there," I say. "Chad *definitely* knows you exist."

Drea shrugs. "It's hard, you know. We're still close, but I feel like there's so much more competition now . . . so many girls. So confident. So pretty. Always hanging all over him."

"Yeah, but they're not *you*."

Drea shrugs again. "You must think I'm some insecure brat." She wipes at her eyes and looks away.

I shake my head. "I know you better than that, remember?"

"I miss you," she says again.

I lean over and give her the biggest hug. When it breaks, I grab a tissue and help her blot at her eyes.

"Thanks," she says, with a blow to her nose.

"What are friends for?"

"I mean it," she continues. "You're the best friend I've ever known."

"And I mean it, too—you and Chad belong together."

Drea smiles slightly and we begin to reminisce—about our late-night chocolate binges, the time Amber mooned one of Hillcrest's landscapers on a dare, and how we always used to do spells together, including the one we did to help Amber's boobs grow an extra cup (except that spell never worked).

A couple minutes later, Chad knocks on my window, startling me. I roll it down.

"What's going on?" he asks. "There's just so long I can watch PJ and Amber going at it in their handcuffs."

Drea and I say our goodbyes, complete with hugs, kisses, and promises to call each other more often. I step out of the Jeep to say goodbye to Chad as well.

"Thanks for coming," I say, giving him a hug.

"Don't worry about it," he says. "I'd do anything for you."

Our hug breaks and we just stand there, looking at one another, for several seconds.

"I'm sorry if I've been an ass," he says. "I just worry about you."

"I'll be okay."

"I know," he says, touching my forearm. "You always are." Chad kisses my cheek and hugs me once more. "Call me if you need anything."

"Thanks. I will."

A second later, Drea honks the horn. I wave them goodbye as they pull out of the parking lot, knowing in my heart that they're two of the best people I know—and that they truly do belong together.

Shell

It's snowing even harder now. Mason leads Shell inside his cabin. There's a room in the back that Mason keeps for meetings among the leaders and for private talks with campers—like this.

Shell clenches the fabric of his empty pocket, wishing the pentacle rock were still inside. He fears for Brick even more than for himself, wondering why Brick would ever confront Clay that way—wondering what Clay will do now that he knows Brick is on to his stealing.

Mason closes the door behind them. It's a tiny room with four benches set up in a square, and no windows. He gestures for Shell to take a seat. "How are you getting along?"

"Fine," Shell says, taking another deep breath.

Mason nods, sitting down across from him. "I've been pleased with the progress you've made. I think you have great potential here."

"Thank you, Mason."

"But I've also noticed you're very quiet . . . very observant. I often wonder what you're thinking."

"Nothing," Shell says, swallowing hard.

"Surely, you must be thinking something."

Shell shakes his head, wondering if Brick betrayed him by saying something. Or maybe someone spotted the two of them on the beach last night after hours.

"I've noticed you've gotten close to Lily," Mason continues. Shell nods.

"Good," Mason says. "Lily's a nice girl. She's very passionate about our group. I thought you two would make a good match; that's why I suggested it."

"What do you mean?"

"I mean, it was my idea. She originally had her heart set on Clay, but I had a little chat with her and steered her in your direction."

Shell's mouth drops open, completely taken aback.

"Surprised?" Mason asks. "I did it to make you more comfortable here. You've been through a lot . . . abandoned on the streets like that. Plus, with your lack of memory . . .

I just thought you might like the extra attention. She's quite beautiful, don't you think?"

Shell nods, his mind racing with questions. It's like a blow to his gut. Why would Mason do such a thing? Why would Lily agree to it?

"Just tell me how I can make your life more pleasing here, and I'll see what I can do," Mason continues, "as long as you do for me and the group in return."

Shell clenches his teeth, remembering how Lily told him she loved him, how she kissed him so passionately. Was she lying? Or does she believe it purely because Mason tells her to?

"Are you okay?" Mason asks.

Shell nods, though he wants to be sick. "Is Clay upset?"

"He'll get over her. Clay's resilient like that. Maybe Daisy would be a better match for him anyway—more of a challenge. What do you think?"

"I think he probably cares for Lily."

"Don't worry about that, my friend," Mason says, scratching the silvery tuft of his beard. "Clay knows he has to do what's best for the community; we've spoken about it in some detail. What's important is that you understand I'm always looking out for my campers; I'm always trying to improve the quality of everyone's life here. We have a very special community amongst us. But it doesn't just happen on its own. We, as individual members, have to work together in our mission of love, peace, and harmony. We can't just think about ourselves. We have to make sacrifices for each other—only then will we achieve ultimate peace."

Shell nods, wanting more than anything to leave this room, to leave this camp—and never look back. "Is that all?"

Mason shakes his head. "We need to be loyal to one another here, is that clear?"

Shell nods, wondering what he's insinuating.

"Loyalty is the key to a successful community, don't you think?"

"Of course." Shell nods.

"And so, when someone isn't loyal, it can have a detrimental effect on the group as a whole. Disloyalty has its consequences."

"Consequences?" Shell swallows hard.

"Tell me about your memory," Mason says, narrowing his pale blue eyes on him.

"What about it?"

"Have you started to remember anything about your old life?"

"No."

"Are you lying to me?"

Shell shakes his head and looks away, completely aware that he's a terrible liar—that for each lie there's a karmic penalty to pay times three.

A second later, the camp air horn sounds, indicating a problem.

"What now?" Mason sighs.

There's a knock on the door, sparing Shell from further interrogation.

"Come in," Mason says.

It's Rain. "The police are here," she whispers. "They want to talk to you."

Mason apologizes to Shell for having to cut their conversation short and then heads out to attend to business.

Shell

Shell pretends to gather fire logs from the stack that he and Brick chopped recently. He arranges several logs in the crook of his arm as he looks over at the two officers who question Mason. He's way out of earshot, but it appears as though the officers are being rather laid back about things. They casually glance about the place as they ask questions.

Mason looks far from nervous, talking with his hands and laughing aloud a couple times. Shell makes eye contact with Mason and quickly looks away, pretending to be highly engrossed in gathering wood for the kitchen fire.

"Need some help?" Brick calls out to him.

Shell nods and Brick makes his way to the stockpile. "Why did Mason want to talk to you?" Brick whispers.

"Did you know about Lily?" Shell asks him. "About how Mason told her to give me special attention?"

"What are you talking about?"

Shell shrugs, continuing to sneak glimpses at the officers. "Lily loves Clay, doesn't she?"

"She used to," Brick says, "until you came along. Why? What did Mason say to you?"

Shell shakes his head, reluctant to get into it further at the moment, especially with Mason still looking on.

"Don't worry about them," Brick says, regarding the officers. "Cops drop by here every so often. They just like to check things out . . . make sure our group isn't doing anything weird."

"Nothing weird here," Shell whispers under his breath.

They carry the wood into the kitchen and sit down to eat. Lily takes the seat right next to him. "Good morning," she beams.

Shell nods, picking at his scrambled eggs with his fork, trying his best to ignore her.

"Are you okay?" she asks, resting her cheek against his shoulder.

"Fine," Shell says, peeking up at Clay, who's sitting just across from them, watching the whole thing.

"Not hungry?" she continues.

Shell sighs, hoping she gets the message. He feels awkward getting her attention like this, especially right in front of Clay. And yet, he's almost sure that Lily herself *believes* she feels something for him. He wonders how long she's been living at the camp. How long does it take someone to become so brainwashed?

"Is everything okay?" Clay asks, perhaps noticing Shell's discomfort.

Shell nods yet again, noticing that the questions have caused him even more attention. Some of the elders at the end of the table gaze up at him from their plates.

"I'm looking forward to our trip into town," Brick says, changing the subject. "What will we be shopping for?"

"We need to have a little talk," Clay tells him, ignoring the question.

"Sure," Brick says, his eyebrows furrowing slightly. "When?"

Clay glances a moment at Shell and then resumes eating his breakfast. "When I say so, that's when," he says, finally. "When I know you're alone."

Shell's heart quickens at the words, suddenly overwhelmed with an enormous sense of déjà vu. He remembers the nightmare he had about the old man from the cottage—how, in it, the old man had whispered into his ear "I know you're alone."

Shell looks to Brick, knowing full well the topic of Clay's little talk. He'll want to question Brick about what he said earlier about the platinum necklace.

Brick frowns and looks back down into his plate, perhaps finally realizing the gravity of his boldness.

"I hope we get some free time to wander about," Lily chirps. "I love watching the people."

"Me, too," Daisy says. "I like to see what they're buying, what kids our age are interested in these days."

A second later, Mason comes in. Rain stands from the table and goes to his side. "Is everything okay?" she asks.

"Everything's just fine," Mason announces to the table. "I don't know why they feel compelled to check up on us so often."

Shell nearly chokes on his toast. He wonders what the police really know about their group, if maybe they have suspicion about the looting. But they obviously can't have too much proof; otherwise they would have gotten a search warrant.

Shell studies Mason a moment, watching as Rain serves him his breakfast and sets the napkin on his lap just so. Surely Mason knows what he's doing with his mind games. Surely he must take pleasure in forcing needy, desperate people into stealing and working for his own livelihood. He makes campers feel like there's no way out, like they need him and this community in order to survive. But, like those who broke out of the camp—those whom no one is allowed to speak of—Shell is determined to leave.

Shell

After the morning chores and a quick lunch, Clay announces that he's leaving for town and orders Brick, Shell, Daisy, and Lily into the community car. Members of the camp normally head into town at least once a month to pick up the necessary supplies that can't be acquired at the trading field.

The town square is about thirty minutes from the camp. They stick close together as they walk down Main Street, stopping at a pharmacy for things like aspirin and cold formula, and at a gas station to fill gasoline containers for the generators.

They drop off their purchases back at the car and then head into the grocery store at the end of the street, each with a short list of items they're responsible for picking up. It's a medium-sized market with about ten aisles, a small produce section, and meat, fish, and deli counters at the back. While Clay keeps watch at the exit door, the rest of the campers disperse in pursuit of their assigned items.

Shell wants to get Brick alone, to talk to him about his boldness earlier with Clay. What was Brick thinking? And now Shell himself is guilty by association, having been right there during the whole stolen necklace conversation.

But he can't get away from Lily. She sticks close to him as he makes his way down an aisle in search of tuna fish and canned Spam. He suspects she purposely had Daisy whisk Brick away as soon as they stepped inside the store.

"Are you mad at me about something?" Lily asks.

Shell shrugs, focusing away from her, toward the grocery shelves.

"What did I do?" she continues.

"Nothing," he says. "Forget it."

She pulls at his arm, trying to snag his attention. "I *can't* forget it," she whines. "Why are you being this way?"

"Don't you have some shopping to do?" he asks.

A moment later, Clay appears at the end of the aisle, having obviously heard them from where he was standing. "What's going on?" he asks.

Instead of answering, Lily scurries off down the aisle, her eyes full of tears. Clay gives Shell a glaring look. "We'll talk about this later," he snaps, and then follows Lily down the aisle.

Leaving Shell alone.

Shell looks toward the exit doors, wondering if he'd be able to dash out without being caught. But what about Brick?

He hurries across the length of the store in search of him. With Lily keeping Clay occupied, there's a good chance they could both escape. He spots Daisy first. She's filling a shopping basket with boxes of matches. "Where's Brick?" Shell asks her.

"He went looking for you," she says.

Shell turns on his heel, dashing in the opposite direction, hoping that he doesn't bump into Clay. He moves toward the front of the store and spots Brick by the registers.

"Finally," Brick calls out, rushing in his direction. "I've been looking all over." Shell glances over his shoulders. There's still no sign of Clay. "Come on," Brick says. "I have something to show you."

"Let's go," Shell whispers. "We can leave . . . *now!*" He gestures toward the exit doors.

Brick looks at the doors, seemingly tempted, but then shakes his head. "This is more important."

"What is?"

"Come on," Brick urges, grabbing Shell by the arm. "My spell worked."

A knot forms inside Shell's chest. He glances back at the exit doors, wondering if he's making a big mistake. But he follows Brick anyway, still wondering where Clay and Lily have gone.

Brick leads them down the dairy aisle, stopping to hide behind a large display. "There," Brick says, pointing toward a mother shopping with her teenage daughter.

"What?" Shell asks.

"That's her," Brick says. "The girl from the trading field . . . the one with the wings."

Shell takes another look. Even though the girl looks similar, with her long blond hair and light silvery eyes, there's something different about her. "I don't know," he says, finally.

"Are you blind? That's *her*; I'm telling you. Just go up and ask her."

The two women move farther away, down the aisle. "*Do* something," Brick says.

At the same moment, the girl gazes over her shoulder, pausing a moment at Shell and Brick. She makes eye contact with Shell and smiles slightly before turning away.

Shell approaches her slowly from behind, eager for it to be the same girl, even though she looks so different in her plaid school uniform and hooded overcoat. "Excuse me," he says, softly.

The girl turns around to face him, and so does her mother. "Do you know this boy, Angela?" her mother asks, a biting tone to her voice.

"I don't think so," the girl says, shaking her head.

"Are you the girl from the trading field?"

"Trading field?" Her face scrunches slightly.

Shell swallows hard, continuing to study her. Seeing her up close like this, watching her expressions and hearing her voice, he's almost positive now that this is the same girl. "Yesterday, at the trading field," he repeats. "By the pond . . . you were telling me about my broken wings."

"Trading field?" her mother asks, taking a step closer. "You haven't been hanging around with those drifters again, have you, Angela?"

The girl shakes her head, taking a step back. "I'm sorry," she says. "But I have absolutely no idea what you're talking about. I was at school yesterday, and then I went to the library."

"Are you sure?"

She nods and glances sheepishly toward her mother, her cheeks pinkening over. "I mean, I think I'd know if I went to the library or not. You must have me confused with someone else."

Shell lingers a couple seconds, noticing that the mother is getting more agitated by the moment—her arms folded and her mouth tightened into a scowl. "Sorry," Shell says, a thickness in his chest. "You're right. It's my mistake."

He turns and walks quickly away. A few seconds later, the girl calls out to him. "Hey, wait," she says.

Shell turns back around.

"You dropped something." She takes several steps toward him, away from her mother, and then scoots down as though to pick something up off the floor.

Shell furrows his eyebrows, sure that he didn't drop anything.

"You wouldn't want to lose this," she whispers, placing the object into his palm.

Shell looks down at it and feels his heart quicken. It's a silver pin in the shape of a pair of angel wings.

"She's looking for you," the girl whispers.

"Who is?"

She draws an X on her neck with her finger. A moment later, she's called away by her mom. The girl meets his eye one last time, and then hurries away.

Stacey

After class the following day, I stop by the room to gather some spell supplies and then head straight over to Porsha's house. This time she invites me into her room right away.

"How are you doing?" I ask her.

She shrugs, but she looks a whole lot better—less angry, more centered. I sit beside her on her bed, noticing how she's wearing the onyx bracelet. "It looks good on you," I say, pointing at it.

Porsha shrugs again, repositioning the bracelet on her wrist so that the clasp is at the back.

"You know the onyx stone helps promote strength."

She doesn't respond.

I take a deep breath and reach into my backpack, pulling a healing-receiving crystal from the inner pocket. It's a broad, flat piece that I bought this past fall in hopes that its properties might help empower me a bit. But I was never able to unclench my crystal cluster rock long enough to give it a chance.

"Have you ever used crystals?" I ask. She shakes her head and I place the crystal into her palm. "This one will help you draw in and receive energy. It's also good for self-healing."

"Why would I need to receive energy?"

"It might help you with your mom—so you won't be afraid next time she sends you a message."

Porsha nods, pressing the crystal into her palm. "Thanks," she whispers.

"Sure."

"So, now what?" She sighs and pulls a strand of her long blond hair down in front of her eyes.

"I thought we might talk about your dreams."

"Do you think I'm crazy?"

I shake my head. "No. Do *you* think you are?"

She shrugs, dragging another strand of hair in front of her face. "Everybody else seems to."

"But do you?"

"Sometimes. Sometimes it's easier to just become what everybody expects of you."

I reach out and pat her back, allowing her head to rest against my shoulder, knowing in my heart that she isn't crazy and hoping she knows the same.

After several seconds, she lifts her head up and lets out another sigh.

"Are you ready?" I ask.

"For what?" Her eyes are just visible through the long strands of hair.

I reach back into my bag for some spell supplies—a small pillowcase; tiny bags filled with cinnamon, nutmeg, and vanilla beans; a bottle of orange oil; some lavender incense; a travel bowl for mixing; and some pillow stuffing I bought at the craft store.

"What's all that?" she asks.

"I thought we might do a spell together. Did you know I practice Wicca?"

She nods. "My father told me."

"So, do you want to try it . . . the spell, I mean?"

Porsha shrugs, but I can tell that she wants to. She reaches out to touch the velvety fabric of the pillow.

"I bought that last spring, as soon as I got the acceptance letter to come here. It was sort of a pre-dorm-room present to myself. I thought the purple color would be cool for the room."

"Are you sure you want to use it for this?" she asks, eyeing the bottle of orange oil.

"Definitely." I light the incense stick, place it on a holder, and then run all the spell supplies through the smoke.

"What does that do?" Porsha asks.

"It charges the materials, making them sacred; they work better that way." I sprinkle the cinnamon three times into the bowl and then ask Porsha to do the same with the nutmeg.

"It smells like apple pie," she says, a tiny smile forming on her lips.

I smile too, removing a vanilla bean from the bag, feeling an extra tingle over my fingers as I do. "Vanilla beans are good for intuition," I say. "The cinnamon will help increase your psychic awareness and the nutmeg will help you deal with your nightmares better—so you aren't afraid of them."

"How did you learn all this?" she asks.

"My grandmother, mostly. Some I've learned from my mother. A lot of my spells come from old relatives; and then some I make up on my own."

"That's cool," she says, wiping a strand of hair from her eye.

I drop the vanilla bean into the mixture of cinnamon and nutmeg and then add in droplets of the orange oil, concentrating on the orange's ability to enliven the spirit. I ask Porsha to close her eyes and stir it all up with her fingers, meditating on her dreams, imagining them awakening her senses.

She opens her eyes several seconds later and I direct her to fill the pillowcase with the cotton stuffing, still concentrating on her dreams. "Now add in the dream pillow mixture," I say, handing her the mixing bowl.

Porsha scoops it all out using her fingers. "Can I add something else?" she asks, opening her night table drawer and pulling out a journal.

"Like what?" I ask, impressed that she's taking initiative.

She flips the journal open to the middle and tears out a page. "Just some of my thoughts—some of the stuff I dream about. I like to write it down sometimes."

"A dream journal," I say, thinking of Jacob. Actually this whole scene reminds me a little of him—of us—doing a spell together.

"So now what?" Porsha asks.

"Zip the pillow back up, run it three times through the incense fumes, and repeat after me: 'May this dream pillow enhance my dreams while I sleep; may the visions be clear and may I hold them so deep.'"

Porsha repeats the chant, passing the pillow through the smoke.

"So mote it be," I whisper.

"So mote it be," Porsha repeats. She hugs the pillow into her middle and picks up the healing-receiving crystal, pressing it into her palm. "Do you want to talk about my nightmares now?" she asks.

"Are you ready?"

She nods. "I think I am."

stacey

While Porsha knots her hair back in a rubber band, I grab a notebook and pen to get down to business. She seems a bit more relaxed now after the dream pillow spell. Still clutching the pillow into her middle, she sits on the bed facing me. Lavender incense rises up in long, grayish tendrils from atop her desk.

"Do you want to tell me about the letter T?" I ask her.

Porsha rolls up her sleeve, revealing a T burned into her arm the size of a thumbprint. "I did this after I first dreamed about the boy."

"What does it mean?"

She shakes her head. "I think it might be his initial."

"His initial?" I repeat, thinking of Tim, telling myself that it can't be true—the T must stand for something else, something related to Jacob.

Porsha nods. "I keep dreaming about him in the woods. He's not alone. There's some other guy there and he's angry at the boy. He's punishing him."

"For what?"

"Knowing too much, I think. It's like he's smarter than everybody else—or at least he thinks he is. The guy is showing him that he's wrong."

"How is he punishing him?"

"They start out just talking, but then it gets heated. The boy is defensive, which makes the other guy blow up."

"And what happens?"

"There's a fight. I see a gun. And then I see blood," Porsha whispers. "All I see after that is blood."

"Do you know *where* these woods are . . . or when all of this is supposed to happen?"

"Here," she whispers. "Massachusetts. I've seen a car in my dreams—a big, clunky one. It has a Cape Cod sticker on the back with a picture of a crab."

"The Cape?" My heart jumps.

"Yeah," Porsha says, squeezing the crystal I gave her. "Why?"

"Can you see the boy you're dreaming about?"

She nods. "He looks around my age—fifteen or sixteen. He has blond hair . . . sort of longish on the top, and he isn't very tall."

"Are you sure about the age?" I ask, anxiety high in my voice.

She shrugs. "I think so. Why?"

My chest tightens. My face feels like it's sweating. I take a deep breath to calm myself down, but it's like I can't get enough air, like my heart has just shattered into a million glass pieces.

"Stacey, are you okay?"

Is it possible that she's wrong about the age? That Jacob dyed his hair blond? That she's mistaken about his height?

I bite my bottom lip to keep from screaming out and do my best to nod like everything's okay, even though it isn't. Nothing will ever be okay again.

Because the boy she's dreaming about isn't Jacob.

"Are you okay?" she repeats.

I clench my teeth, telling myself that it has to be okay, that I have no choice. "Just go on," I tell her, my voice barely more than a whisper. It suddenly occurs to me as an afterthought that, given Porsha's description of the boy, it isn't Tim either.

"He's involved in some commune or clan or something," Porsha continues. "I keep seeing the ocean and a fishing boat . . . and people living in these rustic cabins—no TV, limited electricity, people getting water from a well . . . "

I nod some more, trying to focus, trying my best to make sense of it all. Why would she be dreaming about some boy on the Cape—a place where I just spent the worst months of my life? "When is all of this supposed to happen?"

Porsha rolls her other sleeve up, where she's got tomorrow's date written on her forearm in thick black marker.

"Do you know the time of day?"

"Morning, I think."

"But you're not sure?"

She shakes her head. "It's dark, but I'm pretty sure it's early morning because I saw the sun rise up through a webbing of trees. But I almost feel like, by that time—sunrise—it's too late."

"We need to go there," I say.

"*Where?*"

I shake my head, realizing that it'd be almost pointless to head down to the Cape without doing a little research first. "I need you to get some sleep," I say, standing up from the bed. "Keep the pillow clutched against you and tell yourself that you're going to dream, that the dreams will point us in the right direction. Try asking your dream questions."

"Excuse me?"

"You're in charge of what you dream," I explain, "at least to a point. Remember that."

She sighs. "What does that *mean?*"

"It means you need to ask your subconscious questions —Why am I here? Who are you? Where am I?"

"Easy." She fakes a smile.

"Not easy," I correct. "It takes practice, but it's a useful tool if you want to know more. In the meantime, I'm going online to see if I can find some info on any cultish communities on the Cape."

"Let me come with you."

"No," I say. "I need you to have another premonition. Call me as soon as you wake up. We don't have time to waste."

stacey

I leave Porsha's house and bolt over to the library to do a little online research, grateful for the distraction. I spend at least an hour Googling mainly C-words: Cape Cod communities, communes, cults, camps, and crab bumper stickers.

But instead of pulling me away, it brings me back—seeing all the promotional pictures of beaches and cottages, remembering how happy we all were to rent our own place there last summer. It tears me up, remembering those last few months—Amber and me in the cottage on our own, her trying to convince me to keep on living, but me just wishing that I was dead.

I take a deep breath and try to refocus, continuing to plug away at my search. I spend an additional half-hour taking all kinds of notes, clicking on links that look even a little promising. In the end, I wind up with evidence of four cultish groups, all with cryptic details about their provincial ways of life, just like Porsha described, but none with any specific details about their whereabouts.

I let out a sigh and head back to the dorm, suddenly feeling more depressed than ever. Maybe the whole reason that I'm destined to help Porsha is to see that Jacob really *is* gone—just like my ability to hope.

When I get back to the room, PJ and Amber are there. They're sitting on her bed, tangled up in each other's limbs and making out hardcore—there's even visible tongue.

"Hey," I say, in an effort to be polite.

But they're obviously too busy to respond. Several seconds later Amber breaks the liplock, her sunny golden lipstick smeared all over her mouth. "We missed you at dinner," she says. "Slimy noodles with clear glaze."

"Sounds delectable."

"Did you meet with Porsha?"

I nod.

"How's it going with her?"

"Good," I say. "I think we're on to something."

"Can I help?" she asks, blowing out a lime green Bubble Yum bubble.

"Or me," PJ asks, snatching the bubble up with a finger and cramming it into his mouth.

"Not now," I say, "but I'll let you know."

Amber stays locked on me for a couple more seconds before PJ tackles her down, stuffing the gum back into her mouth with his tongue. While the happy couple resumes their bubble gum swapping, I lay back on my bed. There's a part of me that wants to ask Amber for help—to cry on her shoulder and help me figure things out. But I don't. It's not that I don't think she'd drop everything to spend time with me; it's just that she seems so happy right now and maybe one of us should be. Maybe, when it comes down to it, I need to let Jacob go, once and for all.

I open my night table drawer and grab his dream journal. In it, he writes about the nightmares he was having—nightmares that predicted his own death. He wanted me to have the journal; the last entry says that if anything happens to him, I'm to get it. He even inscribed it to me—"To Stacey, forever, with love."

I run my fingers over the inscription, feeling a tingling sensation pulse through my skin. The phone rings a few seconds later, interrupting me. I snag the receiver, eager for it to be Porsha, with some insightful news about her dreams. Instead it's Hayden looking for Janie. I take a message and then dial Porsha's number. Apparently she's still asleep, but Tamara promises that she'll have Porsha call me just as soon as she wakes up, regardless of what time it is. I give her Amber's cell phone number, just in case I decide to go out for some air, assuming Amber's a little too preoccupied with PJ to mind if I borrow her phone for a while.

I hang up and glance over at Janie's side of the room, catching sight of the book she's got sitting on her bed—*The Complete Idiot's Guide to World Religions,* with a bookmark sticking out the middle. It makes me smile slightly. I continue to look around, my gaze wandering to the window and the waxing moon, and then to PJ and Amber going at it on her bed. It's like life is happening all around me—people are moving on, things are changing—but I'm still in the same place, in the world of the dead, when all I really want to do is feel alive again.

I fight the urge to turn another page in Jacob's journal, closing it up instead, and snag the phone to dial Tim's number.

"Hey," he says. "I was just going to call you. Are we still on for studying tonight?"

Studying? Tonight? A tiny croak escapes my mouth. I completely forgot about our study plans.

"Is everything okay?" he asks.

"I guess I'm just a little on edge."

"Sure," he says. "No problem. Maybe tomorrow night would be better?"

I pull at the fringe on my pillow, wondering how to phrase it, how to get the words out without sounding completely desperate. But then I just say it. "Maybe we could just hang out? I could come over."

"Sure," he says, a smile in his voice. "I rented a bunch of flicks."

"Great." I smile too. "I'll be there in a bit."

stacey

Before leaving the room, I try to tell Amber that I'm borrowing her cell phone, but she's still too preoccupied with PJ to care. I also end up borrowing a little of her makeup—courage in the form of mascara, lipstick, and blush.

When I get to Tim's dorm, I'm anything but confident, wondering if maybe I should turn back before it's too late. But instead I knock on the door.

Tim is all smiles when he sees me. "You look great," he says, inviting me in.

"Thanks. So do you." I take a deep breath, trying to swallow down the guilt I feel just being here.

"I'm glad you called me," he says, taking my coat.

"Yeah. Me, too." I look away and walk past him into the room. He's got a stack of movies piled high on his desk—mostly science fiction flicks.

"Can I get you a beer?" he asks.

I shake my head, but then reconsider, trying to remind myself to relax, that I have every right to be here, and that I can't keep living in the past. "Sure," I say.

"Great." Tim pulls two cans of Bud from his fridge. He opens mine and then hands it to me.

"Thanks." I take a big, long sip and look up at him. He looks perfect—hair disheveled to perfection, a mustard-colored Abercrombie sweatshirt, and khaki pants with just enough wrinkle.

"So," he says, "do you want to watch something?"

I shake my head, since I know I couldn't possibly concentrate on a movie right now.

"Are you okay?" he asks. "You seem a bit distracted."

"Yeah," I say, taking another sip and looking around the room. The setup kind of reminds me of Jacob's dorm room at Hillcrest—bed against the far wall, night table beside it, and faux-wood desk in the far left corner. There are piles of dirty laundry strategically littered about the floor, out of step, and there's a bunch of posters on the walls—sporting stuff mostly . . . the Red Sox, the Bruins, the Celtics. It's also apparent that PJ has moved in. There's a bed in the corner piled high with junk food wrappers and pizza boxes.

"Hungry?" he asks.

I shake my head. "I'm sorry. There's just a lot on my mind, I guess."

"Care to unload on me?"

"You're so nice," I say, suddenly feeling even guiltier.

He nods and smiles again. He smells like fresh musk and grapefruit, like he just stepped out of the shower. "I'll have to agree," he jokes.

"Maybe we could just sit for a while," I ask, gesturing to his bed.

"Sure." Tim arches his eyebrows for just a second, perhaps surprised by the suggestion.

Before giving myself the chance to overthink it, I take a seat at the foot of his bed, noticing right away how comfortable it feels.

"So what's going on with you?" he asks, plopping down just inches away from me.

I shrug. "What do you mean?"

"Why are you so nervous?" He nudges me with an elbow. "We're just hanging out."

"I know."

"Then what?"

I avoid the question by looking around the room for some divergence, something to talk about, my gaze finally falling on a pair of PJ's SpongeBob boxer shorts thrown over a chair. "How are you and your new roommate getting along?"

"It could be worse," he says, frowning toward the stack of pizza boxes piled high on PJ's bed. It appears as though there's a fuzzy glob of cheese melted to the top of one of the boxes.

"I guess you did sort of get pressured into letting him stay with you."

"It's not so bad." Tim shrugs. "I mean, aside from having to stock up on stuff like Lysol and air freshener. He isn't here that much."

"I know." I sigh.

"Is that a bad thing?"

More shrugging. "It's just that he and Amber have gotten really close all of a sudden."

"And you're not happy about it?"

"No. I mean, I *am* happy—for her, for them. It's just . . . when did all of this happen, you know . . . the two of them back together after all this time?"

"Are you upset because she didn't talk to you about it first?"

I shake my head, knowing that it's more because I didn't see their quickie reunion coming. I mean, what's wrong with me?

Tim strokes my back, making me feel all jumpy inside. It's just so weird—having someone else touch me like this, someone who I know has intentions beyond just being a good friend. "Life happens," he whispers.

I nod, telling myself that nothing could be truer.

"Do you want another beer?" he asks.

I shake my head and force myself to look into his eyes. "I just want to forget."

"Forget *what*?"

But instead of answering, I lean into him, pressing my lips against his. It takes Tim a moment to digest what I'm doing and kiss me back. The next thing I know, our beer cans hit the floor with a clank and my mouth mashes harder against his, my tongue pushing through his lips.

"Wait," he says, pushing me away slightly. "Are you sure you want to do this?"

But I ignore him, forcing my eyes to close. I straddle him on the bed, going in for more kisses, telling myself to just go with it, to like the way it feels.

And to forget that I'm not with Jacob.

Tim glides his hands up and down my back as I work at his shirt, pulling it up over his head.

"Wait," Tim repeats, forcing me to stop.

"What?" I hiss.

"Slow down. What's the rush?"

"Just be quiet," I whisper.

Tim allows me to kiss him once more before stopping us again. "We need to slow down. It's not that I don't like you, it's just—"

"Forget it," I say, knowing that he's absolutely right and that I've made a huge mistake.

"I'm sorry," I say. "I don't know what I'm doing."

Tim tries to sit up in bed and I move myself off him. "I should go," I say.

"You don't have to."

"I do." I grab my coat and head for the door, feeling increasingly embarrassed by the moment.

Stacey

It's just after nine when I get back to the room. Amber and Janie are out. I sit down at the edge of my bed, trying to mentally get a handle on what an absolute idiot I am. I mean, what was I thinking?

I get up from the bed to look at myself in the mirror. My lipstick is smeared across my mouth and my mascara has run a bit; there are a few tiny flecks across my cheeks. I take a deep breath and pluck a tissue from the box, cleaning myself up as best I can, noticing Amber's No Screw With You eyeliner pen in teddy bear brown. If only I'd used that instead. I take it and unscrew the cap, smudging my finger against the tiny paintbrush. Instead of applying it to my eyelid, I unzip my coat and draw an X across my neck.

Just like that night.

When Jacob and I first started getting close, we did a trust spell together with henna. We dipped our fingers into the brown paste and drew on each other's skin. Mostly clues . . . stuff that was going on at the time . . . stuff to help us figure out why I was dreaming about my own death.

But then Jacob drew the X across my neck. He knew even then that we were meant to be together always.

A second later, there's a knock on the door.

"Who is it?"

No one answers.

"Who is it?" I repeat.

Still no response.

I cap the eyeliner, toss it back with Amber's stuff, and then hurry to the door, wondering if it might be Porsha.

It's Sage. She's standing on the other side of the door crack, dressed in camouflage pants and a tight black top. Her hair is separated into two thick, black braids. "Can we talk?" she asks.

"Now? I'm not really feeling well."

"It'll just be a minute."

Against my better judgment, I open the door wide to let her in.

"I think maybe you got the wrong idea about me before." She stands in the middle of the room with her arms folded.

"Really," I say, feeling the surprise on my face.

"I'm not a fake, if that's what you're thinking."

I close the door back up and turn around to face her.

"I want to learn about Wicca," she continues.

"Why?" I ask, noticing how she's staring at my neck—at the X. I try to nonchalantly cover it over by rubbing at my throat.

"Because," she shrugs, "it seems so cool. All the spells and stuff."

"It's a lot more than spells. The spells are pointless if they're not purposeful—if they're not backed by good intention."

"I know that."

"You do?"

"Well, I *want* to know."

I let out another sigh and then direct her to my bookshelf. I pull out some of the reference books I have—my copies of *Teen Witch* and *Elements of Witchcraft*. "Here," I say. "Read these."

"Seriously . . . I can borrow them?"

"They're good for getting started, for seeing if Wicca is your thing or not."

"Thanks."

"Sure." I take a deep breath and sit down at the edge of my bed, continuing to rub at my neck, seeing if I can wipe the X away, though it seems this screw-proof eyeliner lives up to its name.

"Are you okay?"

More nodding.

"What's wrong with your neck?" Sage takes a couple steps closer to look. "The rune for partnership, right?"

I nod, somewhat surprised that she recognizes it.

"I'm not a *complete* fake," she says. "I do know *some* of this stuff. So who's the boy?"

"It's kind of a long story."

"Does he go here?"

I shake my head, wishing she'd take her books and leave.

"So I take it you guys have one of those distant-relationship things?"

"He's gone," I snap.

"*Gone?*" Sage sits down beside me, clearly sensing my angst —which only makes it worse. I feel my eyes well up. A couple tears slip down the creases of my face.

Sage doesn't ask me any more. She just wraps her arms around me and rubs my back. And all I can do is let her.

stacey

As soon as Sage leaves, I mentally pick myself up off the floor and wipe away the proverbial dust.

Before I call Porsha again, I dial Tim's number, leaving what feels like a full-five-minute apology on his voicemail. I plead temporary insanity, tell him how sorry I am, and say that I had no right to try and use him like that. I babble on, telling him that all I wanted to do was right everything that's gone wrong in my life, but that I was pushing too far, moving too fast, and going in the wrong direction. I tell him that maybe I'm just not ready for everything to be so right. And then I apologize for not making any sense.

But at least it makes sense to me.

After that, I hang up and dial Porsha.

"She's sleeping," Dr. Wallace tells me.

"*Still?*" I sigh.

"How are your sessions going with her?" he asks, ignoring the question.

"Good," I say. "I think we're making progress."

He asks me to give him concrete details about our meetings—who and what we talk about, as well as undeniable proof that she isn't as unstable as everybody thinks. But all I can manage to get out at the moment is "I don't think she's crazy."

I make a promise to fill him in more at another time, and then make *him* promise to have Porsha call me ASAP. I hang up, reminding myself that it would be stupid to have him wake her up now, possibly interrupting one of her premonitions—even though time is really of the essence here.

I sit back on my bed, noticing a long rectangular package sitting on the floor. I pick it up and read the labels. It's addressed to me, from my mother. Amber must have picked it up along with her stuff. I open it up, peeling away at least three layers of tissue paper until I get to it—a thick red candle.

"For remembrance," I whisper, feeling badly for what I said to her before, how I accused her of wanting me to forget everything—to forget Jacob—when it's obvious that she wants me to remember him.

I get back on the phone and call her.

"Did you get it?" she asks, before even saying hello.

"I did. Thank you."

"I want you to remember, Stacey. You wouldn't be who you are if you didn't."

"I know. I'm sorry for blowing up before."

"Don't worry about it," she says. "Just be happy—don't dwell on memories; appreciate them for what they are and for the person they've helped you become."

"Thank you," I repeat.

"Don't thank me," she says. "Just light the red candle and remember him. Remember to have hope."

"Hope for what?"

"For whatever makes you happy."

"What if there is no hope in getting what makes me happy?"

"There's always hope," she says.

I let out a small sigh, feeling anything but hopeful. Still, after we say our goodbyes, I grab the red candle and consecrate it with olive oil and lemongrass incense. Then, using a razor blade, I carve the rune for partnership (the X) into the side. The crumbling red wax sparkles beneath my fingertips. I set the candle down on a ceramic plate that's been cleansed and bathed in a full moon's cycle. Then I reach into my night table drawer and pull out the white candle stump. It's the remainder of the candle that Jacob and I lit when we silently declared our love for one another. Jacob's uncle, who taught him most of what he knew about magic, told him to save the candle for his one true love. And so we lit the candle one night, each holding a starter candle, sitting on the floor of my dorm room at Hillcrest.

I press the stump against my nose. It still smells like rose oil from when we consecrated it. I light the red candle and use its flame to ignite the stump's tiny wick, careful to keep my fingers away from the fire. "For remembrance," I whisper. I drip the stump's wax over the red candle, thinking how the individual droplets look like tears, and then I place the two candles side by side on the plate. The hot red wax drips down over the white stump, gluing the two candles together so they become one.

After the stump's wick finally burns out and there's a giant pink globule of wax at the bottom of the red candle—the product of the two parent candles—I lay back on my bed, tempering the urge to take a tranquilizer by running my fingers over the X on my neck. It takes over an hour before the urge finally dies, and even longer than that for the red candle flame to go out. I roll over in bed, wondering when Porsha is going to finally wake up and call me, feeling myself drift off as well.

The next thing I know, the phone rings, jolting me awake. I snap out of bed and glance at the clock. It's after eleven. "Hello?" I say, picking up the receiver.

"It's me, Porsha."

"How are you?" I ask. "Did you have another nightmare? Did our spell work?"

"We need to talk."

"Is there something wrong?"

"I need to see you," she says. "I'm in your dorm. I tried to sneak in through the back, since I don't have an ID, but I ended up in the basement and now I can't get out. The doors only open one way. Can you come get me?"

"I'll be right down."

I hurry down the hallway and take the back staircase all the way down to the basement. I edge the basement door open, noticing right away how completely dark it is. "Porsha?" I shout, my voice echoing. I stick my hand inside, feeling around the wall for a light switch. I find one and click it on, but I don't see her anywhere. It's absolutely vacant down here—just one long concrete hallway with brick walls.

"Porsha?" I call again, looking behind me, toward the staircase, wondering if maybe she managed her way upstairs. But how could she if, like she said, the doors only open up one way? I look around for something to wedge into the door crack, and end up slipping off my sneaker and using it to hold the door open instead.

I begin down the hallway, noticing how much colder it is down here. I fold my arms to stifle the chill, picturing the hallways of dorm rooms stacked above me. There are doors to the right and left. I call Porsha's name a couple more times, wondering if she might have gone into one of them, maybe looking for an alternate route.

I stop suddenly, hearing something coming from behind me—a rhythmic sound, like the ocean, like the tide pulling at the rocks. I turn to look, just as the basement door closes.

Locking me in.

"No!" I shout out. I run to the door and try pushing it back open, but it won't budge. I pull at it, kick it, and smash my fists up against it. But it's no use. "Porsha!" I shout again, noticing that even my sneaker is gone now.

"Here," a voice whispers from somewhere down the hallway.

I begin in that direction again, listening hard for her voice. "Where?" I ask.

"Here," she repeats. Her voice is coming from the room on the right. I knock on the door, but there's no response. I wrap my hand around the knob. At the same moment, all the lights go off.

"Come on in," the voice whispers.

My heart pounds. My jaw shakes. I take a deep breath and turn the knob. "Porsha?" I say, stepping inside. There's a wall directly in front of me, preventing me from moving any farther. I go to take a step back, but the door closes, boxing me in.

I move my fingers over the walls, searching for a door handle. But there doesn't seem to be one. I reach up and feel the ceiling; it's just above my head. It's like I'm trapped in a closet of some sort, only it's smaller than a closet—more like a casket.

"Hello?" I whisper, trying to be brave.

"I'm here," she whispers back.

"Who?"

A scratching sound comes from outside the box, like someone's clawing to get in. I bang at the walls, trying to get out, but it's so small inside here that I can't get enough momentum in my arm.

"Help me!" I shout.

"How does it feel to be dead?" she asks. "*Dead, dead, dead, dead, dead.*"

"Porsha?"

"No." She giggles. "It's Jessica, Porsha's mother."

"Where are you?" I ask, noticing how my head feels dizzy, how I'm starting to sweat.

"I'm right behind you," she whispers.

I try to turn around, but it's too crammed inside this box.

"Ever wonder what it feels like to be buried alive?" she asks.

"Why are you doing this?"

"*You're* the one who's doing it. This is *your* dream, remember?"

I swallow hard, conjuring up all my strength, reminding myself that this *is* my dream and that I have the power to change it. I close my eyes and concentrate hard. A few seconds later, the door cracks open and a slice of light shines in.

Jessica is there. She wraps her arms around me and kisses my cheek. "Much better on this side, isn't it?" She's wearing a silky white robe with huge bell sleeves that remind me of angel wings.

"Is that what death is like?" I ask, gesturing to the box behind me, the one I was standing in.

She shakes her head. "Not for most of us."

"What do you mean?"

"I mean, thank you for helping me pass on to the other side."

"You're passing over?"

She nods. "I know my daughter will be okay now . . . now that you're helping her. I feel like a whole truckload has been lifted from me. You can't pass on with all that extra baggage." She smiles, her pale gray eyes squinting slightly. "Thank you for all your help."

"But I haven't done that much yet."

"You have . . . more than you know."

She leads me out to the hallway. The basement door is wide open now, my sneaker sitting and waiting for me on the floor.

"Can you just answer one question for me?" I ask.

She nods, somewhat reluctantly. "Just one."

"Why is Porsha dreaming about this boy on the Cape? What is her connection to him? What is her connection to *me*?"

Jessica smiles. "I'm surprised you haven't already figured out the answers to some of those questions."

"How would I?"

"By using your intuition—what you've learned, what you sense in your heart to be true. Why do you think *you're* connected to Jacob?"

"Why do I think I *am* connected to him?" I ask, noting how she chose to use the present tense. "So he isn't on the other side? He's still alive?"

"I said I'd answer only one question."

"But you haven't answered anything, really."

"I have to go." Jessica looks down at her watchless wrist. "I keep forgetting that time doesn't exist on the other side. Oh, well." She shrugs and turns in the opposite direction of the exit door, toward the blazing light at the end of the corridor. Her wheat-blond hair blows back from the intensity of the glow. She stops just inches from the light and turns to me—a little girl again, like when I first met her. She waves to me, a bright and contagious smile across her ten-year-old face.

I wave back, watching as she turns around and continues into the light. I turn away, too, eager to find my way back upstairs.

But I'm no longer in the basement. I'm at the beach. The tide is coming in, bringing with it a new sense of hope. I sink down into the sand, breathing in the warm, salty air, feeling the sun blaze down over me. The waves roll in and crash against the surf, just a few yards from my feet. After several seconds, I notice something in the water. It bobs up and down a couple seconds before surfacing completely. I stand and clasp my hands over my mouth, watching the figure swim toward the shore—toward me.

Jacob.

I'm trembling all over. "Is it really you?" I gush.

He nods and I run to him, half-crying and half-laughing—trying to catch my breath. "I love you," I whisper in his ear.

Jacob sweeps me up in his arms and I feel more complete than I ever thought possible.

A couple moments later, I wake up with a gasp—in a sweat. Amber's cell phone is vibrating in the pocket of my jeans. "Hello?" I say, scrambling for the volume.

"Hi, Stacey? It's me, Porsha. Are you okay?"

Still trying to catch my breath, I tell her that I am okay, noticing the lingering sense of hope in my heart. "How are *you*?" I ask. "Did you have another nightmare?" I sit up in bed and glance at the clock. It's 3:15 in the morning.

"I need you to come right away," she says. "The spell worked. I know where the boy is."

Shell

During the ride home from the shopping trip, during his late afternoon chores, and all through dinner, Shell can't stop thinking about the girl he met in the grocery store—about what she said to him and how she drew that X on her neck with her finger, telling him that someone was looking for him.

Shell knows it must be someone from his past—his soul mate—only he doesn't know who she is. He sits back in bed, smothering his head in the pillow, frustrated with his own mind, with why it's keeping things from him. Why is it that he's able to remember his uncle, but he isn't able to remember his one true love?

He lets out a giant sigh and then releases the pillow to his lap with a plop. The subtle noises stir Brick, who turns over in bed and peeps an eye open. When he notices that Shell is awake, he sits up in bed. "Why aren't you sleeping?" Brick whispers.

"Sorry I woke you," Shell says. "I have a lot on my mind." Shell thinks how ironic the statement is—since his mind is the thing that's failing him.

"Hey, was anyone in here earlier?" Brick asks, rubbing at his sleepy eyes. "Lily or Daisy, maybe?"

"No, why?"

Brick shrugs and then laughs at himself. "Must have been dreaming. I could have sworn I heard a girl's voice whispering in my ear."

"Whispering *what*?"

Brick shrugs again. "She just kept asking me where I was."

"Did you answer?"

"I think I did. I think I said Brutus, but I'm not sure. You know what's weird, though?" Brick says, chuckling. "She kept calling me by my real name."

"Your *real* name?"

"Yeah, you know, my pre-community name, the one I had before I came here."

"Which is?"

"Trevor." Brick lets out another chuckle. "Not as cool as Brick, is it?"

"It suits you," Shell says, taking the information in. "I wonder if it means something . . . the voice you heard."

"Come on," Brick moans. "Tell me you haven't dreamt about girls before. If I hadn't been so rudely awakened, maybe my dream could have had a happy ending."

Shell laughs. "Let's not go there."

Brick reaches under his bed for Shell's pentacle rock. He gives it back to him and then sits at the foot of Shell's bed. "So why *are* you up? What's bothering you?"

Shell shrugs, reaching under his bed for a red candle. He snuck it from the kitchen at dinner, while everyone was cleaning up.

"What's that for?" Brick asks.

"Remembrance."

"Seriously?"

"My uncle taught me the meaning of candle colors."

"You really want to remember more about your past, don't you?" Brick asks.

Shell nods, glancing over at the empty beds in the corner, where Oak, Teal, and Horizon usually sleep. "Where are they tonight?"

"Punished. They're sleeping in tents outside."

"It's got to be ten degrees out at best," Shell says.

"Blame it on Clay."

"Why, what did they do?"

"They were making fun of him during chores, I guess. They were supposed to be peeling potatoes, but they were playing around, imitating him—his nasally voice, his hunchback posture, and the way he's always narrowing his eyes at everybody." Brick squints his eyes extra hard to demonstrate. "Anyway, he walked in from behind and saw the whole thing."

"That sucks."

"At least it won't happen to us." Brick grins.

"Why not?"

"I told him I knew about what happened on trading day, how he stole the jewelry from Rain's table." Brick smiles, the tiny gap between his two front teeth barely visible. "I did it right after dinner while I was clearing the plates . . . just a few feet from Mason. You should have seen Clay's face." His grin widens.

"Did Mason hear you?"

Brick shakes his head. "I doubt it."

"Why would you do that? Do you know for a fact he's the one who took it?"

"I do *now*. The scab didn't deny it."

"You shouldn't have done that."

Brick shrugs. "I'm sick of him controlling my every move. At least *this* gives me a little leverage; I don't have to be afraid of him anymore."

Shell nods, but he has his doubts. "What if he makes things more difficult for you now?"

"No way," Brick says, raising his eyebrows and grinning. "He already told me that he wants to set some time aside tomorrow so we can talk—just the two of us."

"Alone?" Shell asks, remembering the words from his nightmare.

"Naturally," Brick shrugs. "He said we should *discuss* a couple things . . . I'm thinking he wants to let me in on his looting . . . you know, so I won't say anything. Either that or he wants to give me a little more clout, make me a big shot around here. What do you think of that?" Brick hikes up the sleeve of his T-shirt to flex a muscle that isn't really there.

"I don't know," Shell says, shaking his head.

"I'm kidding, of course." Brick rolls his sleeve back down.

"No. I mean, I don't think you should be alone with him; make sure other people are around."

"You're being paranoid," Brick says. "I *need* to be alone with him. How else is he going to crawl inside my trap? Believe me, there's nothing I'd like more than to bring that scab to his knees. Plus, If we're alone, there's a good chance he'll confess the whole thing . . . maybe even show me cold, hard proof. Then I could go to Mason and tell him everything."

"Promise me you won't be alone with him," Shell insists, remembering the conversation he and Brick had on the beach—how Brick told him that Clay has a gun.

"Why? What's with you?"

"I have a bad feeling about this."

"*Why?*"

"Because . . . it just doesn't make sense to me."

Brick sighs and looks away. "Nothing makes sense to you. Clay wouldn't try something stupid, if that's what you're thinking. Mason wouldn't allow it."

"Don't be mad," Shell says, brimming with doubt. "Just don't be alone with him. Don't cut any deals. Okay?"

"And how am I supposed to avoid it?" Brick asks, running his fingers through his hair in frustration. "What am I supposed to say when he wants to pull me aside?"

"You'll come up with something," Shell says, reaching out to bop Brick in the arm.

Brick nods, but Shell can see that he's clearly disappointed. "You won't be sorry," Shell says, bopping his arm one more time.

Brick pulls his arm away to roll his sleeve back up. "Yeah, I'll be sorry. And you will be, too. We could've been *big.*" Brick flashes his muscle again, making Shell laugh.

Shell

After Brick returns to his bed, Shell remains awake. He reaches into his coat pocket for a handful of parsley that he was able to save from his salad at dinner. He somehow knows that parsley has the ability to cleanse and, since he wasn't able to sneak into the cupboard for a bottle of olive oil—on top of the candle he was already snatching—he needs it for its purification properties.

He rolls the parsley between the tips of his fingers before applying it to the candle's base. The tiny green leaves bead up as he glides the sprig down the candle's length, concentrating on the idea of purity. He touches the top end of the candle. "As above," he whispers. Then he touches the bottom. "So below." He continues to consecrate the candle for several more moments before unclasping the safety pin from his belt loop. Using the point, he carves a giant X into the side of the candle and then sets it down on a plate. "With the power of the moon and the strength of the sea," he whispers, "I wish, I want to remember thee. Please tell me, Dream. Please make it clear—how did I end up living here?"

Shell positions the candle and plate on a safe spot on the hardwood floor and then lights the wick. He watches the wax droplets drip down the side, reminding him of tears. The flame flickers slightly with the draft in the room. Shell pulls his covers tightly around him and clenches his pentacle rock, lounging back in bed, willing his mind to remember.

After several minutes, he feels himself start to nod off. He extinguishes the candle with a few droplets of water from his cup, and then allows himself to fall asleep.

. . .

The ocean is absolutely freezing tonight. Shell swims through it, holding his breath underwater, trying to find his way out. It's completely black below sea level. Not even the moon's light can help him under here. Still, he keeps moving forward, trying to preserve his breath as best he can; his lungs feel like they're filling up.

"Over here," he hears someone whisper.

He turns and sees Angel. She's floating a few feet away, dressed in a long white gown that floats upward. There are beams of light emanating from her skin.

"She's up there," she says, pointing toward the surface of the water, struggling to keep her dress down.

Shell looks up, but it's just so dark.

"Here," she says, removing an extra set of angel wings from her back. "You can pay me back later."

Shell takes them. "Thank you," he says.

"No sweat." She helps Shell fasten the wings to his back and, as soon as they're in place, he becomes illuminated as well. "Pretty cool, huh?" Angel says.

Shell nods.

"You almost drowned, you know," she says.

"Right now?"

"No, silly." She laughs. "Before . . . when you fell overboard. Don't you remember yet?"

Shell feels his face mess up in confusion.

"Oh yeah, that's right; people with amnesia don't remember anything, do they?" She laughs again.

"Amnesia?"

"Oh, like it's such a big secret." She huffs. "Tell me you didn't know. I mean, it's so completely obvious. Why else can't you remember anything from your past?"

Shell nods, knowing in his heart that it's true, but that he didn't want to label it. He's heard somewhere that amnesia can last for months, if not years.

"So what are you waiting for?" She throws a piece of sea kelp toward his head. "Don't you *want* to remember?"

He nods.

"So get going, you goose!" She points upward again, toward the surface of the water.

Shell swims in that direction, his lungs so much stronger now, less constricted. After several seconds, he reaches the surface and breaks through it.

To his complete surprise, it's daylight now. How long has he been lost at sea? He treads a few moments in the water, trying to get his bearings. There's a long stretch of beach on both sides of him. He swallows hard, noticing the girl sitting alone in the sand. She stands when she sees him, taking several steps forward until they're only a few yards apart.

She's more beautiful than he'd ever imagine—long hair, the color of dark chocolate; golden brown eyes; and a heart-shaped face. There's a large dark brown X over her neck. Somehow he knows that he's the one who drew it there—with henna, he's sure.

The girl is trembling. She clasps her hands over her mouth. "Is it really you?" she asks, her voice cracking slightly.

Shell nods and the girl runs to him, sobbing uncontrollably, unable to catch her breath.

"I love you," she whispers, over and over again.

Shell embraces her, noticing right away how she smells like lavender, feeling more complete than he ever thought possible.

Shell

Shell wakes up in a sweat, his sweatshirt damp with perspiration. He forces his eyes closed, trying to retain his dream —her face.

He can still feel her—the way her fingers clasped around his neck, the way she pressed herself against him, her heart beating fast against his chest.

And what Angel said—how he has amnesia. It's not like it comes as a big surprise to him; it's just that the word makes it more real. There's a past out there waiting for him—a whole life—and yet he has no idea how to find it.

Keeping his eyes closed, he remembers how she also said that he fell overboard, that he almost drowned. He wonders if that's why he felt so uncomfortable sitting on the dock, near the water. He concentrates hard on the image, imagining himself falling from a boat and plunging into the sea.

That's when he remembers. The cruise. The railing that came loose. And tumbling backwards through the air. His head had smacked hard against something—the side of the boat maybe. After that, everything went black.

He remembers several hours later—or maybe it was days. Someone was whispering to him, rubbing a warm cloth over his face. He thinks it was Sierra. He remembers her brittle voice—how she sang to him and told him stories. She fed him chicken broth and herbal tea, even though he was barely conscious, and nursed him back to health. He remembers her telling him how lucky he was, that his neck could have snapped in the fall. She told him that all things happen for a reason—that that's why Clay and the others were on a taking mission that night. They'd been following the cruise boat he was on and saw the accident—his fall.

He wonders why Mason or Clay never mentioned all this, if the only reason Sierra told him was because she thought he might never wake up. But then he thinks how it's obvious that they didn't want him to know. Because then he might want to go back.

He opens his eyes, eager to tell Brick all about his dream, but he isn't here.

Shell showers and dresses quickly, stuffing the pentacle rock in his pocket, wondering where Brick might have gone off to so early in the morning; it's barely 5 AM.

"Have you seen Brick?" he asks Teal, on his way in from sleeping outside.

Teal shakes his head, pressing a handkerchief to his nose, having most likely caught a cold from sleeping out in ten-degree weather.

Shell wonders if Brick might have been assigned an early morning chore. He heads to the dining cabin, hopeful that he might learn something from one of the other campers.

And he knows just who to ask.

Lily is standing at the kitchen basin, washing potatoes. "You're up early," she says, looking outside. "The sun isn't even out yet."

"Have you seen Brick?" he asks, ignoring her remarks.

Lily looks over her shoulder at Rain, who sets the table only a few feet away. "No," Lily says, shaking her head.

"Are you sure?" Shell asks.

"Sure, I'm sure. What kind of question is that?"

"Where's Clay?"

Lily shrugs and resumes scrubbing the potatoes.

"I know you're lying," he tells her quietly so Rain can't hear. "I know how close you and Clay are; he tells you everything. Are he and Brick together?"

Lily peers back at Rain. "Is everything okay?" Rain asks, her long black hair spilling down over the bib of her apron.

"Just fine," Lily says, trying to smile.

"Tell me," Shell whispers.

"Tell you *what*?" She splashes her hands in the water a bit, trying to lamely drown out their voices maybe. "You haven't been very nice to me lately."

Shell clenches his teeth and takes a deep breath. "I need you to help me outside for a second," he says.

"I'm busy," she says. "Breakfast is in an hour."

"Please," Shell insists. "I need you to hold the door open for me while I bring in some wood." He narrows his eyes on her, hoping she gets the message.

"Well, why didn't you say so in the first place?" She smiles.

Shell nods to Rain, but she barely has time to acknowledge their exit because she's called away by Sierra, who's looking after the children in the adjoining living room.

Shell leads Lily outside, over by the chopping station and the stockpile of wood. He pretends to gather a couple logs in the crook of his arm. "Just tell me," he says. "Where's Brick? I know you know something. Is he with Clay?"

"First, *you* tell me," she says with a huff. "Why have you been so distant with me lately?"

Shell takes another deep breath, silently counting to ten. "Because I know you don't care for me the way you think you do."

"Of course I do."

"No," he says. "I know that Mason told you to give me extra attention."

"No, he didn't."

"You're denying it?"

Lily shrugs and looks away.

"Do you think that's normal?" Shell continues. "Do you think you're supposed to be told who to love?"

"Mason knows best," Lily whispers, her eyes welling up. "Plus, it doesn't mean that I *don't* love you."

"You know as well as I do that if I never came here, if Mason never told you who to care for, you'd be with Clay right now."

Lily shrugs again, but she doesn't deny it.

Shell puts the logs down and reaches out to touch her forearm, allowing her to fall into his arms. After several seconds, he breaks the embrace, noticing a group of campers look in their direction en route to the bathroom. "You need to help me," he whispers. "I think Brick might be in trouble. If you know where he is, you need to tell me."

Lily takes a step back, wiping at her eyes. "He's fine." She sighs. "He went with Clay."

"Where?"

"Ask Mason. I'm not getting in trouble over this."

Shell feels his chest tighten. He clenches the pentacle rock in his pocket, reminding himself of strength. "Where is Mason?"

"Where else *would* he be so early in the morning?" she huffs. "His study."

Shell turns on his heel, hurrying off to Mason's cabin. He knocks a couple times on the exterior door, but no one answers. He tries the knob. It turns. "Hello?" he calls, easing the door open. "Mason?"

He takes a couple steps inside and looks toward the door to Mason's study. It's open a crack and there's a shadow flickering on the wall, from a lantern he assumes. "Mason?" Shell calls again.

The floorboards creak. Shell swallows hard, preparing what to say.

"Shell?" Mason says, stepping into the doorway of his study. "Is everything okay?"

Shell shakes his head. "I'm looking for Brick."

"I see." Mason tightens his grip on the book he's holding. "Why don't you step inside a moment and we can talk."

Shell hesitates but then joins Mason in his study. They sit opposite one another on the benches, much like their last meeting. Mason closes the door behind him and rubs at his eyes, a long sigh blowing out his mouth. "What do you need Brick for so early in the morning?"

"I'm just looking for him. I don't need him, per se."

"He's with Clay."

"Where?"

Mason narrows his eyes on Shell. "How much do you know about Brick?"

"Enough."

"Enough to know of his betrayal?"

Shell feels the surprise on his face. "What betrayal?"

"He's been stealing from the group. Taking without first considering the worth an object has to its owner is stealing."

"Wait," Shell says, shaking his head. "What do you mean?"

"I mean, there were some missing things found under his bed . . . jewelry trinkets, mostly. He's been betraying us. I'm sorry to have to be the one to tell you."

"Wait," Shell repeats, his mind whirling with confusion. "You have it all wrong. Brick isn't the one who's stealing."

"When you betray one of us, you betray the entire community," Mason continues, ignoring Shell. "You betray our mission here. We can't allow such behavior to go on unnoticed."

"Clay's the one who's stealing," Shell says.

"I wouldn't be surprised if that's what Brick told you, but I have reason to believe otherwise." Mason lets out another disappointed sigh, tossing his book to the floor. "This isn't the first time that Brick has betrayed the entire community. He's also been involved in witchcraft nonsense, even after he'd been warned against it. Our minds need to be pure if we're to conduct good work here."

"Mason," Shell says, standing up, heat rising to his face. "It isn't true."

"I'm sorry he's betrayed your friendship as well."

Shell clenches his teeth, knowing that there's no point in trying to convince Mason now. He has to find Brick.

"Where is he?" Shell asks.

"Clay is taking care of things."

"What does that mean? Will Brick be okay?"

Mason gets up and goes to the door, holding it open for Shell's exit. "He needs to learn that what he did was wrong. That's what we do here—teach."

"Mason, please," Shell insists.

"I have to go now," Mason says, grabbing the lantern and swinging it back and forth, as though a warning, as though he might strike Shell. "I'm driving some of the elder men into town. We have a little business to attend to and probably won't be back until early tonight. We can talk more then if you wish."

Shell nods and leaves, knowing more than ever now that he has to find Brick—and that they have to get out of here.

stacey

I jump out of bed and grab my coat, pulling on a pair of boots as I plop down on Amber's bed. "Wake up," I whisper, shaking her slightly.

She wipes her eyes, still a little disoriented from sleep. "What's going on?"

"I need to borrow your van."

"Why?" she asks, sitting up. "Is there something wrong?"

I nod. "It's Porsha. She knows where the boy is . . . the one who's supposed to die."

"Can I come with you guys?"

I shake my head. "You have class."

"So do you. What happened to the good old days . . . when you used to let me help you fight crime?"

"I hope to be back later tonight."

"Ho hum." She sighs, clearly disappointed that I won't be taking her with me. Amber grabs the keys from her Hello Kitty lunchbox of a purse and hands them to me. "Take my cell phone, too," she says, scrambling through the contents of the box to find it.

"I kind of already did," I say, pulling the phone from my pocket.

Instead of griping about it, Amber nods. "Good," she says. "Call me if you need anything or just to let me know you're okay."

"Of course," I say, giving her a giant hug. It is sort of sad that she isn't coming with me . . . that Drea isn't here, too, and that everything is changing so fast.

Amber's vintage Volkswagen van is parked in the back of our dorm. I climb in, start her up, and crank the heat. It's 3:30. It's probably going to take us close to two hours to get down to the Cape from here, maybe more. Part of me is hoping that her prediction about the sun rising is wrong, that it's dark in her dream because it's nighttime rather than early in the morning. I'm just not sure we'll make it other-wise.

I pull out of Beacon's Drive and across the street to the president's house. Porsha is already waiting for me in the driveway. I unlock her door and she hops in, dressed for the occasion in shades of black and charcoal.

"Let's get out of here," she says, peering out the windows. "My father's still asleep."

"Did you tell him you were going out?"

"Yeah, right," she says, fastening her seatbelt. "I left Tamara a note that said I was with you. That should keep him quiet for a while."

I shake my head and pull out onto the road, the van sputtering a couple times from the cold. "So where are we going?"

"Where else? The Cape."

"Yeah, but *where*?"

Porsha pulls a few sheets of paper from her bag. "A town called Brutus."

"*Excuse me*?" I gasp. Brutus is only one town over from where we were staying this past summer.

"Yeah," Porsha says, referring to the sheets. "Your spell worked. I dreamt about some place called Bargo Tower." She flashes me a picture of a tall brick tower positioned high on a hill. "I looked it up online and found it. Here are the MapQuest directions, by the way." She places them on the console.

"Okay," I say, taking a giant breath, trying to get everything straight. "So, this boy—"

"Trevor," she corrects. "That's his name. He told me so in his dream. And then he asked me if I was his guardian angel."

"What did you say?"

"I told him I was." She shrugs. "I mean, when you think about it . . ."

"Wait," I say. "Is he going to be at the tower?"

She shakes her head. "I told you, he's at some camp, but it's near the tower."

"How near?"

"I'm not sure, but Brutus is pretty small." She rechecks the map. "It shouldn't be hard to find a camp commune like theirs . . . you know, so primitive, near the woods, overlooking the ocean. I bet people in the town will know about it."

"That's it? So we're just supposed to ask? You didn't see anything else?"

"I saw a fence."

"What kind of fence?"

"A chainlink one, like they have at parks, but with barbed wire at the top."

"Like a prison?"

She nods. "There was a hole in the fence, too—toward the bottom—like it had been cut and pried open, and there was a lot of overgrown brush around it."

"Was there anything else around it? Any structures . . . some landmark we might be able to recognize?"

Porsha shakes her head. "It might be near something bee-related."

"B, as in the letter *B*?"

"No." She shakes her head. "*Bee* as in the kind that buzzes."

"You saw *bees*?" I ask, feeling the surprise on my face.

"No, but I heard them buzzing in my ear." She sticks her finger in her ear as though she can still hear them.

"It's the middle of winter," I say, turning onto the highway. "Are you sure it was bees and not something else buzzy?"

"What can I tell you?"

I shake my head and glance at the clock. It's almost four; we only have two more hours before the darkness starts to lift.

"Didn't I do good?" she asks.

I nod. "Better than good."

"Thanks," she says, gripping the healing-receiving crystal I gave her, reminding me more than ever of myself.

stacey

We don't say much on our way down to the Cape. I'm just too tense for words. I keep my foot pressed firmly on the gas the whole way, over the Sagamore Bridge and past the *Welcome to Cape Cod* sign. We pass several Cape towns on the highway as we continue into the Brutus/Dalmouth area.

"We're doing good on time," Porsha says.

I nod, grateful that there isn't much traffic at this time of day, that it only took us an hour-and-a-half to get here. I take our exit a little too fast, almost sending the van on two wheels.

"This sucker's got steam." Porsha pats the console, which makes the glove compartment drop open. A red lacy bra and Catwoman mask fall out. "I won't ask," she says, closing the compartment back up with the tip of her finger.

I smile slightly and click on the overhead light to read over the MapQuest directions.

"Thank you," Porsha says, just out of nowhere.

I glance at her. "You're welcome."

"I mean, you didn't even have to help me. What's in it for you?"

"More than you know." I take a deep breath and continue to turn down several more streets. "We should probably talk about what we'll do once we get to the camp."

"Save Trevor," Porsha says. "What else?"

"No, I mean, I find it hard to believe that such a primitive-type camp is going to let two young girls go waltzing in there without a word, especially a camp where actual killing is about to take place."

"Good point," Porsha says. "How about we just say we're looking for some place to stay?"

I bite my bottom lip, losing confidence by the moment.

The MapQuest directions bring me through downtown Dalmouth. It looks much as I left it—the brick streets and touristy shops. Only now it's covered with patches of snow.

"Are you okay?" Porsha asks, obviously noticing my sullen state.

"I will be," I croak.

"This is where it happened, isn't it?" she asks. "Where you lost your love?"

I nod.

"Sorry," she says.

I shrug, fighting the urge to break down.

"Sucks, doesn't it?" She sighs.

"Which part?"

"Coincidence. You lost your love here and now I'm bringing you back."

"I don't believe in coincidence. Everything happens for a reason."

"So what do you think the reason is?"

I shake my head and bite my bottom lip, wondering about the irony of the situation, wondering if maybe Porsha's nightmares are sort of like the ones Jacob was having about me. He didn't even know who I was and yet he felt compelled to find me—to save me. Because we were soul mates.

Maybe Trevor is Porsha's soul mate and that's why she's been dreaming about him. Maybe that's how she and I are connected. I'm helping her find her soul mate, so that I can finally put mine to rest.

We enter Brutus and spot the Bargo Tower right away. It's in full view, high up on a hill, highlighted by street lamps.

"It's a little past five," Porsha says.

I nod. "It'll only be dark for another hour."

"Right, so we need to hurry up." Using the street map, she directs me toward the ocean, telling me how it appears as though it meets patches of woods in several places.

"We need to ask somebody," I say, noticing some guy dragging his trash out to the curb of his driveway. I pull over and roll down the window. "Excuse me?" I shout.

The man turns from his trash and takes a couple steps toward my window. He looks much older up close—maybe seventy at the least—with wiry gray hair and a skinny build.

"We're looking for a campsite," I say.

"For RVs or tents?" He takes a second glance at the van.

"No," I say. "We're looking for a camp where our friend is staying. It doesn't have electricity and they use well water." I shake my head, thinking how ridiculous I sound.

"The commune?" the man asks.

"Yeah." I nod. "I think so."

"You've got a friend staying at that place?"

More nodding.

"They should shut that damn place down." He shakes his head and lets out a sigh. "The problem is the leader's too damn slippery. He's got a loophole for everything."

"Can you tell us where the camp is?" Porsha asks, leaning closer to the window.

"That commune is no place for two young girls like yourselves."

"Please," Porsha insists.

"Can't do it," the man says, repositioning his cap. "I'd never forgive myself later."

"We need to get our friend," Porsha says. "He isn't safe."

"If he's at that place, you can bet he isn't safe." He sighs again and thinks about it for several seconds. "Okay," he says, reluctantly. "I'll tell you."

stacey

The man gives us directions to the camp, telling us how careful we need to be and how we shouldn't listen to any of the leader's "mumbo jumbo." Being such a small town, we're actually pretty close to the place and, when he mentions that it's just past a honey farm, I almost leap out the window and kiss him.

"*Bees*," Porsha whispers, a bit surprised by her own prediction.

We arrive in what appears to be an undeveloped part of town—no houses, sparse streetlights, and tons of trees. Once we pass the honey farm, the road turns from pavement to gravel.

The camp is just up ahead, a barbed wire fence around it. I drive toward the entrance just as a couple flashlight beams shine in my direction from what appears to be a small guard shack.

"What do we do?" Porsha asks, her eyes widening.

I bite the inside of my cheek, noticing two people standing at the gate. I take a deep breath and park the van. "Are you ready?"

"What do you mean?" Porsha asks.

Instead of answering, I work quickly, removing the ignition key from Amber's key ring and shoving it into my sock, just in case I'm forced to give up my keys. Now, only the trunk key and what appears to be a key to an old gym locker remain on the ring. "Let's go," I whisper.

"Wait," Porsha says. "What are we supposed to say?"

"Just follow me," I whisper and open the door, almost wishing Amber were here to break the proverbial ice. Porsha follows as I head to the entrance, my heart pounding, my teeth chattering from the early morning chill.

The two boys keeping guard are actually pretty young—around fourteen or fifteen at most. They're dressed in regular street clothes, but it's clear from their stance that their job is to keep people from entering, and so I wonder if they're carrying weapons. "Excuse me," I say, resting my hands against the fence, noticing the sharp metal spokes that jut off the winding wire at the top. "My friend and I are from out of town. We were wondering if maybe you could give us a place to stay."

The two boys exchange a look and then one of them shakes his head.

"Please," Porsha whines, joining me at the gate. "We don't have money for a motel and we're practically out of gas. It's freezing out here."

"We can do work in exchange," I offer. "Is there somebody in charge we can ask?" I look through the fence. Despite the darkness, I can see that there are a bunch of cabins lined up in the middle. I glance from right to left, searching for someone who might be able to get us in. But the place looks almost vacant. There's a parking spot just beyond the gate; I can tell from the tire tracks. There's also a chopping block and a stockpile of wood piled high near the opening of the forest and a pathway that seems to veer off toward a beach.

"Where is everybody?" I ask. "Is everyone still asleep?"

"You need to leave now," the taller of the boys tells us. He reaches inside his pocket, as a warning I think. There's definitely something in there. It's not big enough to be a gun; I figure it might be a pocket knife or a bottle of pepper spray. Still, it's nothing I want to protect myself against— not yet anyway.

I take a deep breath, remembering how Porsha said she saw an opening in the fence in her dream. I glance toward the forest, noting how she also said there was brush and overgrowth surrounding it.

"Okay," I say finally, taking a step back from the fence. I nod to Porsha and then gesture toward the van. "Let's go."

Shell

After Mason leaves for town, Shell continues to scour the camp for Brick. No one will give him any inkling as to where Clay may have taken him, though he's not convinced the other campers even know.

Except Lily. After searching the beach and checking that the fishing boat is still docked, he decides to take one more look in the forest before heading back to the dining cabin and insisting that Lily tell him where Clay and Brick have gone.

He figures he'll go deeper into the woods this time. He passes the chopping station and takes just a couple steps down the dirt-covered trail that winds into the trees.

That's when he spots it: Brick's pentacle rock. It's sitting faceup in the middle of the path, practically glowing because of its whiteness. Shell picks it up, remembering the time he and Brick scratched on their rocks and wished for peace, knowing that Brick would never be so careless as to misplace it like this. A sick feeling creeps up Shell's throat, like he's going to be sick.

There's no doubting it; Brick dropped the rock on purpose—in hopes that someone would find it and come looking for him. Because he's in danger.

Shell picks up the rock and hurries into the forest, trampling over fallen branches and dead brush, shouting Brick's name until his throat stings. But no one answers him. He stays firmly on the trail, relying on its steadfastness to guide him through the early morning darkness, wondering why he didn't think to bring a lantern.

After several minutes, he begins to feel extra guarded and uneasy. His heart constricts. He stops a moment to catch his breath and get his bearings, the frigid morning breeze biting at his skin. He thinks he hears some noises up ahead. He squints to try and see something, but it's just too dark; the sun has yet to rise.

He moves quickly again, almost tripping over a log, trying to trust his instincts and where they're pulling him—farther and farther away from the camp. It must be a good twenty minutes now that he's been gone. He wonders if the other campers have noticed, if they'll tell Mason when he gets back from town. Surely there'll be hell to pay. But it doesn't matter. He has to find Brick.

He quickens his pace even more, his heart tightening into a ball. The farther he gets from the camp, the thicker the trees and brush become, and the narrower and more obscure the trail gets. It's like a web of dead branches all around him, scratching at his arms and legs.

His mind races, wondering if this is how Rock and the others escaped—if they did it early in the morning when everybody was still asleep, if they waited until Mason and Clay weren't around. He sees the barbed wire fence that surrounds the camp property up ahead, making his heart pump extra hard. His mind jumbles even more. He wonders if he could scale the fence, if he could make it without getting caught up in the wire—if he could escape this place once and for all.

But how could he abandon Brick?

Shell lets out a sputter of a breath, wanting to scream out of mere frustration. He begins back in the direction of the camp, veering slightly off the path this time. He passes a thicket of dead bushes, doing his best to shield his face so he doesn't get scratched.

That's when he finally sees them—in a clearing up ahead. There are lanterns hanging from tree branches, highlighting their movement. Brick is crouched on the ground, his back facing Clay. Shell hurries toward them, noticing that Clay is holding a gun, pointing it toward the back of Brick's neck.

"Stop!" Shell shouts, just a few feet away now. "Drop the gun!"

Clay pauses and looks back, a grin crawling up his face. Shell tries to catch his breath, assessing the situation and what to do. Brick peeks back at him, a trickle of blood running down the side of his face.

"Are you all right?" Shell asks him.

Clay turns back, meeting Brick's eye. "I told you!" Clay shouts at Brick. "Don't move! Not unless I give you permission."

Brick swivels quickly back around and Shell notices how blood is running from his ear.

"Let him go!" Shell shouts.

Clay shakes his head. "He needs to be punished! He's betrayed our mission here."

"By catching you?" Shell asks. "You're the one who's been stealing."

"Maybe you need to be punished as well."

Shell ignores the threat, crouching down beside Brick to help him up.

"I told you not to move!" Clay shouts at Brick. Brick squats back down, clearly terrified by Clay's threat. "Move away from him!" Clay orders, pointing the gun at Shell. He pushes the barrel deep into Shell's throat, making him choke. A sputter sound escapes his mouth. Shell takes a couple steps back and raises his arms, as though to surrender.

"Turn around," Clay tells him, cocking the gun.

Shell motions to turn but, instead, grabs the gun and tries to pry it out of Clay's hands. He twists Clay's wrist, hearing a popping sound, almost able to snag the gun away. Clay recoils slightly, letting out a pant. His fingers loosen from the barrel but he won't let go. A second later, a shot goes off—in the direction of Brick—causing Shell to lose focus. His grip on the gun slips.

Panting, Clay gains his footing. The gun pressed firmly in his hand, he uses its weight to pistol-whip Shell. Shell goes reeling to the ground, landing flat on his back, and Clay pounces down on him. He pushes the gun into Shell's neck, pinning Shell in place.

Shell chokes, his mouth agape.

"Think you can beat me, don't you?" Clay breathes. "You want to take my place, don't you? You want to get on Mason's good side and take over—and take Lily."

Shell wants to deny it, but he can barely manage more than a gasp. His mind whirls, wondering what to do—how he can fight back. He goes to raise his arms up slightly, but Clay only pushes the barrel in deeper.

"No!" he hears Brick shout. Brick is standing now, just a few feet away. More blood runs down his face. His eye is blood red as well.

"Back!" Clay shouts, looking slightly over his shoulder—one eye on Brick, the other still on Shell. "Get back and sit down, or your friend here is dead. You'll be right after him."

Brick obeys and Clay focuses back on Shell. "Ready to surrender now?" Clay asks him.

Shell nods, his mind still scrambling, unable to give up. He wants to tell Clay that he has no interest in Lily—to remind him that it was Mason's idea for the two of them to get together. But he can't speak. Clay bears the gun deep into his throat.

Clay releases the barrel a bit from Shell's neck and scoots back. Shell gasps, grasping around his neck and trying to breathe—to get enough air.

"Turn around," Clay tells him. "And don't move."

Dragging himself up to a crouched position, Shell obliges, wishing his guardian angel were here to save him now.

stacey

We drive away from the camp, taking a side road that enables us to follow the barbed-wire fence. I rest my foot on the accelerator, tapping it just enough to keep us moving forward, trying to go as slowly as possible so that Porsha is able to keep a careful watch for the opening she saw in her dream.

"It's going to be hard," she says, reminding me how the opening was covered by brush, how the fence appeared to have been cut, the metal torn away for someone to crawl through.

I shine the high beams, but it's still hard to see. The road is narrow and the trees—some of them at least thirty or forty feet in height—are only a few yards away, towering over us, the fence tucked just inside, with brush and overgrowth all around it.

After a few minutes, the road comes to a dead end but the fence continues, stretching through what appears to be salt marshes. I park the van and switch off the lights.

"What now?" Porsha asks.

"What do you think?"

Porsha nods and we exit the van, continuing to follow the fence on foot. The ground is frozen, allowing us to traipse fairly easily through the marshes, instead of sinking into what would otherwise be thick and sopping mud. After several minutes, Porsha's pace starts to lag a bit.

"Are you okay?" I ask, looking back at her.

She shakes her head. "I don't know."

I turn around to face her, my breath visible from the cold. "What do you mean, you don't know?"

"I mean, it's freezing. I'm tired. There's got to be at least another half-mile of fencing."

"Meaning *what*?"

"Meaning, I don't know," she repeats. "What if this is all just a big fat waste of time? What if my nightmare didn't predict correctly? What if there *is* no opening in the fence?"

"You need to have more confidence in your dreams than that."

Porsha nods, letting out a sigh. She adjusts the onyx bracelet around her wrist and then reaches for the crystal in her pocket.

We continue on, trying to work fast before the sun breaks. I run my fingers over the links of the fence, trying to sense something. That's when I feel it. It's like my whole hand has warmed over; the skin at my fingertips tingles, radiating up my arm.

"What is it?" Porsha asks, obviously noticing how I'm shaking all over.

"We're close," I whisper, the anxiety mounting in my chest.

"How do you know?"

"I just do." I *feel* it—there's something in this forest that I need to see—to find. "The opening's around here somewhere."

Together, Porsha and I scour the individual sections of fence, pushing at the brush and overgrowth to get a better look. Porsha lets out a frustrated sigh but continues to follow my lead. Several sections later, both hands now tingling with warmth, I find it. "Here!" I shout.

We push away the brush that surrounds the hole—a rusted tear in the fence where the metal has clearly been cut away—and crawl through. A loud bang fires in the distance. Porsha and I exchange a look, probably wondering the same thing—if it was a gunshot.

If we're already too late.

At the same moment, the sun pokes its way up through the trees, signalling that it *is* too late.

"No!" Porsha shouts.

My chest constricts. My head feels suddenly dizzy. I remove the knitted scarf from around Porsha's neck and tie it to the fence, just above the hole, so we're able to find our way out. "We can't stop now," I say.

There's a ringing in my ears that grows more piercing with each step. I hold my fingers over the sound and stumble along, following a narrow dirt path that leads us through the woods. The sun's light slices across the dried out trees and brush, making it easy to see. I pause a moment to look back at Porsha, trying to keep pace with me. Her mouth is moving, but I can't hear what she's saying. The high-pitched ringing in my ears is blocking everything else out, making my head feel even dizzier.

I turn back, trying to keep stable, trying to avoid the branches that stick out in my path. After only a couple minutes, I see movement up ahead—a group of boys, I think. One of them is pointing something—his arm's extended— and so I'm guessing it's a gun. I move closer, just a short distance away from them now.

That's when I see him.

Kneeling on the ground, he turns to look in our direction—at me. I shake my head and look harder, feeling my skin tingle. It *can't* be him.

But it is. I know it is.

My mouth trembles. My body turns limp. He looks away like I don't even matter.

The ringing screeches in my ears and my head spins. I think I scream. I think my legs begin to wobble. Colors swirl in front of my eyes. I want to look at him again, but I can't— I feel sick. My body feels limp. A haze of hands—Porsha's, I think—swoops around me. But it's too late. I've already hit the ground. All the lights have gone out.

Shell

Still crouched on the ground with his back to Clay, Shell hears movement behind him in the woods. He turns to look. There are a couple girls heading toward them. One of them stares at him, her body swaying from side to side, like she's going to pass out.

Shell shifts his focus to Clay, who's glaring at the girls, the gun dropping slightly in his grip. Shell plunges into Clay's middle, fists first, sending Clay reeling to the ground.

The gun flies from Clay's grip, into a throng of bushes. Brick runs to retrieve it.

Meanwhile, Clay is able to roll himself out from under Shell. Clay struggles to his feet; Shell manages to stay in a kneeling position. Clay goes to kick Shell in the face, but Shell intercepts, grabbing Clay's foot and throwing him off balance. Shell springs up just as Clay falls backward. His head slams down hard against a rock slab. Shell pins him to the ground, a stick pressed into Clay's neck, but it appears as though Clay is unconscious.

Shell glances over at the girl who fainted. She's positioned on the ground away from him, her dark hair spilling out over a patch of snow. "Is she okay?" he asks her friend.

The blond girl nods, waving a hand over the fainted girl's face and unzipping her coat, trying to revive her. "She's starting to come around."

Empty-handed, Brick moves from the bushes to stand over Clay. "He isn't moving," Brick says. "Is he . . . ?"

"Dead?" Shell asks. He crouches down farther, so that his cheek hovers just above Clay's mouth and nose. "No, he's still breathing. He's just unconscious. He hit the rock pretty hard."

"Maybe he's faking," Brick says.

Shell doesn't think so, but he checks anyway. He jams the point of the stick into Clay's palm a few times, but Clay doesn't so much as flinch. "Let's get out of here . . . before he wakes up."

"We have a van," the blond girl says.

"Where?" Shell gets up.

The blond girl points behind them, toward the dirt trail. "There's a hole in the fence back there," she says.

Shell nods and moves to help them up. "Give me a hand," he tells Brick. He goes to lift the fainted girl. That's when he notices—when he's close enough to see how familiar she looks. He recognizes her from his dreams—the girl on the beach.

His soul mate.

Shell

Shell lifts the girl into his arms while her friend leads them to the fence, out of the forest.

"Jacob," the girl whispers. Her eyes are still closed, as though only half-conscious. "Am I dreaming?"

Shell doesn't know what to say and so he just focuses forward, trying to move quickly, noticing the bright yellow scarf tied to the fence, just above a hole. The girl unties the scarf, wrapping it around her neck and scooting through the hole feet-first. "Now you," she says, pointing to Brick. "We can help pull her through."

Brick crawls through the hole and Shell kneels down, sliding the girl toward the opening. A moment later, he hears a shifting sound in the brush behind him.

"Hold it!" Clay shouts.

Shell looks back. Clay is still a distance away but charging at him at full force.

Shell works hard, pushing the girl through the hole, while Brick and her friend pull from the other side.

Finally through, Shell stands back up. Clay is there, a long, thick branch held high above his head. He moves to pound it down on Shell's head, but Shell ducks and dives into Clay's middle, knocking him to the ground. The branch flies from Clay's grip. Shell straddles Clay, slugging him across the jaw a couple times.

By the time Brick has scurried back through the hole to help Shell, Clay is already down, knocked unconscious again. Brick and Shell dive through the hole and jump into the van, the doors already open, the motor already running. No sooner do they close the doors back up than the van peels out and they're gone: finally free.

Shell

The van jolts from left to right as the blond girl tries to steer backwards through the gravel on the dead-end street. When she gets to the end, she backs into a clearing, the tires spinning as she shifts into drive, stepping down on the accelerator. "Where should we go?" she asks.

No one answers. Shell tries to catch his breath, figuring that Brick is probably doing the same, probably just as confused and relieved as he is.

"Maybe we should go to the hospital," the girl continues. "You guys look pretty banged up."

"No way," Brick says. He's sitting beside her in the front seat.

Shell knows it's because Brick's a minor that he doesn't want to go; the hospital would surely ask about his parents and find out soon enough that he's a runaway.

"Then where?" the girl asks. "I mean, I know this probably sounds totally random right now, but I don't exactly have my license yet and—"

"Who are you?" Brick asks, interrupting her. "I mean, where did you come from? Why were you in those woods?"

The girl shrugs. "It's sort of a long story."

"Do I know you?" Brick asks, shifting in his seat. "Because I kind of feel like I do."

"It's Trevor, right?" she asks.

His mouth falls open. "How do you know my real name?"

"Your *real* name?"

"Nobody's called me Trevor in years."

"Well, I've been dreaming about you," the girl says. She reaches into the glove compartment for a couple Wet Naps. She tosses one to him—for his face—and another to Shell. "My name's Porsha, by the way."

Brick nods, ignoring the wipe, as though completely rapt by this girl—this girl who's been dreaming about him.

Shell remembers the dream Brick told him—how a girl's voice came to him in the middle of the night. The girl knew his real name and asked him where he was. A shiver runs down the back of Shell's neck. He's sure now that there was more to that dream, that somehow Porsha and Brick have a connection—maybe sort of like the connection he has to the girl sitting beside him.

He glances at her just as her eyes flutter open. "How are you feeling?" he asks. Instead of answering, she slides in closer and embraces him. He can feel her tears dripping down his neck.

After several moments, she breaks the embrace, perhaps sensing how distant he seems. He takes the opportunity to study her—her long dark hair, her golden brown eyes, the X on her neck. "I know you," he whispers.

The girl is trembling. She clasps her hands over her mouth, more tears streaming down her face.

Shell doesn't know how to respond. "What's your name?" he asks, noticing how he's trembling as well, how Porsha is watching them in the rearview mirror.

The girl looks confused; her eyebrows furrow and her mouth forms a tiny frown.

"What's your name?" he repeats.

The girl shakes her head, her lips puckering up like she's going to be sick.

"Are you okay?" Shell asks.

"It's Stacey," she whispers. "Don't you know me?"

"I dreamt about you," he explains, wiping her tears with his thumb.

"Jacob," she whimpers, pulling him closer, resting her forehead against his chest.

Shell pauses at the name, knowing somehow that it's his.

"Jacob?" Porsha gasps. She turns to look back at him, the van swerving to the right. She has to grab the wheel to regain control.

Stacey kisses his cheeks and whispers into his ear—how much she loves him and misses him, and how he's never to leave her again.

He allows her to continue for several more minutes before finally pulling away. "I remember *some* things," he whispers.

The girl nods, beginning to understand maybe. She reaches into the pocket of her coat and pulls out a crystal rock. She places it into his palm. "Do you remember this?"

He clenches it, reminded of his pentacle rock. "I don't know," he says. "Maybe. I'm feeling a bit of déjà vu, I guess."

"You gave this to me for protection and strength," she explains.

"I want to remember," he whispers, looking at the X on her neck.

The girl takes his hand and places it there, running his fingers over her skin. "We need to get you home," she whispers.

Shell nods, wanting more than anything to know what home is.

stacey

My heart races. My mind won't stop reeling. I want to scream at the top of my lungs—*Jacob is alive! Trevor is safe! We're out! We're free!* But it's comatose-quiet in the van now. I think even my heart is beating louder.

All I want to do is hold Jacob. I want to jump into his lap and wrap my arms around him until my arms break. But instead I lean back into the seat, sensing how uncomfortable he is by my affection.

I wipe my tears—a mix of elation and sadness—and try to catch my breath, grateful that my head has stopped whirring, that the ringing in my ears has ceased as well.

"Maybe we should go to the police," I say, ever eager to delve back into my role of responsibility.

"No!" Trevor says. "No police."

"Maybe we should just get a little farther away first," Jacob says.

I nod, my heart roiling at the sound of his voice after not hearing it for almost five whole months now.

Porsha makes an attempt to turn on the radio, but the sound is all fuzzy and she ends up shutting it off. I glance over at Jacob again. He tries to smile but then looks away, making my heart squelch.

I know this is uncomfortable for him, but it's also hell for me. I mean, why aren't we talking? Why does my skin itch for no reason? Why can't I get comfortable in my seat?

I take another deep breath, telling myself that it's quiet because nobody knows quite what to say. What *do* you say? What words will make it real, make it all make sense, do justice to everything we've been through?

I look over at Jacob again, waiting for him to meet my eye, but he doesn't. Instead, the van ends up swerving to the left and I feel my cheeks get fireball hot.

"I'm really not comfortable driving the highway," Porsha says, shifting the van into park.

I look out the window, noticing that we're sitting in the middle of an IHOP parking lot. "What are we doing?" I ask her.

"Pulling over; what does it look like? Does somebody else want to drive?"

"Let's go inside," Trevor says, wiping at the blood on his face. "We can get cleaned up and order some food."

Jacob agrees and we go.

While the guys head off to the bathroom, Porsha and I get seated at a circular table by the window. She asks me about Jacob and I tell her that it's true. It's him. He's alive.

"How can that be?" she asks, her face a giant question mark. "I mean, are you sure it's him?"

I nod. "They never found his body."

"That's insane," she says, looking half as dazed as I feel. "I mean, it's crazy."

"Crazy or not, I don't believe in coincidence," I remind her. "We were meant to come here. I was meant to help you—for so many reasons."

Jacob and Trevor join us a couple minutes later. The waitress gives us our laminated menus and we order platefuls of pancakes, hashed browns, and scrambled eggs. But I can't even think about eating. There's a rusty taste in my mouth and my eyes sting, like I could cry at any second.

I take a deep breath, relieved that my awkward energy hasn't smoldered Porsha and Trevor's conversation. They've been chattering away for the past fifteen minutes at least.

I open my mouth to say Jacob's name, to start up some form of conversation, but Porsha interrupts me, announcing that she's going out to the lobby to call her dad. After she leaves, it's quiet again.

"Hungry?" Jacob asks, after a few moments of uncomfortable silence—even more uncomfortable than inside the van.

I shrug and bite my bottom lip, wondering what happens next. I mean, Jacob is *here*, sitting next to me, and yet this feels so anticlimactic.

"I'm starving," Trevor says, grabbing his stomach.

"Me, too." Jacob smiles at me. "I haven't had pancakes since I can't remember when."

"A comedian." Trevor laughs.

I feel myself smile as well, grateful for the break in tension. Porsha returns to the table a few seconds later. "How's your father?" I ask. "Was he upset? He must have been really worried about you."

Porsha shrugs. "He'll get over it. Besides, I told him you'd be over to explain everything." She smiles at me and then focuses back on Trevor. "He said you could stay with us for a little while," she tells him. "He's got friends who work in Social Services; he'll work out all the legal stuff. Besides, our place is huge. We have tons of spare rooms."

"Sounds great." Trevor smiles, a tiny visible gap between his two front teeth. "Now, if I can only get used to being called Trevor."

"We could rename you," Porsha suggests, "but I request that it be something that begins with a *T*."

"How come?"

Porsha hesitates and then rolls up her sleeve, revealing the burn mark. Trevor's mouth drops open. He shakes his head and gazes into her eyes, not knowing what to say. "I feel like I've been looking for you forever," she tells him.

It even gives me tingles.

I smile at the two of them, happy that they've found each other—and that he's finally safe.

Our food arrives and Jacob and I make insignificant small talk. He tells me how good the pancakes taste, how at the camp he mostly got cold cereal and rice for breakfast. I talk about my coffee—how I've been drinking it black lately, how I no longer like the flavored kind. At least I think these are things that I say. I'm not really thinking about food. I'm wondering what's going to happen now. I mean, where do we go from here?

I fake a bite of scrambled egg and watch Jacob as he enjoys his pancakes. I want to ask him about his parents—when he plans to call them, if he's looking forward to seeing them, if he even remembers who they are. "Your parents and I have been in touch a few times," I say, finally. "I could call them for you . . . you know, so they know this is real."

Jacob doesn't respond right away, and so I feel bad about the suggestion—like maybe I'm pushing too much and trying too hard. But then he finally looks at me and smiles. "That would be great," he says, his voice barely above a whisper.

I smile too, continuing to push my food around on the plate, noticing a huge pit growing in my stomach by the moment. I know I should be happy—and I am—but there's a sadness, too.

This just isn't how I thought it would be.

"I hope being with my parents and seeing stuff from my childhood will help me remember," he says.

"They live in Colorado," I say, accidentally dropping my fork. It clangs against the plate. I snatch it back up and do my best to muster a smile. It just never occurred to me—that Jacob would be leaving me again.

"I'm not leaving you," he says, as though reading my mind. "I want to spend time with you as well. I want you to fill me in on stuff—what we did together, all our old memories."

My heart does a somersault inside my chest, reassured that we're obviously still connected. A part of me wants to jump up and down. But there's another part that can't help feeling sorry for myself. He looks at me with those slate-blue eyes and I just want to crawl up inside him and stay there forever.

But he doesn't know who I am.

He doesn't remember the time we drew henna on each other, or when we first kissed. Or that night on the boat in his room when I first told him I loved him.

"Are you okay?" Jacob asks, obviously sensing my funk.

I nod and bite down on my bottom lip, fighting the urge to cry.

"I *will* remember." He touches my shoulder, sending tingles down my back. "I want you to help me remember."

I touch his hand, fighting the urge to tell him how much I love him. "I'd like that," I say instead. A stray tear rolls down my cheek. Jacob wipes it with his fingers and I stop myself from kissing his hand.

But then I kiss it anyway.

Jacob reaches into his pocket and places the cluster crystal rock into my palm—just like old times. I clasp it for strength, running my fingers over the smoothened edges—where the crystal has healed itself over.

"It's going to be okay," he whispers.

"I know."

"Are you sure?"

I nod, knowing that Jacob and I are destined to be together, that nothing—not time, place, or lack of memory—will ever keep us apart.

epilogue:
Stacey

It's been two months since I found Jacob, and nearly seven weeks since I've seen him last. His parents ended up flying out here right away. They couldn't have been more shocked or elated to see him. His mother especially was a huge gush of emotion. But Jacob didn't remember them.

They stayed at a bed & breakfast just down the road, trying to get reacquainted with the son they thought they'd lost. But then they took him back home—to Colorado—only a few days later.

Now that he's there, he's started recalling bits of his childhood—where he went to kindergarten, a tree fort he built with his dad, and the time he made vanilla brownies with his mom; how they ate all but the entire pan before his dad even got home, how they both ended up sick for hours after.

Before his parents took him back, he told us about his experience at the camp. He told the police about it, too—about the stealing and the brainwashing; how there are runaway minors living there; and how campers are kept captive. It was a little crazy here after the news came out about his survival, but the irony is that, even though Jacob ended up turning the camp in, he also feels grateful for it—for them. He knows that if it wasn't for the campers following the boat and pulling him out of the ocean after the fall, he wouldn't be here right now.

And so I'm grateful for the camp as well.

It nearly kills me not being with him now, but we've been talking on the phone, e-mailing incessantly, and writing each other letters. I didn't follow him out to Colorado because I wanted to stay and continue school. I wanted to give him time to remember.

And now he has.

He called me the other day, telling me that he remembered our white candle spell—every inch of it, from the rose oil to the moment we kissed. He also remembered the first time he told me he loved me—one night in December when all the stars were out and we lay in the snow, making snow angels and laughing at each other's stupid jokes . . . his impersonation of Keegan, the hippy resident director of my dorm at Hillcrest.

He asked me if I'd consider coming out to Colorado for spring break. *Consider it?* I almost hung up on him right then, eager to call a travel agency to book a ticket.

I'm just about finished packing. My flight leaves in three hours. Amber is going away, too. So is Janie. They're actually vacationing in the same place. A group of about twenty Beacon students, including PJ, Tim, and Janie's boyfriend Hayden, are headed to Cancun. I'm glad Tim doesn't hold anything against me after my stint of temporary insanity. He's actually been a really great friend.

So has Porsha. She's doing so much better now; her father couldn't be more pleased—*so* pleased that he finagled Trevor a place to stay. Having taken in foster kids in the past, friends of the president, who live just down the road from the college, welcomed Trevor into their home and gave him his own room. Sadly, Trevor's real mother has no interest in being a part of his life, and his birth father couldn't be found.

I hope I've taught Porsha enough so that she's better able to deal with nightmares if and when she gets them again. But it seems now that her nightmares have stopped, the possibility of having more is the furthest thing from her mind. Instead, she and Trevor have been enjoying just being normal again—going to school, going to the movies, practicing magic—practically joined at the hip.

It reminds me of how Jacob and I used to be . . . how I hope we'll be someday soon.

Last night I had a dream about him—that we were sitting up in one of those ski lifts, looking down over the slopes. It was daylight out, but you could still see the stars and the new quarter moon, like they were just beyond our touch. Jacob took off his glove and drew the rune for partnership over my lips with his finger. And then he kissed me and it tasted like apple cider mixed in champagne—all sweet and bubbling inside my mouth. It felt like I had fallen out from the bottom of my chair, that I was tumbling through the sky, past the mountains, toward the earth below. But, when I opened my eyes, we were still sitting in the lift and he was still kissing me. And it was nighttime now—as if we'd been kissing all day, as if our world had just stopped while everybody else's kept moving forward.

I run my fingers over my lips, still feeling a tingle there, hopeful that my dream is a premonition for what's to come.

THE END